FIRE DANCE

4-30-11

MIKE SIROTA

Fire Dance

ZOVA BOOKS

LOS ANGELES

$ZOVA$ BOOKS

First ZOVA Books edition 2011.

Printed in the United States of America.

For information or permission contact:
ZOVA Books
P.O. Box 21833, Long Beach, California 90801
www.zovabooks.com

ISBN 9780982788059
eBook ISBN 9780982788066

Cover design © Daniel Pearson

To Jacqueline,
my wife,
my best friend.
We have been
through it all…
together.

CHAPTER ONE

Concordia

1

Outside the adobe walls of the sanitarium the eerie, primordial beauty of the southern California desert went ignored by the wandering inmates.

No matter that it was April, the time when desert wildflowers blossomed, painting a landscape that contradicted the majority of opinions regarding the bleak, arid world of sand and scrub. The inmates of Concordia Sanitarium, in their white, shroudlike gowns, did not see the patches of magenta monkey flowers, the yellow blooms of the creosote bush or the burroweed. The fiery red tips of the ocotillo cactus were invisible to them, and so too the purple-blue buds of the indigo bush.

Jacob Owen liked this time of year, and he took a moment to observe its subtleties, as a connoisseur would study a fine work of art. Once, he would have felt no differently than the rest of the inmates.

Once, he had been like them.

If not for Dr. Everett Cooke he might still be walking in their shrouds.

Good Dr. Cooke.

Twelve years ago: the spring of 1866, when Jacob had been admitted to the Connecticut State Hospital for what the doctors called *dementia praecox*. He had been twenty-six years old then. An incurable case, they said. He'll stay here, safe, and won't be a burden to anyone for the rest of his natural life.

The odds had been against him, Jacob now knew. Earlier in the nineteenth century, mental institutions had been torchbearers in reforms for treatment of the insane. But by 1866—and even now, in 1878—they had deteriorated into little more than custodial facilities for hiding an undesirable social problem.

But Dr. Everett Cooke was hardly a conventional practitioner. Indeed, he would have been quite at home during the ill-fated reform movement. In addition to his many duties at the hospital, he made Jacob his personal project. Within a year Cooke's peers were forced to acknowledge the fact that the funereal-looking Jacob had been restored to a "far more agreeable mental condition."

Ever since then, Jacob had served Dr. Cooke faithfully. He would have followed him anywhere, as he'd done to California ten years ago.

Dr. Cooke's first four years in California had been at the prestigious Livermore Sanitarium, up north. He had done fine things there, and had won the respect of his colleagues.

So in 1872, when his dream of becoming the medical supervisor of his own facility turned into reality, he was provided with excellent references by the Livermore administration. Concordia Sanitarium filled up quickly.

Lots of folks criticized its location, Jacob recalled. Such an odd place: the bleak desert across the mountains from the harbor town of San Diego. Miles off the stagecoach route between Los Angeles and Yuma, the same route that the Spanish explorer, Juan Bautista de Anza, had followed over a century ago when he opened the trail to California. But after the first couple of years, even the harshest critics had to admit that it seemed to be going well.

Standing two hundred yards from Concordia's walls, Jacob watched the dust cloud rising on the rutted trail that led to the facility.

Dr. Cooke was due back today after spending over a week in San Francisco. Jacob hoped this was him.

But soon the wagon was in sight: not Dr. Cooke's fine coach, but the old prairie schooner, long ago stripped of its bows and canvas. It was Tom Semple, returning from a mail run to the way station at Diablo Wash.

The young attendant waved and reined the tired-looking horses to a stop near Jacob. He never pushed the animals, Jacob knew; but although it was only April, the temperature was already in the eighties, and it was bone-dry.

"Anything of interest?" Jacob asked.

The slow-talking Tom replied, "Letters, the usual things . . . uh, and the shipment of . . . drugs we was expecting. You want . . . a ride back in?"

"Thank you, I feel like walking."

Tom left. Jacob turned, started back then stopped to again take in the breathtaking sweep of Concordia's surroundings.

This was the northern end of a broad valley, ringed by impressive mountains. Concordia Sanitarium had been built near a twisting creek that emerged from the mouth of a canyon. Thick, ten-foot-high adobe walls enclosed the two-story main building, which made it look like a fortress. The only way in or out was through a set of massive wood doors, which were set into a sculpted entryway. At the moment these doors, which faced the creek, were open. Inmates walked around outside. Some knelt by the creek under a broad canvas canopy. Attendants kept close watch on their charges, diverting them from any painful cactus plants.

Jacob set off again. Twenty yards from the entrance a slight, gray-haired woman with a smooth, laughing face waved a butterfly net in the empty air. Three times, a glance into the net, then she would pirouette a few yards and repeat it. Near her, another old woman moved along the sand on all fours, stopping upon occasion to sniff, then dig a hole. The butterfly-chaser ignored Jacob; the dog-woman, tongue lolling, rose on her knees and waved frantically.

Two bearded men, similar in features and dress, panned for gold in the tributary. Once, there had been gold in Bighorn Creek, but most of it had been taken out years ago. The inmates—original forty-niners—were content to do this from morning till dusk.

Passing through the gate into the courtyard, Jacob thought of old *ranchos* he had seen in California. Much of the labor on the outer walls and building had been done by mission Indians employed on *ranchos* to the south, or from *asistencias* in the nearby mountains.

There were more patients here, mostly elderly. *Senile dementia*, where would we be without it? Dr. Cooke had once joked. Some wandered aimlessly; walking ghosts, Jacob thought as he stared at their pale gowns. Others sat cross-legged on the sand, motionless. A man with long white hair and intense eyes drew pails of water from a small well—the underground runoff of Bighorn Creek—and frantically poured the contents into barrels, often spilling some.

"Good work, Mr. Witherby," Jacob called, "good work."

A girl of fifteen or sixteen squatted by the front door. Her pale, dirt-streaked face was not unattractive, but her wide, haunted eyes were unsettling. A hand reached out for Jacob's pant leg.

"There, Sarah, you let me pass," Jacob said, gently removing her hand and patting her head. "That's a good girl."

The building was u-shaped, though neither of the two wings had been part of the original construction and were only a single story. It too was made of adobe, as well as pine from the mountain forests to the west. Adobe was cool in the summer, and retained heat for the cold winter nights. The walls, flecked with straw that had been added to the mud plaster as a binder, were between three and four feet thick at their base. Heavy timbers were used for the inner partitions and the flat roof, these solidly bound with rawhide thongs. There were many small windows along the first floor, each discreetly barred in such a way as to hardly be noticeable to an inmate looking out.

Jacob walked down the lengthy main corridor. Its hardwood floor was covered by a woven, floral-patterned floorcloth. There were attractive tapestries on the walls. And candle sconces, widely spaced, each positioned just below the twelve-foot ceiling.

The doors of the patients' rooms lined the corridor. Each room was small, modestly appointed, but clean and comfortable. Some were occupied, most empty.

Patients were encouraged to stay out of their rooms during the day. At the other end of the hall was a well-stocked library. No fiction; Dr. Cooke didn't want to confuse their minds further. There were other things for the patients to do in the communal hall, which doubled as a dining room. Sometimes birthday parties were held there, or dances. Dr. Cooke believed those were good things for his patients.

A middle-aged woman stood rigidly against one wall. Every few seconds she thrust her head forward and made an odd, mewling sound. Farther along, an obese man in his twenties rolled about on the floor, grinning like a Cheshire cat. Jacob stepped gingerly around him.

The clinic was located at the far end of the hallway. Dr. James Lassiter, young but weary looking, worked there, assisted by a nurse named Ellie Foster. Two of the six cots in the clinic were occupied by inmates with minor afflictions.

Jacob noticed that the heavy door on the far wall of the clinic was slightly ajar. Tom Semple or someone must have gone down into the "dungeon."

The place where they kept *the thing*.

In addition to the proximity of Bighorn Creek, Dr. Everett Cooke's choice of location for the sanitarium had to do with an underground tunnel left over from the valley's brief gold rush. A miner had discovered a thin vein and had assumed it to be part of the elusive Mother Lode. Time and the changing desert had reclaimed much of the shaft. But a single chamber was left, strongly shored up, accessible only through the door in the clinic and down a flight of wide stairs. Intractable patients were sometimes confined there, even shackled, until they had calmed down. Owing to the nature of Concordia's mostly senior inmates—and Dr. Cooke's liberal policy regarding tranquilizers—the room was seldom used.

This was where, over three months ago, they brought the thing called Bruno Leopold.

Jacob had always been uneasy about what went on below. Even during the past nine days, with Dr. Cooke away and most of the administrative concerns on his shoulders, he had left the work in the dungeon to Tom and Dr. Lassiter and the others. Not that he wasn't curious about Cooke's progress . . .

In any case, it would all be over in a little more than a month, thank the Lord.

"Tom's already brought the new medicine to you?" Jacob asked the nurse.

Ellie Foster nodded. "He's an efficient young man."

"No sign of Dr. Cooke yet?" Lassiter asked.

"No. But there are still a few hours of daylight left. He'll be here."

2

Forty minutes later Dr. Everett Cooke arrived at Concordia Sanitarium. This bleakest of outposts, according to so many, was home for him, and he was always glad to return.

The days in and around San Francisco had been the closest thing to a vacation in years. Business and pleasure both, of course. "Absence of occupation is not rest, a mind quite vacant is a mind distressed," William Cowper had said about a century ago. Some time at Livermore, where he was always welcome. But there had been the opera, theater, the stores and fine restaurants . . . the women.

Cooke's four-seat Concord coach, built by the Abbot-Downing Company in New Hampshire, was engulfed by inmates and staff as it pulled up in front of the building. The "good doctor" (they all called him that) greeted every one by name. There was a rakishness about him, the aura of a Mississippi riverboat gambler, more impish than menacing. He was forty but looked younger. In spite of the heat he was comfortable in an expensive, high-buttoned frock coat.

Business: Cooke had brought back two new patients, a man in his sixties, a woman of nearly eighty. He had given them meprobamate, a mild tranquilizer, to help through the trip. Attendants assisted the pair down; inmates surrounded them with benign curiosity. The newcomers were bewildered.

The last passenger to step down from the coach was an attractive middle-aged woman, finely attired in a striped muslin day dress and carrying a lace-edged parasol. Mrs. Lucinda Blair was among the social elite of Los Angeles. Six months earlier Lucinda had committed her mother, Elizabeth Cuddy, to Concordia Sanitarium. The poor woman, in her seventies, had been suffering from *senile dementia* for some time now and was both an embarrassment and a burden to the family. Since becoming a patient, Mrs. Cuddy had not been visited once by her daughter—not an uncommon situation, but one that had caused Lucinda some guilt of late.

Looking around disapprovingly, the woman said, "I'd like to freshen up before I see my mother. Please take me to my room."

Cooke nodded. "Tom will see to your comfort."

Tom Semple, straining with Lucinda's heavy suitcase, led the woman around the back of the sanitarium to the facility's only outbuilding, a small, seldom-used guest bungalow. Cooke watched them off, then turned.

Sarah squatted at his feet, looking up at him. Her body trembled as she tried to smile. Slowly, she hiked the hem of her gown up over her knees.

"There, Sarah, that's a good girl," Jacob Owen said as he pulled the hand free and smoothed down the garment. "Why don't you go with the others and make the new people feel at home?"

The girl moved away reluctantly, her eyes still on Cooke. The doctor nodded at his associate.

"Thank you, Jacob," he said.

"Welcome home, Dr. Cooke." Jacob always called him *Dr. Cooke*, despite their long acquaintance and similarity in age. "You had a good trip?"

"Yes, quite good. How did everything go here?"

"Fine, just fine."

Dr. Everett Cooke was a sincere, conscientious crusader in the fight against mental illness. If he had a *fault*—one which he recognized and accepted—it was his above-average taste for the quality of life. Although all his patients came from families that could afford the care, he was adamant about limiting the number to no more than fifty at a time. That was why his fees were exorbitant. But this did not trouble him. Those families, like the Blairs, were more than willing to pay handsomely for concealing their "problem." So why not take advantage of it?

"Everything all right below, then?" Cooke asked.

"Dr. Lassiter says so," Jacob replied.

Cooke smiled. "You still won't go down, will you?"

"Not if I can help it."

"Well, I'd like to make that my first matter of business, as soon as I'm settled in. Jacob, you'll see to Mrs. Blair, won't you? Tom is not exactly possessed of your, ah, social skills."

"Yes, of course I will."

3

The "dungeon" (Cooke hated the staff saying that) was dimly lit. From the top step, Cooke could barely make out the large form huddled against the back wall below. When he started down slowly, the shape moved.

They had brought Bruno Leopold there in a huge crate, wearing leg irons and handcuffs. Last year, in San Francisco, this son of immigrants had murdered his parents, a sister, an aunt, and a neighbor child, most brutally. He'd been sentenced to hang.

But Dr. Everett Cooke, aware of the young man's severe mental deficiencies, had made a request of the authorities. He wanted to "study" Bruno, find out the causes of such a malady, possibly prevent or minimize future incidents. It was the kind of research that stimulated the good doctor, made his caretaking chores with the other inmates more acceptable. Despite resistance, he'd won his argument. A stay of execution had been granted until some time after the middle of May.

And on his recent visit to San Francisco Cooke had again spoken to the authorities, telling them of Leopold's progress and requesting even more time for his work. They would be sending a letter to advise him of their decision, though Cooke felt certain the extension would be granted. Until the letter came, he would refrain from telling the staff.

The hulking man on the straw-littered floor was eighteen but looked older. His dusky, moon-shaped face was frozen in a perpetual scowl. Although of average height he was powerfully built, the thick arms and legs silently bragging of his strength. This immense power had enabled him to kill those five people with only his hands. Also, he had injured three policemen during his arrest; one would never walk again.

Leopold's seeming passivity as Cooke stood over him was due in part to the chlorpromazine, a powerful tranquilizer, which they'd given him from the beginning. The truth of it was, Cooke well knew, his daily dosage had been reduced, and the chains forged to the shackles around his wrists and ankles had been lengthened in proportion to his diminishing intractability. Dr. Lassiter had reported even more improvement during Cooke's absence.

"Hello, Bruno, how are you?" Cooke asked.

Bruno shaped his mouth in a grotesque smile, raised an arm weakly. "Go-od doctor," he said in a deep, slurred voice.

"Yes, it's me, and I'm going to spend more time with you, like before. Today I must see to all my other patients, but tomorrow will be yours. You understand, Bruno? Tomorrow."

"To-morrow," he repeated dully. Lassiter had reported just giving him the largest dose of chlorpromazine all day, which would immobilize him until morning. "To-morrow. Go-od doctorrr . . ."

"Sleep well, Bruno," Cooke said, and he left the dungeon.

4

Lucinda Blair barely responded as Jacob Owen, in his most cordial voice, pointed out the virtues of Concordia Sanitarium while leading her into the main building. Remembering how her mother had been toward the end, Lucinda was reluctant to see her. Mrs. Cuddy could become lost within herself, not recognizing members of her own family for hours at a time. That had been the most unnerving thing of all.

And here, all these pathetic creatures wandering around the courtyard, or the hallway. It was so unnerving, so . . . frightening. But she was a strong woman, and she'd sworn she would follow through.

Elizabeth Cuddy sat on a stool in her room, staring out the window, a vague smile on her face. Years before, she had been the matriarch of one of Los Angeles' most wealthy and influential families.

Now ...

"Hello, Mrs. Cuddy," Jacob said cheerfully. "Look who's here to see you."

"Mother?" Lucinda said.

The old woman turned slightly. There was no hint of recognition in her voice as she spoke: "'I take pleasure in infirmities, in reproaches, in necessities, in persecutions, in distresses, for Christ's sake; for when I am weak, then am I strong.'"

"Mother, it's me, it's Lucinda!"

"'I have been young, and now am old; yet have I not seen the righteous forsaken.'"

"Oh please, Mother, can't you hear me?"

"'If we suffer, we shall also reign with him.'"

Lucinda glanced helplessly at Jacob. "It's no use! She's just like before—"

"Lucy? Is it ... Lucy?" The old woman's vague smile was gone; she stared at Lucinda, wide-eyed.

"Mother?"

"*Lucy! Oh dear God—!*"

They embraced, both sobbing. Jacob smiled broadly. For nearly a minute they clung to each other; then, Mrs. Cuddy's face again grew serenely blank. She pushed her daughter away.

"'When ye stand praying, forgive, if ye have ought against any ...'"

Lucinda was trembling. "I-I must get out of here!" she cried. "I'll come back; yes, I will, but—"

"'... that your father also which is in heaven ...'"

"I must get out!"

"'... may forgive you your trespasses.'"

"I'll go to my room *now!*" she told Jacob.

She ran out into the corridor, Jacob following. There seemed to be many more inmates than before. One of the prospectors from Bighorn Creek grinned a grin of brown rotted teeth. The young girl—Sarah—clutched at the bows on Lucinda's dress with both hands, her lips moving wordlessly. A couple of yards ahead, the obese man rolled along the carpet, his tongue protruding. On the left a tall, skeletal man with skin like parchment emerged from behind a door. He was naked.

Surrounding Lucinda, hands reaching, grabbing . . .

"Back away," Jacob told them gently. "Let Mrs. Blair pass."

Reaching, grabbing . . .

"I'll go to my room now!"

Pulling free of the inmates, Lucinda ran outside. Jacob was sorely pressed to keep up with her.

5

Dr. Cooke's three personal rooms—bedroom, parlor, office—took up a portion of the second floor, where most of the staff resided. The first-floor door leading into a single stairwell was always kept locked; too much for a wandering inmate to get into upstairs. It was for their own good.

By the time night fell over Concordia Sanitarium, Cooke had spent at least a minute or two with each of the patients. Jacob informed him of the incident with Lucinda Blair and her mother. The good doctor took it upon himself to call on the distraught woman. He hosted her at dinner in the privacy of his parlor. By the time she went to bed that night, Lucinda had calmed down greatly.

Later, while making their final rounds, Cooke and Jacob Owen emerged from the clinic. Sarah had been squatting on the floor a couple of doors away. She duck-walked quickly, until she was at their feet. Gazing up expectantly, she pointed between her legs.

Cooke smiled. It had been a while . . . "Yes, all right," he said. "Jacob, please clean her up and bring her to me."

Sarah scampered joyously to her room, Jacob following. Ten minutes later, he brought the girl to Cooke's parlor. Scrubbed clean, Sarah's face was comely, though pale. Instead of the shroudlike garment she wore a white cotton dress, slightly tattered, which fit her well, showing off her curves, the swell of her young breasts. The dress was a hand-me-down from Ellie Foster, who at thirty-five had decided she was too old to squeeze into that sort of thing. Cooke was delighted.

"Well, don't you look lovely," he said. "Thank you, Jacob."

The gaunt man left. Holding Sarah's hand, Cooke led her into the bedroom. The girl smiled; she loved being in his rooms. And this time, she was sure, she'd get to stay until morning.

6

The next day, a Thursday, Jacob rode to the Diablo Wash way station to meet a Yuma-bound stage. On Friday either he or Tom would take Mrs. Blair to the station for the coach to Los Angeles. But that day, Jacob was pleased to notice before he left, the woman had recovered sufficiently to be spending time with her mother. They were walking, arm-in-arm, outside the walls. Mrs. Cuddy's periods of lucidness seemed longer, and even when she was "not quite herself," Lucinda was better able to deal with it. This, Jacob thought, was what Dr. Cooke should be most proud of, *not* what he did down in . . .

That Thursday was special for another reason. Dear Mrs. Virginia McLeod was celebrating a birthday, her seventy-first. The staff had even managed to make her aware of it, although it required constant reminding to keep the woman excited about her party, which would, Jacob had informed everyone, begin at eight o'clock.

Sarah was excited about the birthday party all day. She would wear the white dress again, the one *he* had liked so much. And maybe he would dance with her.

Dance with her.

Late in the afternoon Sarah stood along the edge of Bighorn Creek, a few yards from the prospectors. There were no mirrors on the first floor, and she wanted to look at herself in the water. She stood tall by the bank, swaying gracefully, dancing to music only she could hear.

Tom Semple oversaw the patients outside the walls. He didn't mind the duty, even though the temperature was up near ninety. In another couple of months there would be days in excess of 120 degrees. That often kept the inmates quieter than the tranquilizers did. As usual the air was bone-dry, more so because of the sparse rain all year. Bighorn Creek flowed sluggishly out of the canyon and was about half its normal width.

Tom had been watching Sarah by the creek and realized that he had never seen her stand so straight. Nor did the heat seem to bother her, he also noted, for she was plainly entranced by what she saw in the water.

7

Jacob Owen thought that Hiram Tickner was an amazing man. Most of the time he would recline in the courtyard, staring blankly. But sit him down at the piano in the communal hall, whisper "Mozart's *Divertimento No. 7 in D Major*" or "Schubert's *Impromptu, Op. 142, No. 3*," and there would be lovely music for as long as one cared to listen.

Shortly after eight Mr. Tickner was furiously engaged with the *rondo alla turca* from Mozart's *Piano Sonata No. 11*, not something to which you could dance. Most of the inmates and staff were there. Lucinda Blair had come with Mrs. Cuddy, although the presence of so many shrouded figures had heightened the younger woman's anxiety. Tables and chairs had been pushed back against the walls. Tom Semple stood guard over Mrs. McLeod's birthday cake, which had three large candles stuck in the chocolate icing. Tom was also in charge of dispensing punch and other sweets.

Lucinda had again been invited to dinner by Dr. Cooke. By eight-fifteen, when he had not yet made an appearance, she mentioned it to Jacob, who told her that he would go and find him.

"Please, I'd like to go with you," Lucinda said hastily.

Promising her mother—who did not hear her—that she would be back, Lucinda followed Jacob out of the communal hall. They checked first in his quarters, then the clinic, where Ellie Foster was working.

"He's downstairs, where else?" the nurse said.

Jacob nodded. "I should have guessed. But so late?"

"That's what I told him—an hour ago. Uh, Jacob, would you like me to get him?"

He sighed deeply. "No, I'll go down. Mrs. Blair, please wait here."

Slowly descending the dozen wide steps, Jacob froze halfway. He could not believe what he saw. Dr. Cooke sat cross-legged on the straw, inches from Bruno Leopold, who had assumed a similar position as best he could with the burden of chains. His body was animated with short, jerky movements.

"Dr. Cooke, are . . . you all right?" Jacob asked.

Cooke glanced up. "Ah, Jacob. Come here; don't be afraid."

The gaunt man continued down, stopping on the bottom step. This was as far as he would go. Cooke always left his keys hanging by the door, but Jacob had a full set clipped to his belt.

"Bruno, this is Jacob," the doctor said.

Leopold's scowl made Jacob uneasy. "Ja-cob," he repeated.

Jacob glanced at Cooke. "You have him *heavily* drugged."

"He's just taken his medicine. But heavily? His dosage is almost half of what it was when we first started with him."

"Astonishing," Jacob said. "He's given you no trouble?"

"There were moments, especially at first, but he's progressing nicely. I'm pleased that you finally decided to come down."

"I just came to say that Mrs. Blair is waiting to have dinner with you, and Mrs. McLeod's party has begun."

"Oh damn, is it that late?" He looked at his pocket watch. "Time to sleep now, Bruno."

The man's eyes were sagging under a beetled brow. Cooke leaned forward and patted his shoulder. Jacob tensed. "Go-od doctor," Bruno said, then curled up on a straw mat.

"Yes, my friend," Cooke said, "one day we'll take off your chains. And if you've worked hard, who knows? Perhaps upstairs with the other patients, out in the sunshine?"

Bruno rocked ecstatically on his mat. Jacob was stunned. Why was Dr. Cooke saying that? In another month, Bruno Leopold would be returned to San Francisco and hanged for his crimes.

"Good times ahead," Cooke went on. "Now then, Mrs. Blair. Jacob, will you stay with Bruno until he's asleep? As you can see, he's quite excited."

"All right," Jacob replied vaguely. "Dr. Cooke—?"

He looked at his watch again and started up the stairs. "We'll talk later, Jacob."

8

Sarah didn't like it when so many people were in one place, especially when none of them was Dr. Cooke.

The party was not a prison; patients could still walk around. Sarah had left after Jacob and was in her room, just inside the open doorway. The good doctor would have to pass this way.

She would go back to the party on his arm.

Lucinda Blair was alone in the clinic, Ellie Foster having gone on to the party. Cooke smiled sheepishly.

"I'm sorry; I lost all track of time," he said.

"I understand, Doctor. Having been exposed to some of your wonderful work, I can imagine how busy you are."

"If you don't mind waiting, I can make myself presentable."

"You look fine. Besides, we should dine quickly. The others are so anticipating your presence at the party."

He extended his arm. "Shall we, then?"

The skinny man—Jacob—was keeping his distance, but Bruno didn't care. As the chlorpromazine calmed him more, making his eyelids heavy, he thought about the day.

He thought about *Good Dr. Cooke*.

Bruno wasn't going back. The good doctor was keeping him here. One day he would go upstairs, and he would have friends. Not going back, not back, because they would kill him for what he had done, and Bruno didn't want to die.

Didn't want to die.

Good Dr. Cooke, good doctor . . .

Not go back, not back.

. . . didn't want to die.

9

Hiram Tickner was playing a lovely rendition of Beethoven's *Für Elise*. The melody stirred a lost memory in Mrs. Virginia McLeod, from a time when she and her husband, dead these many years, had been king and queen of the dance floor. Now she was in his arms again, swaying rapturously with the grace of a woman four decades younger.

The skeleton man bumped into Mrs. McLeod and broke her magic spell. He was out on the floor, stepping high, raising each bony leg in turn. Mr. Witherby, the water bearer, and one of the bowlegged prospectors were also moving to the bagatelle. The prospector nearly stumbled over the dog-woman, who was agitated by the activity as she weaved between the others on all fours.

Despite the urgings of the Concordia staff, most of the inmates remained off the dance floor.

When she heard Dr. Cooke's voice in the corridor, Sarah started out of her room.

Then, she heard the woman.

Peering out cautiously, Sarah saw Cooke and Lucinda Blair. They were smiling at each other. *Smiling.* They went into the stairwell; there was a click as Cooke locked the door.

Tears streaming, Sarah staggered along the corridor. With each step she regressed into the posture of her madness, until she squatted in front of the stairwell door. Looking up, she opened her mouth in a silent cry and began hammering a fist at the air, over and over, over and over.

10

Bruno's body lay still. He was turned away from the wall; a twisted smile was visible in the cellar's dim light.

"Pleasant dreams," Jacob Owen uttered.

Pleasant dreams, good dreams, Bruno's brain thought. *Good doctor . . .*

His breathing was heavy, guttural, as it usually sounded in sleep. "You won't be smiling next month, you poor bastard, when they put the rope around your neck," Jacob said softly. "Christ, why is Dr. Cooke dealing in such a lie?"

Good dreams, good doctor . . .
Rope.
Next month . . . poor bastard.
Good doctor, good . . . lie.
Around your neck.
Lie, Dr. Cooke lied.
Didn't want to die.

Bruno was gasping for air, choking. Jacob, on the stairs, turned to see him thrashing. No time to call Ellie Foster from the clinic above. He ran to the supine figure, whose jaw had clamped shut. Fearing that the man had swallowed his tongue, he knelt and tried to pry his mouth open.

"Bruno, what—?" he began.

Massive hands encircled his throat. Fighting through the strong drug, Bruno strangled Jacob, ending his resistance by snapping his neck. Standing now, still holding Jacob, Bruno pulled the keys off his belt, then flung the corpse to the floor.

Find the right key; fit the key in the hole. Bruno was not good at this. But he . . .

Didn't want to die.

. . . so he kept at it, still shaking off the haze, drawing strength from having killed again with his hands. Luckily, one key fit all the brackets. He cast the irons across the dungeon.

Dr. Cooke . . . good doctor.
Lie.
Around your neck . . . poor bastard.
Lie lie lie.

Bruno Leopold started up the steps.

11

The bagatelle had flowed into a Chopin waltz. Other inmates

were on the dance floor now, twenty-five or so, half the census of Concordia Sanitarium. Dr. James Lassiter knew how much they wanted to get at the birthday cake for dear Mrs. McLeod, but he wouldn't allow it until later, when Dr. Cooke appeared.

So he and the attendants exhorted, cajoled, led them onto the floor, and the number grew to thirty, then thirty-five. The fat man crawled to the center, his tongue lolling in time to the music, like an obscene metronome. They formed a circle around him, no two dancing together, not touching, other than an accidental bump. Around and around, a slow, hypnotic caucus-race out of the same impossible tale that had bred the Cheshire cat.

Around and around . . .

Sarah was still hammering at the air when Bruno loomed over her. "Dr. Cooke?" he grunted.

The girl glanced at him, then pointed at the door, thrusting her arm forward and back. He tried the door, hunted for the right key, found it quickly. Pushing Sarah aside, he started up.

Recovering, Sarah scampered into the stairwell ahead of him. She knew, after all, where Dr. Cooke would be, and this man did not. Seeming to understand this, Bruno followed her.

They were at his quarters. Another key let them into his office. Holding a finger to her lips, Sarah glided across the room, past the doctor's exquisite, tambour-front William IV desk, to the parlor door. Bruno's passage was less stealthy.

Cooke and Lucinda were helping themselves to the still-warm food under the lids of the sterling silver platters when Bruno threw the door open. He was on them swiftly, a hand around Lucinda's throat cutting off her scream.

"What are you doing?" Cooke exclaimed. "How—!"

Bruno drove a balled fist into the doctor's face; Cooke spat out blood and broken teeth. Before drifting into a thick haze his eyes fell upon Sarah. She had leaped, catlike, onto a Chippendale window bench and was grinning as she silently exhorted Bruno on with her twisting body.

The squirming woman was an annoyance. Bruno snapped her

neck and dropped her down on the table. But the *good doctor*, what to do with the *good doctor*? He deserved more, *more*, because he had . . .

Lied.

What to do! The *medicine* was still inside, and even without it his brain did not work so quickly, because he was not like everyone else, and he couldn't think, *couldn't think* . . .

Throwing the limp Cooke over his shoulder, he hurried downstairs. There was the sound of a piano from somewhere, but the corridor was empty. Nor was the bent creature, who had shown the way up, with him anymore. He was still unsure what to do. But quick, it had to be *quick*. Couldn't stay much longer.

Didn't want to die.

The dark place. Instinct sent him back to the dark place in the ground. In the clinic he found the prybar, claw hammer and pliers that Tom Semple had used to add the links in his chains. *Chains*. Although not sure why, he grabbed the tools, carrying them and Dr. Cooke down into the dungeon, closing the heavy door.

Chains, he thought again. He hated the chains.

When Dr. Cooke regained consciousness a minute later, he was chained to the wall.

Bruno Leopold's face was two inches from his. "You lied."

Cooke stared in horror at Jacob Owen's body. "I—don't know what you mean, Bruno. Why do you say I lied?"

"You'll send me back . . . they'll hang me."

"Bruno, that's not true!" Cooke exclaimed. "You—!"

"Didn't want to die!"

"Bruno, you weren't going to—!"

"Lies lies lies!"

A hand encircled Cooke's throat and squeezed. Eyes bulging, mouth agape, the medical supervisor of Concordia Sanitarium silently pleaded for his life.

Bruno's other hand closed upon the pair of pliers. Clamping down tightly, he pulled Dr. Cooke's tongue out of his head.

12

Sarah was going to follow the man downstairs, to see what he would do with Dr. Cooke. But she held back because of . . .

The woman.

The outsider, who had smiled at her earlier and had been so nice. Probably laughing at her all the time; *laughing*.

Jumping off the window bench, Sarah squatted by the table and hammered Lucinda Blair's corpse with a fist. Over and over, feeling no satisfaction. It wasn't hurting the woman, wasn't making her cry out.

An ornate, brass-based peg lamp burned on a satinwood server. Sarah picked it up, held it over the table, tilted it slightly so that some of the kerosene spattered on the body. The Tam O'Shanter shade began sliding out of its holder. Grabbing it, she burned her hand. The lamp fell as she staggered back.

Flames consumed the linen-covered table in seconds, Lucinda's body sitting atop the pyre like an honored Valkyrie. Sarah cowered by the wall, terrified, but also fascinated by what she had caused.

Drapes took the flames; now their spread was beyond control. Furniture, tapestries, walls ignited in the tinder-dryness, the roar like that of a long-confined dragon set free to belch its deadly breath. Dr. Cooke's exquisite Persian rug carried the flames to Sarah, who tried to move, but not quickly enough. Her dress was set ablaze; her efforts to swat it out were futile.

Mouth open in a silent scream, Sarah waded across the sea of fire to the door. Flames pursued her through Dr. Cooke's office, engulfing all patient records and his fine collection of books. Down the stairwell, exploding into the corridor moments after she staggered away, nearly blind now, the dress burned off, hair and flesh carrying the destruction. Lurching into one wall, another, flames consuming the floorcloth and hardwood, the tapestries, these in turn igniting the dry walls of the sanitarium.

The shrouded caucus-race was circling the communal hall to a mazurka from Delibes' *Coppelia* when the blackened, flaming thing that had been Sarah burst in. Before Dr. Lassiter could turn she leaped on his back, the crisping flesh from her grasping hands adhering to his white lab coat. He screamed, tried to shake her off, could not.

A few inmates followed the attendants into the corridor, but most remained in the caucus-race, oblivious to the fire spreading through the hall. Hiram Tickner did not get up from the piano, although his music now was a single, atonal chord struck over and over, loud enough to be heard above the crackle of flames. This did not put the dancers off balance.

Only one way out. Ellie Foster, Tom Semple and the staff tried to reach the front door, but the hallway had become a tunnel through Hell. Adobe melted, flowing like lava; windows imploded.

Dr. James Lassiter's flesh became one with the charred creature on his back.

Old Mr. Witherby, the water bearer, poured invisible buckets onto the flames.

The caucus-race went on to the tune of the discordant note.

13

Dr. Cooke had lost consciousness. *Water*, Bruno's dull mind remembered, *if you splashed water . . .*

Bruno wanted the good doctor awake when he killed him with his hands.

No more water here, but maybe in the clinic. He hurried up the stairs.

When he opened the door, a loud jet of flame threw him down. Intense heat filled the chamber; the matted straw caught, along with the bone-dry timbers that shored up the old shaft.

Dr. Everett Cooke, coughing thick gobs of blood, was incinerated in his shackles.

Bruno Leopold's death was longer and more painful, and even when half his body had been burned away he continued to crawl toward the steps, although for the most part those steps no longer existed, but he had to keep going, because he . . .

Didn't want to die.

A few days later, a letter for Dr. Cooke arrived at the Diablo

Wash way station. It was from the authorities in San Francisco, granting him an indefinite extension for his work with Bruno Leopold, the convicted murderer.

Eventually George Tucker, the stationmaster, returned the letter to its sender, along with the rest of the mail and other things that could no longer be delivered to Concordia Sanitarium.

Smoke Tree, Summer 1994

1

66 A re we there yet?"

The whiny poser of every kid on a car trip longer than one hour. If Tracy Russell had thought her son was serious, her reply might have been as tritely condescending as all the eighty billion or so that came before it.

But she knew Joey better. The kid hardly ever let himself get bored, a rarity for a nine-year-old. Since leaving St. Louis they'd driven two full days, and part of a third, and Joey had managed to keep himself busy most of the time—with an occasional digression into being a pain-in-the-butt. Having along two shoe boxes crammed with baseball cards, a hand-held *Star Wars* game and the latest issues of *Game Pro* and *Nintendo Power* magazines didn't hurt. And he'd brought books, too: *The Hobbit*, his favorite, and a bunch of old adventure novels his grandfather had given him last Christmas. At times he'd read out loud to help his mother ward off the boredom of the endless interstates.

"Are we there yet?" he repeated in an abrasive voice, rendering a near-perfect imitation of Bart Simpson.

"Actually, I have some bad news," Tracy said in mock solemnity. "We went the wrong way."

"We did?"

"What do you see outside?"

He pressed his nose against the window. "Sand dunes, brush, lotsa cactuses."

"Cacti. Yeah, that confirms it; this is definitely *not* I-10 in southern California."

"It's not? Then where are we?"

"Rhode Island. It was probably that exit we missed in Oklahoma City. We got turned around."

"It said on the last sign that Palm Springs was in thirty-something miles."

"That's right: Palm Springs, Rhode Island." Tracy flashed him a thumbs-up. "Nice town."

"Oh. What do we do now?"

"We can't go back cross-country. Big traffic jam in Bee's Knee, Iowa; cow on the road."

Joey maintained a great deadpan. "How about Canada?"

"Uh-uh, we can't risk the Toyota being dented by a stray hockey puck."

"What about south, around Cape Horn?"

"Yeah, the way people used to get to California! Good call. I wonder if we can rig the car with sails and pontoons."

Joey laughed. He had one of those infectious little-kid chuckles they used to put on the laugh tracks of sitcoms before they were shot in front of live audiences. Tracy loved his laugh.

And she loved *him*; God, did she love this kid.

It was hard to believe she had ever loved his father as much. But there *had* been a time . . .

"Mom, is Grandma really dying?" Joey suddenly asked. "Is that why we're driving out so fast, without stopping to see anything?"

Tracy never sugar coated things for her son. "You know Grandma's been sick for a long time."

"Uh-huh. Her . . . lungs, right? That's why they moved to

California."

Tracy nodded. "The warm, dry climate. Doctor said it might give her some more years."

"But it didn't!"

"That's not true, champ. They've been out here over three years. She might not've had *that* if they'd stayed in St. Louis." She glanced at him, smiled. "Besides, we don't really know what's happening yet. Your grandma's a tough lady; she may be around to see you graduate *summa cum laude* from MIT."

Joey shrugged and fell into a thoughtful silence. Tracy remembered her father's call last Friday, the barely concealed urgency in his voice when he'd "suggested" they come straight here from St. Louis, no sightseeing on the way, which had been the plan. No, she hadn't taken a turn for the worse. It was just that she wanted so much to see her daughter and grandson, kept asking when they'd be there . . .

Terminally ill people know when their time to die is near, don't they? Tracy thought. They take care of any business, summon all dispersed family members for a final visit—tie up the "loose ends."

They know when it's time.

Tracy stopped for gas off Highway 86, south of Indio, even though her six-year-old Toyota Cressida still had over half a tank, and Smoke Tree, where her parents lived, was less than thirty miles away. She'd been behind the wheel for a long time and wasn't about to show up at Mom and Dad's door without first having a look at herself in the mirror.

Well, could be worse, she figured as she stood in the rest room behind the Four Palms Store. She'd washed her peppery blond, shoulder-length hair in the motel last night and it seemed to be holding up. Face looked a little pale (she *was* tired), but some makeup would cover that. Couple of new lines; nothing she could do about it, even though she knew her mother would notice. Not much got by that lady.

Overall, the effect did not displease Tracy. Earlier this year she'd turned thirty-three; but anyone far enough down the hall of the high school where she taught might still mistake her for one of the students. Mrs. Russell was a favorite fantasy of many adolescent boys. Yeah, so her tits could've been bigger, and 5'4" wasn't exactly *statuesque*; but looking like a cross between Jodie Foster and Michelle Pfeiffer was OK.

Joey had finished pumping the gas and was sitting on the hood of the car, eating a Ding Dong, when Tracy returned. "Come on, kiddo, don't spoil your appetite," she said. "I'm sure Grandma has a great dinner for us."

"It's only three o'clock," Joey replied. "I'll be hungry when we eat."

Yeah, he will, she knew. For a kid who always looked like a Third World poster child, he could pack it away.

"You ready?"

"Uh-huh." He gestured across the highway. "What's that big lake over there?"

"It's not a lake. That's the Salton Sea."

"The *what*?"

Tracy had noticed it on one of the Triple A maps: a *sea* in the middle of the desert? She'd been curious herself. "It's been there less than a century. Happened by accident, when the Colorado River overflowed its banks and filled up an ancient sink. The water carried lots of salt deposits right along with it. Would you believe its *surface* is over two hundred feet *below* sea level?"

"How do you know all this stuff?"

"I'm a teacher, I know everything."

The boy nodded. "Yeah, right."

They continued south, then turned off Highway 86 and headed west on S22, designated on Tracy's map as the Borrego-Salton Seaway. Once again the stark, silent desert pressed up against both shoulders of the road. Tracy still found it unsettling, even though it had been like this for most of the way since west Texas. From the vast emptiness a town would suddenly be there, even a city; then, just as quickly, it was gone, and the desert again had them.

"Mom, what's a smoke tree?" Joey asked.

"A tree with a nasty habit, I guess."

He looked at her wryly. "That was *bad*. Really, how come they call it that?"

"I—don't have a clue."

"But you're a teacher, you know everything."

"*Touché*. Anyway, I teach drama and art, so there."

"Remind me to ask Grandpa; now *he* knows everything."

They kept it up for a while, and Smoke Tree appeared quickly.

2

Stirrings. The first tentative cognizance of *being*.

No, not the first time, because he had lived before. He had *been*. The reality of that came to him even in those initial seconds.

He had *been*.

But nothing else came as quickly. There were images, yes, but vague, desultory; different colors, sometimes distinct in variegated streaks, then coiling together in an unfathomable serpent's ritual. Frightening him, these colors, though not nearly as much as the blackness that would remain when they suddenly flickered out, because the blackness was so empty, so cold . . .

So seemingly infinite.

And yet not irresistible, because he did not feel its hold upon him, and he could move away from it, move away. He knew that now, and the fear diminished, but did not cease.

Move away. Not up, or down, or to the side, because movement was all the same, and any movement took him away from the blackness, and that was good.

An interminable, sluggish passage through the womb, which was not a liquid womb, but rather . . .

Sand.

A womb of sand, this birthplace of his new being.

Move away from the blackness, move through the womb of sand before it became a granular sepulcher, because he had *been*, and now he *was* again, and he didn't want to die.

Didn't want to die.

3

The man had ordered Johnnie Walker Black on the rocks and had nursed the drink until most of the ice was melted.

Mark Alderson hadn't seen him before. Not that seven weeks tending bar at the Smoke Tree Country Club's Arroyo Lounge had exposed him to every one of the town's twenty-five hundred or so residents; but it had come close.

The bar was quiet, usual for a Wednesday afternoon. A few golfers scattered around inside, or on the patio. Soon the early bowlers of the ladies' league (the country club had four lanes) would stop by for their daiquiris and wine coolers. And for sure it would be busy after five-thirty, when they opened the adjoining restaurant, the Cottonwood Room, which served until nine.

Mark had talked with the stranger a while; part of the job, but it was OK. The man was in his mid- or late fifties, *barely* old enough for residency in Smoke Tree. He was a manufacturer's rep from Philadelphia, a Willy Loman-type with a line of groundskeeping products he had earlier presented to the buyer at the country club. A good listener, Mark had let the man prattle on about the economy, why we should *never* trust any of those Aay-rab countries, his family, why the Phillies sucked.

Then, he'd said to Mark, "It don't seem like you should be tending bar. You sure your name ain't Richard Kimble?" And he had laughed.

It had been said before, with minor variations on the theme, a number of times since Mark Alderson had come to Smoke Tree, California.

In the sixties the late actor, David Janssen, played in a popular television series called *The Fugitive*, about a man, Dr. Richard Kimble, wrongly convicted of murdering his wife. He escapes, and is pursued back and forth across the country by an obsessed cop. Every week, wherever he is, he finds work (rather easily, for a man with no references) as a welder, hospital orderly, forklift operator—bartender. People who take a liking to him all say the same thing, that he just doesn't belong there.

Which was why so many of the old-timers in Smoke Tree, who remembered the show fondly, said the same thing to Mark Alderson.

Had they only known how close to the truth it was . . .

"Sorry," he said, "my name's Mark Bradley."

The salesman eyed Mark curiously. "Nah, you're probably too young to even remember the show," he said. "What are you, thirty or so?"

"Thanks, I'm thirty-six. And I *did* see the movie that they made last year."

"Not the same, no way." The man climbed off the barstool. "Christ, will you look at that!"

Sooner or later all newcomers to the Arroyo Lounge drifted over to one corner to check out the jukebox. The Wurlitzer Model 1015, manufactured in 1946, was the pride of Mark's boss, Jerry Zirpolo, a managing partner of the country club. It had color wheels in its sides, and bubble tubes running from its base to its arch. All of it was original equipment.

"I don't believe this music!" the salesman exclaimed. "Are we in the Twilight Zone, or what?"

There were songs from when Dorothy Collins and Snooky Lanson sang them new on *Your Hit Parade*, and before. Songs by Les Paul and Mary Ford, the Andrews Sisters, Johnnie Ray. Rosemary Clooney's "Mambo Italiano;" "You, You, You" by the Ames Brothers; Bing Crosby crooning "Dear Hearts and Gentle People." And the big band sounds of Artie Shaw, Ray Anthony, Les Brown and his Band of Renown, with a lead singer named Doris Day offering a sultry "Sentimental Journey." The good people of Smoke Tree, where the median age was 74.3, loved Jerry Zirpolo's magic jukebox.

But, as Mark had first observed seven weeks ago, it didn't play a thing after 1954. Skip the King, forget the Fab Four, screw The Boss. Led Zeppelin? Yeah, some weapon the krauts used in World War I. Jefferson Airplane? One of them cheapo commuter lines down south.

Yeah, well, it was all right, Mark figured. He liked all the seniors, and Smoke Tree was OK.

And for the first time in a while he had stopped running. It had been over a month since he'd last thought of emptying the cash register and getting back on the road.

The salesman finished his drink and left without even sliding in a quarter for three selections. Mark was glad; he had sworn that, the next time anyone played Frankie Laine's "Mule Train," he would demolish the prized Wurlitzer.

Mrs. Ivy Hutchinson and her friends came into the lounge a few minutes later. This same foursome played nine holes every Monday, Wednesday and Friday. They took a table by a window overlooking the fairway. Rita Vasquez, the cocktail waitress, was on the patio, so Mark went over for their order.

The women were especially fond of Mark, who stood six feet tall with a lean, well-proportioned body. His rugged face, though not strikingly handsome, was appealing; in the past kids had mistaken him for Wayne Gretzky. His gray-blue eyes always met the gaze of others strongly.

"Oh, isn't he cute?" Mrs. Hutchinson exclaimed, pinching his cheek. She always did that. "If I was thirty years younger—"

"You'd still be too old, dearie," her best friend, Molly Forsythe, said good-naturedly.

They bantered in loud voices, and Mark held back a laugh. He liked this bawdy foursome.

As he fixed their drinks, Ivy Hutchinson punched up three songs on the magic jukebox. The first to come on was the bullwhip-snapping "Mule Train."

Mark thought about how well this foursome tipped, and decided to wait until next time to take a baseball bat to the Wurlitzer.

4

The Spanish-style home of Vivian and Carl Singer, Tracy Russell's parents, was in the Mortero Hill section of Smoke Tree Estates. They had invested in it eight years earlier on the advice of the Findleys, their best friends, whose son was a real estate broker in San Diego. Now, the same homes were going for five times as much. Some of the fairway was visible from the living room window, and there was a breathtaking view of the Borrego Valley and the Santa Rosa

Mountains from the large patio in back.

The Singers never had a great deal of money. Carl had been a factory worker all his life, but had always taken good care of his family. The frugal Vivian, a department store sales clerk, had set aside a good nest egg for their retirement.

It was after they'd made their investment that the troubles came. First, there had been Vivian's long illness, which—even with their insurance—had cut into that nest egg. Then there was Don Russell, Tracy's husband, who had gambled away everything they owned before running out on Tracy and Joey when the boy was five, leaving his wife in debt. The Singers had done all they could, uncomplaining, although Tracy had quickly re-established a life for herself and Joey to relieve her parents of that burden.

When it became judicious to leave the cold, damp Midwest for Vivian's health, the "winter home" in Smoke Tree became their permanent residence. Bert and Muriel Findley were already living there. Carl and Vivian, who had lived and loved together over forty years, were happy in the southern California desert. They enjoyed golf; sometimes, Vivian swore it was the only religion she had. And they now had time to read some of the countless books they had collected during their marriage.

Carl had been waiting for Tracy and Joey out front. *God, not too long*, Tracy thought, *it's so hot*. A robust man, always a little overweight, his hugs had always been real "bone-crushers."

Happily, they still were.

"I'm ready for you this time, pal," Carl told his grandson. "Got every new edition of Trivial Pursuit that's out there. You'll probably take me on the one with all those Disney questions. But I'll get you on the old stuff, and the sports."

"Don't count on it, Grandpa," Joey replied.

"Dad, where's Mom?" Tracy asked as her son started emptying the car.

"Asleep, she's . . . asleep. All the excitement of waiting for you two, I guess. She sleeps a lot these days."

"Dad, is she . . . ?"

Carl took her hand. "The lungs seemed OK for the longest

time. And hell, it's been six, seven years since she had a cigarette. But lately—just lately—they started going real bad again. Doc Hoberg says it . . . won't be long."

"Damn," Tracy said softly, biting her lip. "I want to see her now."

"OK, princess; but listen, she's . . ." He hesitated.

"What?"

"The last couple of days . . . I don't know; I didn't think a problem with the lungs would do this to her."

"What do you mean?"

Carl Singer pulled a handkerchief from his back pocket and wiped his eyes. "You know your mother, the way she's always been. Hell, you're just like her! But there's something wrong now. She's . . . *different.* I can't explain it, princess. You'll just have to see for yourself."

Suddenly Tracy wanted to be with her mother even more than before. She glanced at Joey, who was taking their bicycles off the Foldarack. "Dad, can you . . . ?"

"The boy and me will handle things," Carl said. "Go on in."

No food smells inside. Cooking was Mom's passion, *especially* when it was for Tracy and Joey. *Nothing* had ever prevented her from fussing most of a day over one meal.

The house was comfortably air-conditioned. Vivian Singer lay on top of a pastel quilt. She wore a flannel robe that Tracy remembered from when she was a girl. Other than perhaps thinner, Tracy thought she looked no different than she had when they'd come to St. Louis last Christmas. Her pale, unlined face seemed peaceful, a slight smile creasing it. Vivian, at sixty-seven, was still a striking woman. But her long hair was unkempt, which surprised Tracy, for her mother had always taken special care of it.

Tracy leaned over and kissed her mother's cheek. "Mom, it's me," she whispered.

Vivian's eyelids fluttered open. Her smile remained as she gazed up at Tracy, but the eyes were vacant.

"'When I am old and grayheaded, O God, forsake me not,'" she said dully.

"Mom? It's Tracy. Joey and me are here."

"'Despise not thy mother when she is old.'"

"Mom!"

She turned to one side; her eyes closed. "So tired, Lucy. Must rest. Big night tonight; big doings . . ."

Vivian was asleep again. Tracy, her hand over her mouth, ran out of the bedroom. Carl was waiting for her.

"She didn't know me!" she cried. *"She . . . called me . . . !"*

Carl nodded. "That's the way she's been . . . not all the time, though. And if it matters, she doesn't seem to be in pain when she's like that."

"I . . . guess that's good." She was trembling and didn't want Joey to see her this way.

"Never thought you could get . . . *senile* so fast." He could hardly say the word.

She hurried away to help Joey—and herself. An hour later they were in the kitchen, Carl and the boy fixing sandwiches, Tracy sitting at the table, trying to understand.

Vivian appeared in the doorway.

Her face, more pallid than before, was twisted in pain from her efforts. But the eyes were clear, intense.

"Tracy?" she said. *"Oh, my baby!"*

"Mom?" Tracy stood. *"Mom!"* She fell into Vivian's arms.

"Let me look at you," Vivian said, sparring at tears. "Why didn't you wake me? I couldn't wait for you to come!"

"Mom, I . . ." Tracy glanced at her father, who put a finger to his lips.

"And who is this very tall young man here?" Vivian said. "Do you have an exceptionally sloppy hug and kiss for your old grandma, kiddo?"

"Sure do!" Joey exclaimed, racing toward her.

"Carl, what are you feeding them?" she asked. "That won't do. Let me get a roast ready, or some lasagna. They love my lasagna . . ."

She was having trouble staying on her feet. They helped her back into bed. She took Tracy's arm, pulled her closer.

"This sucks, baby, it really does," she whispered painfully, then was asleep.

Tracy Russell was tired from three days of driving, and didn't have to cry herself to sleep that night. But she did.

5

A few years after the end of World War II, Dexter Jones found a gold nugget of some size in Bighorn Creek.

To this day he could still take you to the exact spot where he first saw the blasted thing. It was where the creek cut through Madhouse Canyon, about three hundred yards in from the canyon's mouth, which was another hundred or so from those old adobe ruins. Not much flow in mid-autumn, and the nugget had been protruding from the east bank just above the water line. Raised a few eyebrows with that rock, Dexter Jones did.

Fifty years later, Old Dex was still looking for the second nugget.

He'd lost an eye over there in Europe, where he'd gone to fight as a teenager; had a leg busted up pretty bad too. The government still sent him disability pay. Some say he left a bit of his mind on the battlefield. But hell, Dexter Jones never worried about what folks thought, because he always did whatever he wanted to do, just so long as it pleased him and didn't hurt nobody.

Shortly after the find he'd picked himself up a big piece of land, dirt-cheap ("sand-cheap," he used to joke). It was off Bighorn Creek, starting about three-quarters of a mile southeast of Madhouse Canyon. He built a home out of brick and wood and any other material he could get his hands on at the time. Nice place, if you didn't mind all the junk in the yard. Powered everything with a gasoline generator for the longest time, before they ran lines in.

Since then Old Dex had explored every inch of Bighorn Creek more than once. From its source, a deep spring north of Madhouse Canyon, all the way to the Borrego Sink, where it emptied. Sure, he'd found lots of "color" in the creek bed, and sometimes what he thought was the tip of a vein.

But the only time Dexter Jones struck gold was fifteen years after settling in the Anza-Borrego Desert. That was when the big development company from San Diego put up its first billboard for Smoke Tree Estates along the county road. He sold them all his land, except an acre for himself; got a pretty penny for it, he did.

The ruins between his place and the canyon interested Old Dex. What was left of some old *rancho*, he guessed. Maybe a bomb-testing area during the war. He had looked into it, and discovered the truth. Christ, a looney bin, of all things! Not a lot written about it, other than it had operated briefly back in the 1870s. No wonder they called it *Madhouse* Canyon. He'd always figured it was because you had to be crazy to live out here.

Through the decades Old Dex had been to the ruins many times. Sitting there, slightly elevated, he could see the numerous turns of Bighorn Creek, could hear the eerie sound of the wind as it cut through the canyon like a scythe. It was one of his favorite spots.

But until two years ago Old Dex had never sat amid the ruins of Concordia Sanitarium at night. "Daytime was God's time," he said. "Night belongs to that pointy-tailed sonofabitch." Maybe it had to do with all those bombs that fell during one endless week of nighttime raids over there. Whatever. Old Dex had *always* been content to stay home at night, watch CNN and tapes of Oprah and *Wheel of Fortune*.

It was on a restless night that he was drawn out by the stars and the cool air and the distant howls of coyotes, and he'd wandered along the creek to the familiar place. Or maybe it was something else that called him.

Since that night, Dexter Jones's life had not been the same.

6

Jack Redmond was a creature of habit.

Every day at five o'clock—give or take a few minutes—he would settle onto the same barstool at the Arroyo Lounge and start on the first of two San Miguel beers. By six o'clock he would be gone.

Every day.

Jack Redmond was Smoke Tree's most famous resident. (*Infamous*, he preferred.) Next to the late Louis L'Amour, he was— arguably—the best-known and prolific writer of westerns in America.

His stories contained an undertone of mystery, as well as a fair dollop of romance, enough to titillate without getting sleazy.

These nightly sessions were—sometimes—tantamount to holding court. Aloof most of the time, Jack was accessible during his "reality hour," as he called it. Folks talked to him, had him sign copies of his books, which were sold in the country club's gift shop, and in other places around town.

Mark Alderson was a fan. In the orphanage, the foster homes—and later, in prison—Mark had found escape in books: the adventure tales of Edgar Rice Burroughs, the graceful prose of Ray Bradbury's fantasies—and the works of Jack Redmond. His favorite character (he and a few million others) was Jed Stockton, hard-nosed sheriff of Dragoon, Arizona, who appeared in more than two dozen of Redmond's novels. He had also chased the bad guys on the movie screen a few times.

Now, at seventy-three, Jack Redmond was no longer prolific. One book a year (blockbuster, of course), that was it. Like other Smoke Tree residents, he enjoyed talking to the club's bartender. Recently, he'd told Mark that in his nearly completed novel he was resurrecting Jed Stockton, who had "died" under mysterious circumstances at the end of a story nearly a decade ago. That was good news for all his fans.

"Pretty slow tonight," Jack said as Mark appeared, unbidden, with the writer's second San Miguel. He would nurse this one, after downing the first quickly.

"Not much different than usual," Mark told him. "It'll get real busy later. What's wrong, Jack, no one offer to buy you a drink in the last three minutes?"

Jack smiled wryly. He reminded Mark of Walter Huston's grizzled prospector in *The Treasure of the Sierra Madre*. "Wouldn't do any good if they *did* offer, you know that. Haven't cadged a drink since I was younger'n you."

"Yeah; I was kidding."

"Glad to hear it."

"Hear what?"

"You *kidding*. Sometimes I think your face would shatter like a glass egg if you cracked a smile."

Mark countered with a one-second grimace, then excused himself to serve another customer. Jack Redmond thought, Mark *Bradley*. Yeah, bullshit. A million hours of research for his stories had made him a competent observer of the human animal. He knew Mark was someone else; put up a hell of a front, the boy did. But he was someone else, no question about that.

Jack was still drinking alone when Mark rejoined him. "You see Dexter Jones lately?" the writer asked.

"Who?"

"Old Dex, that one-eyed relic from the gold rush."

"No, not for a while."

"Haven't seen him much either. Seems preoccupied whenever I do." Jack grinned. "Maybe he's got himself a lady."

"Could be."

"You think he's crazy?"

"I think he's—different. Never really talked to him enough to conclude anything else."

"Interesting man, he is. Spent some time with him years back; used him as a character."

"Oh?"

"Remember the old prospector in *Curse of the Dutchman*?"

"The one they were all after for his map to the lost mine? Sure."

"Well, that was Old Dex, verbatim."

Mark nodded. "I guess he is interesting."

Jack stared at him for a few moments. "I like our chats, Mark," he finally said. "Maybe because you're not nearly as close to Boot Hill as everyone else around here. Or maybe . . ." He shrugged. "I never talked about this much, not even to my would-be biographers, authorized or un-. Somewhere—back east, I guess—I have a son. He'd be older than you, ten years, maybe. Probably grandkids, too. I don't know; I fucked that up a long time ago. Booze, women, too much notoriety . . . Talking to you, well, makes me think of the relationship it might've been."

"I'm sorry," Mark said. "Isn't there anything you can do about it?"

Jack shook his head. "I left that boy and his mother with a lot of hate. No, it's better like this. They buried me a long time ago, got me out of their system. I don't need to rip open old wounds."

Suddenly *he* felt closer to Boot Hill than before. It must have showed. "You OK?" Mark asked.

He sipped his beer. "Yeah, sure. Hey, enough of that! You remember we were talking about Probe the other day?"

"The old word game? Sure."

"I can't find anyone in Smoke Tree who plays it. Rosie indulges me sometimes, but it's not her thing. You said it was once your favorite game. Why don't you come over to the house, and we'll see how good you are?"

"I . . . work almost every night. Sometimes I don't get out of here till after ten."

"You have days off, right? Besides, my bedtime's between midnight and one; has been most of my life. Can't sleep a damn before then. And Rosie insists on falling asleep with Letterman, so I can always stand some late company."

"Well . . ."

The writer's steel-gray eyes found Mark's. "Listen to me, son: I've sat here and listened to people trying to poke into your past. But I've never asked you a thing, have I?"

"No."

"Whoever you are, whatever you're running from—Mr. *Bradley*—it wouldn't bother me."

Mark stared at him, surprised. "Jack, I—"

"Hear me out. I'll say this once, then it'll never come up again. Carrying it around must be tearing you up. If you ever want to talk, I'll listen. And whatever it is, it'll never go farther than me. In the meantime, you could use a friend while you're *sojourning* in Smoke Tree, and I could use some competition for Probe. So I'll expect you after ten tonight. Directions to the house are on this napkin; it's in the Estates, you can't miss it." He finished his beer. "Now, I suddenly got the creative muse, and it's dead here anyway, so I'll see you later."

Jack Redmond got off the barstool and started for the door. Mark watched him walk out, too stunned to say anything.

Mark knew the man was right. If he could only talk about it.

But did he dare? How many times had he trusted someone in the past . . . how many times had he paid for his stupidity? If not for two extraordinary people, he might have thought that was the way of the world. And now, even those two were . . .

Did he dare trust another?

There were customers at the bar. For now the question went unanswered.

7

The womb of sand was endless.

As infinite as the void between stars and galaxies. A day might have passed, or a century; there was no way of telling.

He kept moving, because he was free.

Moving away . . .

. . . from what?

He wasn't sure. It was instinct that drove him. But where? Was *this* his world now? If so, maybe he had it all wrong: Not a womb, but . . .

A tomb.

Suddenly, freedom. The sand held him for a last moment, then—reluctantly—spat him forth. Now he was . . .

Somewhere.

Openness, surely more than before, but still closed in, limited. A narrow, finite void this time; across it he could see—more sand. No, he would not go that way. Stay in the center of   the . . .

. . . *tunnel, passageway, burrow, shaft.*

Moving again, moving . . .

Up.

Yes, he could tell now. He was moving up. And he could feel, too; feel the coolness descending upon him through the . . .

. . . *tunnel, passageway, burrow, shaft.*

Moving upward through sharp twists and turns, moving toward the source of the coolness, where the freedom would be absolute; moving toward . . .

A shadow.

Something dark and frightening; immense, filling up the way above him. Moving quickly, the shadow enveloping him, now not a shadow anymore, but . . .

A creature. Something of fur and claws peering with two large black beads that were its eyes, snuffling through the . . .

. . . *burrow.*

Its burrow, its home.

The kangaroo rat stopped, wary. It could not see him, but knew he was there. *A stupid creature!* he thought. Not a monster. No longer huge, but tiny, insignificant. Not something to be feared, but to be . . .

Used.

He knew how simple it would be. Moving again, toward the trembling animal, which did not turn and run. Distending within the burrow, pressing against its sand walls; growing, growing larger than the kangaroo rat as it neared. Expanding almost too much, engulfing the creature, then shrinking, shrinking down, contracting more rapidly than he had grown, seeing the face of the timid animal turn upward, then . . .

Inside the creature, part of it, but separate. Sensing rapid, minuscule thoughts that were meaningless. Dizzying at first, but quickly tolerable.

He willed the animal to turn, and it turned. He willed the animal to move, and it scuttled off through the sand labyrinth, its paintbrush tail dragging behind.

He *was* the kangaroo rat.

Moving faster than before. The air becoming cooler. Then, above, a new blackness, the good blackness of a night sky, stars flickering within it.

Stars. He remembered stars.

Out of the burrow now, not all the way, but enough to see this world.

His world?

The stars were familiar, and in the moonlight he saw outlines of mountains, and these were familiar too. But the sand and the plants with spines and the scrub, these were not of his world. So vast, so . . . empty. He remembered—people, lots of men in fine suits and ladies in long dresses, and buildings, so many tall buildings, and hilly streets crammed with carriages and wagons.

Not this.

He urged the kangaroo rat all the way out of its hole. Instinctively, the creature thumped the ground with its hind feet before emerging. Looking around he saw—nearby—flickering lights close to the ground, and shapes that could not be mountains or hills, and so were probably buildings. Maybe this was the place he remembered; maybe . . .

Close by, the sand was broken by something long and black; a ribbon, a wide black ribbon. No, not all black. A yellow stripe divided it in two. It came out of the mountains and went on to the place of buildings and lights. He had no idea what it was, but sensed that the kangaroo rat was not frightened of it, only wary. Well, then, if this stupid creature had no fear, it must be all right.

He moved onto the asphalt tentatively, sharp claws clicking on the hard surface. He would follow the ribbon toward the place he had seen; he . . .

The ground shook; slowly at first, then with increasing violence. He froze, looked up. From the place of buildings and lights, two giant white eyes appeared. There was a noise, too; loud, growing louder, deafening. Through his own fear he felt the turmoil of the rat. What was this thing coming toward him? Why couldn't he move? *What was this monster?*

Louder, closer, the eyes lighting up this terrifying world. He threw off the lethargy of fear, the powerful hind legs carrying him in a few leaps to the burrow, seconds before the thing on wheels roared past the spot where he had been. Watching from the safety of the hole he saw another pair of eyes—red this time, and smaller—on the back of the monster as it retreated toward the mountains.

So it hadn't been coming for him. The kangaroo rat was no longer concerned about it; he knew this. Whatever it had been, it was part of this world. He would learn more—but not now.

The animal was hungry, tired, having been busy afield since dusk; so was he, because he had chosen to share its body. They descended into the burrow, not far, where seeds and plant stems were stored in a food cache. The food was tasteless, but he felt the animal's strength growing from the nourishment.

Now it was full, and sleepy. It curled up at the entrance of the food cache and closed its eyes. At first he was terrified of joining it, fearful of another endless sleep like the one that had brought him to this place. No, *that* had been different; it would not happen again.

As images of what he had once been became clearer, the sleep took him.

CHAPTER THREE

Night Visits

1

Smoke Tree's sole hospital was the Valley Clinic, a fifty-bed facility in a modern, two-story building, where designers—judiciously—had made generous use of darkly tinted glass. It stood at the end of a long driveway off Las Palmas Road, the main thoroughfare, three-quarters of a mile past the small cluster of stores and offices that comprised "downtown." The homes and fairways of Smoke Tree Estates, a little over a mile to the north, were visible from the clinic's parking lot.

All things medical in Smoke Tree, outpatient services and such, happened at the Valley Clinic. Dr. Wayne Hoberg, the director, was personal physician to nearly two-thirds of the people, a formidable task for a man who, himself, was pushing seventy. Drs. Christine Goodrow and Ronald Porter, his younger associates, handled most of the others. Only a few chose to drive to the Scripps Clinic in Borrego Springs, seven miles farther west on the Seaway.

The clinic's workload was heavy during only half the year. Snowbirds would begin arriving in November and stay until the end of April, during which time Smoke Tree's afternoon temperatures averaged in the low seventies. This would swell the town's population of twenty-five hundred to three times that number. Hoberg always arranged for additional staffing, although sometimes even that wasn't enough in this geriatric wonderland.

Fortunately, May *did* roll around each year, its average temperatures of over ninety degrees sending the `birds packing off to Boise, Duluth, Pittsburgh, or wherever they came from. Diehard locals no longer had trouble arranging green time—as long as nine holes in one hundred-plus degree, bone-dry air was not a problem for them.

The clear, crisp night had long since extinguished the afternoon fires. Dexter Jones, lightly dressed despite the chill, stood on the sand across Las Palmas Road, opposite the Valley Clinic's driveway. He could see clearly across the clinic's well-lit parking lot, where the cars of the night staffers were scattered. Two orange-and-white ambulances flanked the emergency room door. There had been a shift change at eleven, less than an hour ago, and at the moment no one moved in or out of the building. It had been this way during the three minutes Old Dex had been standing there.

Would've been nice, he knew, to just drive his old Jeep CJ7 right up to the front door. But that, of course, couldn't happen. It was now, most of all, that he missed having his vehicle, because—with his work done—he still had a long walk back to his place, and he was so damn tired.

Yeah, but it was OK. Everything had gone real good, and he was happy.

Smiling, Old Dex turned. His flashlight threw a broad beam over the sand as he passed into the darkness through the creosote and brittle-bush.

2

Jodie Arnold was sorry her shift had begun.

Too much had already happened today, on the second shift. But for her the worst of it was an unexpected *code blue* ten minutes after she'd come on duty—heart failure in a patient recovering from a broken hip. They had the woman in the coronary care unit now, and it was quiet, giving Jodie the chance to catch up on paperwork.

Juan Mercado, the orderly, had pushed an empty gurney past the second floor nurses' station a few minutes before on his way to the elevator. Now the floor was devoid of activity. And quiet too, deathly quiet. Regulations. Don't disturb the old folks, they need their sleep. Jodie had a small radio at her station, currently playing Cream's "White Room" in a way it was never meant to be played, barely above a whisper. Two yards away, a person wouldn't know it was on.

One of the widely spaced air conditioning vents was directly above the nurses' station. Jodie imagined the builders of the Valley Clinic standing there more than a decade ago, saying, "Let's put it where it'll freeze their asses, piss them off and probably lower their level of efficiency." Actually, she had less of a problem with it than the other nurses. Even now, her sweater was draped over the back of the chair.

Then, suddenly, Jodie was cold in a way she never thought possible, cold inside, cold outside, the cold of long ice shards, hundreds of them, driven into her flesh with mallets. She looked up, wide-eyed, crossed her arms, thought about reaching behind for her sweater . . . if only she could stop shivering.

Two seconds later—if that long—the shards were withdrawn, leaving the skin horripilations known by the more cunning name of goose pimples.

Rising above what had been graveyard stillness (Clapton and the boys had finished their song, and nothing else had begun), Jodie heard a sound: the soft rustle of silk against silk, or the sliding of a sidewinder across a desert floor, or . . .

Jodie couldn't recognize it anymore.

"Someone there?" she said, still hugging herself as she peered cautiously over the top of her work station, half-fearing to see *something* being dragged, or perhaps dragging itself, along the floor.

The sourceless sound seemed not to stop, but rather to fade away.

As Jodie stared at the recently scrubbed tile floor, one of the elevators opened with a disconcerting *whoosh*. Startled, the nurse stepped back, nearly stumbling over her chair. Juan Mercado, grinning, approached the station.

"Hey Jodie, you okay?" he asked.

Another song had begun on the classic rock station: Fleetwood Mac's "You Make Lovin' Fun." Still shivering, Jodie looked up and down the floor.

"Yeah, fine," she said, not wanting to share her last few moments.

3

Mrs. Ida Maxwell in room 209 would be dead within a day or two. That was a given.

Last Sunday, before slipping into a coma, the eighty-four-year-old woman had begged Doc Hoberg to "…stop with all the medications and disconnect all the damn tubes and electrodes already." The doctor couldn't do that, not if he hoped to practice medicine in the state of California past Monday. But he could see to it that she went with as little suffering as possible. While still in control of her faculties, she'd signed a Living Will. There would be no "heroic measures" to keep her alive. She would die with dignity.

By Wednesday, June 27, Mrs. Maxwell had outlived her husband of fifty-six years by one month and an odd number of days. Doc Hoberg could remember that day last fall when both the Maxwells—until then as healthy as any octogenarians could ever hope to be—had been diagnosed as having cancer of the lymph nodes. Unreal, Hoberg had thought. The same damn thing at the same time! The tabloids would've loved it: *Deathwatch, Week Seven: Husband and Wife with Identical Disease Neck and Neck in Race to Grave.*

Mr. Maxwell had finally *won*, his cancer metastasizing at an alarming rate in his last month. Ida had been with him at the end. *Oh, the pain in his face!* she'd thought. She had prayed for death to take him quickly.

Now, the same pain had twisted her face, despite the coma and the medications, and who would pray for *her*? The staff, fond of the dear lady, could hardly bear going into her room.

Ida Maxwell's eyes snapped open. She looked around then sat up, nearly toppling an IV stand. Gazing toward the ceiling, she raised both arms; this time the stand was dragged closer to the bed, where it leaned precariously. Palms up, she stretched her bent fingers out then closed them in a sort of fist. Over and over, as though capturing something, then releasing it.

A minute later she put her head back down on the pillow.

When the heart monitor for the patient in room 209 went flat, Jodie Arnold resisted the impulse to call a *code blue*. She turned the machine off and hurried to the room, Juan Mercado following.

Mrs. Ida Maxwell was dead. No surprise. But the rictus of pain, frozen upon her for so long, was gone. She had passed on with a gentle smile lighting her face.

Jodie, brushing away some of the tears she reserved for these nice old people who came to her place of employment to die, also smiled. She knew Dr. Hoberg would be relieved.

4

Mark Alderson had paid seventy-five dollars for his old but serviceable eighteen-speed Schwinn High Sierra mountain bike. He'd bought it from Mrs. Ivy Hutchinson, who insisted she was "getting too old for bumping her buns all over the back country." She'd knocked twenty-five bucks off the price for Mark because he was "so damned cute."

During the past three weeks Mark had spent nearly every free morning hour (and some at night) on the bike. Riding the old Indian trails, the dry washes, paralleling the rims of active fault splinters, gave him a joyous sense of freedom that swept through his body like some indescribable high. On his rides in this eerie yet compelling wasteland, he was able to keep his eyes on what was ahead, over the next ridge or beyond the broad elephant tree, because he knew no one was behind him.

The last patrons had left the Cottonwood Room at nine-thirty.

Fifteen minutes later, Jerry Zirpolo shut down the lounge. After cleaning up, Mark had gotten out of there at five minutes past ten.

He still had not made up his mind where he was going.

Most every other night he pedaled the two miles straight home, a small, modestly furnished apartment in Ironwood Terrace, on Carrizo St., which was what the Borrego-Salton Seaway was called (for three blocks) as it passed through Smoke Tree. He'd gotten it cheap after the snowbird exodus.

Mark liked his apartment. Seven weeks was the longest he'd been in one place for some time. But tonight, the thought of going back to the apartment depressed him.

Tonight, he had an option.

What he had been unable to resolve in four hours was now decided in a minute. Mark pedaled toward Jack Redmond's place.

Indigo Lane: the most prestigious address in Smoke Tree. To reach it you went down the hill from the country club and turned left on Oasis Drive, just before the security kiosk. First past rows of casitas and smaller freestanding patio homes, then through the Mortero Hill section. A left on Verbena Road, just before the end of Oasis Drive, and you were briefly in a neighborhood of custom homes on one-third of an acre lots that overlooked the twelfth, thirteenth, and fourteenth holes of the golf course.

Verbena Road turned into Indigo Lane. These estate lots were between two and three acres in size, their elevation offering the most breathtaking views of the surrounding desert. So far, only five homes had been built along Indigo.

Jack Redmond's large, Spanish Colonial home was the last one: two stories tall, with a soft-lace stucco finish and custom arched windows beneath a terra-cotta clay-tile roof. *Better Homes and Gardens*-style landscaping flanked a circular driveway; liberal use of cacti and native rock had been made, as well as Aleppo pines, bamboo and fan palms. Although a three-car garage was attached, a two-year-old Ford Cherokee with the license plate JREDMND stood just off the edge of the drive, near the entrance.

Mark left his bike on the ground near the jeep. Had to be safe here, he figured. He first knocked on the tall, carved-oak door then pushed the bell when he realized no one could possibly hear that. Deep inside the house, Big Ben's familiar chimes echoed. Mark had guessed it might be an abbreviated version of "Ghost Riders in the Sky" or the theme from *Rawhide*.

"Well, hello there, young man. Jack mentioned you were coming."

Mark knew Rosie Shannon from a twice-a-week golf foursome, but until now had not placed her with Jack Redmond. Rosie, sixty-four, was an attractive woman, even in a faded pink terrycloth robe and floppy slippers. She led Mark into a wide, brick-tiled entryway.

"I'm not disturbing you, I hope," Mark said.

Rosie shook her head. "I was just reading. Got over a half-hour to kill before Letterman comes on. Ooh, I love that boy! Come on, I'll take you to Jack. He's in his study."

The buff-colored brick floor continued along a wide hallway with proportionately spaced clerestory windows, its walls lined with exquisite rugs that Rosie had collected through the years: Afghanistan kelim, Mexican serape, Indian Dhurry, and a smiling sun on a traditional Peruvian weave.

Jack Redmond's cathedral-ceilinged study was the ultimate sanctuary. If not for food and drink, a person could survive in here for a long time. No, that wasn't a problem either, Mark realized, noticing a small refrigerator behind a wet bar. Rich maple bookshelves on one entire wall, and half of another, were crammed with thousands of volumes. Most of the other wall space was filled with western paintings, original artwork for the covers of some of Jack's books. A thick leather armchair looked like something that Jack might have been sitting in for the past forty years; the chair had a matching sofa. A display of western bronze sculpture stood on a mahogany mantel above a used-brick fireplace. The centerpiece of the oak hardwood floor was a finely woven Navajo rug.

Jack was sitting on a backless, ergonomic chair behind a 19" monitor when Rosie and Mark came in. His work center was positioned so that, whenever he glanced up from his computer during the day, he had an unimpeded view of the Santa Rosa Mountains through a cantilevered bay window. Noticing the others, he saved his work and shut the system off.

"Damnedest thing, these computers," he said, joining Mark and Rosie. "They save so much time, especially in the later drafts, but I don't know if I'll ever be comfortable with 'em. Used to work on a manual Royal. Hell, must've done thirty books on that antique. Glad you could come, boy."

"Thanks for asking me," Mark said.

"I'll leave you two alone," Rosie said, "unless there's something you need?"

Jack kissed her, his hands gently cradling her face. "Nah, we're fine. Just don't let Mr. Letterman get too *intimate*, you hear, woman?"

Rosie winked at Mark. "I hope you whip his butt at Probe. He's done it to me enough times; enjoys it, too. Of course, I don't think there's anyone on the planet who can beat him."

She left. Jack said, "You want a beer, or maybe something stronger?"

"Beer's fine."

Jack pulled two bottles of San Miguel from the refrigerator (there didn't appear to be anything *but* San Miguel beer in it), then gave Mark a tour of the room. In his "trophy corner" were a multitude of awards from writers' organizations, honorary degrees from more than a dozen universities (Jack had never finished high school), and documents granting him tribal membership in the Hopis, Apaches, Shoshone, among others. Jack was especially proud of the latter. In his books, he had always portrayed Native Americans fairly and compassionately.

A bridge table was set up with the flat Probe racks, two sets of letter cards and the single set of activity cards. Jack clearly had little doubt Mark would be coming. The only other thing on the table was a bowl of nuts.

"Honey-roasted cashews," Jack said, "not that hamster food you have on the bar."

Fluorescent fixtures lit the room as well, Mark thought, as a night game at Shea Stadium. It was probably the bright light that made Jack appear so pale.

Before they started, Jack brought an ashtray and a pack of Marlboros to the table. Twenty-five years ago the crusty writer had done a brief gig as the Marlboro Man, had even worn his own Stetson. Hell, he wasn't Tom Selleck, but he was realistic-looking. Watching him light up, hands cupped around the match, Mark almost expected to hear the Marlboro Country theme music, adapted from Elmer Bernstein's score for *The Magnificent Seven.*

"OK, boy, let's find out how good you are," Jack said, shuffling the activity cards. Mark thought he sounded like a stereotypical western character, the Old Tired King-of-the-Hill Being Challenged by the Brash Young Gunslinger scenario.

Although it had been many years, Mark eased into the game as though he had played it yesterday. In Probe each player chose a word of twelve letters or less, picked out the appropriate cards and placed them face down in the slots of the letter tray. Each slot had a marked numerical value. Blanks could be placed at the beginning or end of a word, as part of the strategy. Then, following the guidelines of the activity cards (*Take An Additional Turn, Player on Your Right Will Expose a Card, Add 20 Points to Your Score*), you tried to guess your opponent's word, letter by letter. Having an extensive vocabulary helped; but sometimes simple words were as hard to guess as exotic ones, depending upon the letters involved and the positioning of the blanks.

Mark lost the first two games handily then was barely beaten on the third, only because Jack had drawn a *Quadruple Your Next Guess* card on a maximum fifteen-point letter. Jack nodded appreciatively.

"You *are* good. OK, we play without the activity cards."

This was the *pro* game, nothing left to chance. Mark won the first one, stumping Jack long enough on *saponify*—with some carefully placed blanks—to guess his word. For the next hour, Mark was victorious in one out of every three games. Jack had never worked so hard; he appeared to be having a ball.

They made small talk the whole time. Jack asked Mark nothing more intimidating than what part of town he lived in, how he liked the country club. Did he get along with Jerry Zirpolo, his boss? How about that Molly Forsythe? Did you ever see a set of knockers like that on such an old broad? Mark, still awed to be in *Jack Redmond's* house, tried not to ask too many dumb-shit fan questions. He was doing OK at it, he guessed.

At first uneasy, Mark gradually relaxed in the warm surroundings, with the familiar game in front of him, and with Jack's unaffected company. He had not forgotten what Jack had said to him at the bar. *Be careful*, he told himself; *be sure*. No, of course this wasn't *Julius*; nobody was. But . . .

Mark didn't care for the smoky room. Jack wasn't a chain smoker, but he did light up every twenty minutes or so. Glancing at him occasionally through the Marlboro-induced haze, Mark clung to the unsettling impression that Jack, despite his robust facade, was not in the prime of health.

At 11:52 Mark Alderson said, "I'm from New York; Long Island. Lived there most of my life."

Jack continued to stare at Mark's partly finished word. "With your accent, boy, that's a given. Same as saying, '*Yes, it does get hot in Anza-Borrego during August.*'"

Mark winced. "That bad, huh?"

"You've worked at losing it. But when you get excited? Like when we were arguing over how to spell *faldiral*? You sound like every Italian kid from Brooklyn in every World War II movie ever made. You got a W in there?" Mark shook his head. "Damn, what *is* that word?"

"My mother worked the streets," Mark went on. "Don't have a clue who my father was. They tell me that when I was two years old, her pimp stabbed her to death during an argument. You got a G?"

Jack, although staring at the letter trays, hung on Mark's words. "Yeah, there's one, right—*Jesus!*"

"What's wrong?"

Jack's face contorted in sudden pain. His body stiffened for a moment as he looked at Mark, then eased. But he was paler; not from the bright lights, Mark knew for sure now.

The writer took a deep breath. "Stomach cramp or something," he said. "Get those once in a while."

"You want me to call Rosie?"

"No, I'm fine; I just—*shit!*"

He grimaced again, reaching for his left shoulder—at least, that was what Mark first thought. Mark helped him to the love seat.

"Jack, what can I do?"

"My sweater." Jack indicated a coat rack. "There's a bottle of pills in one pocket."

Mark retrieved the small brown bottle quickly. It was empty. "I'd better get Rosie."

Jack nodded. "First door at the top of the stairs. She'll know where there are more."

Rosie Shannon responded quickly when Mark rapped on her door. Soon she had slipped a small white pill under Jack's tongue. The writer still held a cigarette between his fingers. Crushing it out, Rosie glared at him.

"You won't learn, will you?" she snapped. "Not until the big one comes."

Jack smiled weakly. "The big *what*, earthquake?"

"Damn it, Jack, I'm not kidding!" She looked at Mark. "He has a bad ticker. Over a year ago, when he was in L.A. consulting on a movie, he had a slight heart attack. *Slight*. Ever since then he's supposed to be doing something about his lifestyle. Yeah, right."

"Is there anything else I can do?" Mark asked.

"No, he just needs rest."

"Sure; I'll go then."

Jack looked up at him. "Damn it, boy, I'm sorry. And it was going good, too."

Mark nodded. "We'll do it again, soon."

"Tomorrow night!" the writer exclaimed.

"Jack, now is not the time—" Rosie began.

"I'll be over to the Arroyo at five, you'll see. We'll firm it up then."

"Good night, Jack, Rosie."

The woman hugged Mark, staying in the study when he said he could find his way out. "Tomorrow night," Jack repeated.

Mark stopped at the front door for a moment, looked back. The frustration he felt at being unable to share his torment—*he had come so close*—was overshadowed by the concern he felt for Jack Redmond.

He shrugged, put on his fluorescent yellow windbreaker, the one he always wore for night riding, and went outside.

CHAPTER FOUR

"The Way Of All The Earth"

1

Without a clock radio to jar her awake, Tracy Russell was a notoriously late sleeper. It was 7:40, Thursday morning, and her eyelids protested as she forced them open. Laying there, looking up at the unfamiliar swirls on the ceiling, Tracy wondered—in that moment when your cognizance is trying to catch up with the rest of you—just exactly where she was.

Then, she remembered, and understood why her eyes still burned.

The smells, that's what had awakened her. Bacon frying, coffee brewing, corn muffins fresh from the oven. *Mom's kitchen.*

Mom.

Deciding to take her shower *after* breakfast, Tracy climbed out of bed with a groan, threw on a robe and went to the kitchen. The wonderful smells that had greeted her mornings for the first two-thirds of her life were stronger. *Western omelets, surely there were western omelets too!* But how . . . ?

Vivian Singer was George Patton and Douglas MacArthur

rolled into one as she directed her troops from a kitchen chair. Carl and his grandson ran into each other as they rushed to carry out her every order. Tracy had no doubt Joey was holding his own. Still, it was a scene right out of *I Love Lucy*.

"Mom?" Tracy said.

Vivian turned. "Hiya, baby. Hey, is this the way to do it, or what! Cooking breakfast without moving anything but my jaw."

Tracy hugged her. "You're feeling better this morning."

"Uh-huh, pretty good."

Her mother wasn't lying, Tracy knew. She probably did feel better than at other times recently. And being involved in something she loved so much was therapeutic. But she still looked haggard, the pain cutting deep lines into her face. She would have difficulty moving from the chair.

"Hey, let's check that last batch of muffins!" she exclaimed. "Wouldn't want 'em turning into charcoal. Come on, kiddo, hop to it!"

"Yes sir, ma'am!" Joey said, snapping a salute.

"And you!" she told Tracy. "What do you think, you're on vacation or something? Let's get this table set. Use the good stuff."

Tracy smiled and hugged her mother again. Vivian smiled back, except the twist of her mouth didn't come out exactly as it should have.

An hour later, stuffed full from the incredible breakfast, Tracy took her shower and did her hair. Vivian, whom Carl had carried back to her bed, slept deeply.

2

Joey and his grandfather were immersed in Trivial Pursuit when Muriel Findley, Vivian's best friend, stopped by around noon. Vivian still slept. To Tracy, who had spent so many of her childhood hours in their home, the Findleys were like family. Muriel, excited, took Tracy by the arm and led her next door to have a look at her "palace in the desert." Joey could not be dragged away from his game. Carl promised he'd call if Vivian awakened.

An hour later, Joey knew Grandpa's heart wasn't in their

contest. Joey was winning too easily, and that was weird, because his grandfather wasn't one of those grownups who let little kids always win at everything.

Joey knew he was worried about Grandma.

"Wanna take a break, Grandpa?" he asked.

"What? No, not unless you do." Carl smiled. "You trying to quit while you're ahead, pal?"

"I was hoping you'd make some of your popcorn."

"The microwave stuff?"

"No way! The Orville Doofendurfer kind you pop in Grandma's big old copper pot."

Joey knew it was *Redenbacher*. But years ago, when he had been little and the word had been too big, it had come out the other way, and Carl had laughed so hard his side hurt. He was laughing now. Joey was trying to cheer him up and doing a good job of it.

"You got it, pal," he finally managed to blurt out.

"Need any help?"

"Nah, just relax."

When Carl returned with an overflowing bowl of buttered popcorn and two cans of Seven-Up, Joey was looking out the front window. "See anything interesting, pal?"

"There's this big guy working on the yard across the street," Joey said. "I mean *really* big."

Carl put the bowl and the drinks down. "Has to be Gary. He works over here too sometimes." He joined his grandson. "Yep, that's Gary Masten."

Joey looked up his grandfather, a puzzled expression on his face. "Uh, Grandpa, is he . . . retarded?"

Carl shrugged. "He has Down's syndrome. Many cases are more serious than his. Gary is nineteen years old but in his head he's about twelve or thirteen. They call that high-functioning. You know, pal, I bet you'd like talking to Gary. He's got one of the biggest baseball card collections you ever saw."

"Really? Bigger than mine?"

"Could be. He and Harry Keller, his guardian, drive over to San Diego a couple times a month during the spring and summer to catch

Padres games. I've gone with them too. They hit the card shops nearly every time. That's where I got most of the ones I sent you."

Joey was impressed. "Can I meet him now?"

"Sure, but just for a minute. Gary takes his work seriously. I can ask him to stop by—"

They heard a sound coming from the back of the house. A sound like . . . singing, or humming. Carl started for his bedroom, Joey following.

Vivian was sitting up in bed. The tune she hummed sounded sort of familiar to Joey. Something by Mozart, or Beethoven, or one of those old guys.

"Viv, are you okay?" her husband asked, sitting on the bed.

She smiled as she met his gaze. "Big doings tonight," she said.

"What?"

She winked at Carl. "They think I don't remember things, but I do; yes I do."

"What are you talking about, Viv?"

"The party; Virginia's birthday party is tonight. Big doings."

Joey stepped forward. "Grandma, what's wrong—?"

His grandfather quieted him, putting a hand on his shoulder. Vivian smiled at Joey. "Such a nice-looking boy," she said warmly. "'Children are an heritage of the Lord: and the fruit of the womb is His reward.'"

"Grandma?"

Suddenly she was somewhere else again. Humming the same tune, she lifted herself off the bed, hardly aware of Carl's helping hand. Joey backed away, still not understanding what was going on. Vivian hugged herself and began a jerky box-step in her bare feet.

Tracy stood in the doorway, hands over her mouth. Muriel Findley, a step behind, shook her head.

Joey looked up at his mother, trying to understand.

Had Carl not been standing so close, Vivian would have toppled to the floor. He helped her back to bed. She looked at him, still smiling, but weak.

"They think I don't remember," she said in a voice barely above a whisper, then was asleep.

Joey bolted from the room. Tracy was torn between going after him and remaining with her mother. She knelt by the bed, where her father already sat, his hand on Vivian's cheek.

"She's breathing OK," he told his daughter. "Go see to the boy."

Joey stood by the window, watching the retarded man—Gary, that's what Grandpa said his name was—ride down Oasis Drive on the biggest mountain bike he'd ever seen. He turned when his mother came in; tears streaked his face.

"Let's talk, champ," Tracy said.

Joey nodded and walked to the couch, where the untouched popcorn sat atop an oak coffee table. His mother followed. He almost didn't want to hear what she had to tell him.

3

Mark had no phone in his apartment. If Jerry Zirpolo needed him to come in earlier or something, he left word with Mrs. Jenks, the landlady. Mrs. Jenks liked the quiet young man in No. 6, who did odd jobs around the twenty-unit complex in exchange for a reduction in rent.

Mark had wanted to call Jack Redmond and find out how he was feeling (Jack had written his phone number on the napkin too, so Mark figured it was all right). But Mrs. Jenks had gone to Indio for the day, and aside from an occasional passing nod, Mark didn't know another soul at Ironwood Terrace.

He could have walked or ridden the two blocks to the phone booth in front of Rusty's Market, on Carrizo St. But the market was next door to the small, boxlike police station. No sense going out of his way to ask for trouble. He'd seen Smoke Tree's lawmen before; in a small town it couldn't be avoided forever. Police Chief Donald Upton seemed a personable sort. But his deputy, Steve Cornwell, was a big, scowling man in his thirties who must have figured the badge he wore was an invitation to swagger. Twice at the Arroyo Lounge, once in Rusty's Market, Cornwell had looked at Mark suspiciously, maybe curious why a young guy hung out in a townful of old folks. Mark wondered the same thing about Cornwell; he would've been more at home busting heads in some inner city precinct of the San Diego or Los Angeles Police Department. But as it was with bullies, Steve Cornwell probably didn't have the balls to stick his neck out.

No, Mark's life had to be structured, until he decided what to do with it. He spent nearly all his time in one of three places: his apartment, atop his bike on some desert trail, or the Arroyo Lounge. It was better that way.

Thirsty patrons started lining up in front of the bar at 10:45. Many twosomes and foursomes had hit the fairways early to play in the comparative "cool" of the morning. Even at that time the thermometer wavered three notches short of one hundred degrees. Jerry Zirpolo would probably open before the "official" time of 11:00; he often did. But before then, Mark headed for the first phone and dialed Jack Redmond's number.

"You checking up on me, boy?" the writer said in his crusty, good-natured way.

"No, actually I was more concerned about our game tonight," Mark replied. "I hope you weren't planning on using the old 'I'm too sick' excuse to keep me from whipping you."

"Now them's fightin' words, you no-account varmint!" Jack bellowed in his best Jed Stockton voice. "Actually, I feel pretty damn good. Keep the beer cold, boy. I'll see you at five."

Mark hung up the phone. His relief over Jack Redmond's proclamation of health was, he realized, considerable. Tonight . . . yes, for sure tonight, he would share the rest of his story.

Relieved, Mark went out to face the onslaught of Smoke Tree's thirsty seniors.

4

Vivian Singer climbed in and out of her bed all afternoon. Vivian Singer climbed in and out of *herself* all afternoon.

Once, when she'd asked, Carl and Tracy had helped her to the patio, where she loved gazing at the stark beauty of the valley, at the changing hues of the surrounding mountains as the sun moved across them. Choking down her pain, she had held Joey on her lap.

She hadn't spoken much, just felt the joy of touching those she loved so much.

Within half an hour, she "wasn't being herself again." After a sudden, short-lived burst of energy and Biblical espousals, Vivian was back in bed.

Looking worse than before, Carl had informed his daughter. *Sleeping harder.*

The cycle repeated itself a couple of times. Tracy, having ridden the emotional roller-coaster for barely twenty-four hours, marveled at the strength of her father, who had dealt with it so much longer.

Couldn't they do something? she had asked. Take her to the hospital, or at least call the doctor? No, Carl had replied. Doc Hoberg had already said all there was to say; so had Vivian. She knew the score, didn't want the agony prolonged, not a chance.

And most of all, she wanted to die in her own bed, looking at her own things, not in some sterile hospital room, with death on all sides of her.

Muriel Findley had discreetly stayed away for most of the afternoon. When she and Bert appeared at 4:30, Vivian had just fallen asleep again. Muriel was appalled at how haggard Carl and his daughter looked.

"You *must* get out of here for a while," she said. "Go on now; I'll stay with her."

Carl started to protest. Bert put a hand on his shoulder. "Muriel's right. You two go up to the club, have a drink. I'll take Joey over to our place, show him my wood carvings."

Tracy knew they were right and nodded at her father. Carl told Muriel, "We'll go for a little while, but only if you promise to call as soon as she wakes up."

Muriel assured them she would. Five minutes later (Tracy needed that long to *put herself together*) they started down Oasis Drive for the short walk to the clubhouse. Even the late-afternoon heat—the temperature had been a constant one hundred and four degrees for the past three hours—did not bother Tracy; it constituted a change from the artificial coolness of the house in which her mother lay dying.

5

At 4:47 Jack Redmond had not yet made an appearance at the Arroyo Lounge.

Not that Mark had expected him there early; still, for the past ten minutes he had glanced at the door a number of times.

The lounge was quiet; calm before the storm. Mark was refilling the bowls of cocktail peanuts when Mr. Singer came in. Mark hadn't seen the Singers for a while, and he had a good idea why. Usually they stopped in after a round of golf, mostly in a foursome with the Findleys. Mark liked Mrs. Singer. Last week Bert Findley had told him that she wasn't feeling well.

The young woman with Mr. Singer *had* to be their daughter. Thirty, thirty-five years ago Mrs. Singer must have looked just like her. Usually, anyone without white or silver hair warranted a second look in the Arroyo Lounge. This woman, Mark thought, deserved a second look *anywhere*.

You should meet my daughter, Mark, Mrs. Singer had said, a few times. *Maybe when she comes out this summer . . .*

They sat in an isolated corner booth. Rita Vasquez took their order—draft beer for Mr. Singer, Seven & Seven for the woman—and gave it to Mark.

"Hey Rita," Mark said, "how about letting me take them over? Tip's yours."

The waitress glanced at the table and winked at Mark. "Yeah sure, OK. Good luck."

Mark could see the weariness in their faces. They had been talking intently as he approached, but now looked up. Mr. Singer forced a smile above the surface of his pain.

"Nice to see you, sir," Mark said.

"Same here," Carl replied. "This is Tracy Russell, my daughter. Tracy, this is the Smoke Tree Country Club's most renowned bartender, Mark . . ."

"Bradley, but just Mark's OK. Actually I'm the club's *only* bartender—full-time, anyway."

"Hello, Mark."

You should meet my daughter . . .

They shook hands. Tracy's gaze held him firmly. He guessed that it was her usual way with people. Lately, it had not been his. But this time his eyes lingered. He smiled at her; although she did not return it, Mark felt it had nothing to do with him.

"Uh, how is Mrs. Singer doing?" he asked Carl.

"Not too well."

"I'm sorry. Please give her my best."

They needed to be alone; he needed to get back to the other customers. He put down the drinks, said that Rita would check on them and excused himself.

At 5:02 Jack Redmond had still not arrived. A flurry of new patrons awaiting the opening of the restaurant kept Mark busy.

But he remained aware of the empty stool at the end of the bar.

A minute later one of those patrons deposited his ample backside atop Jack Redmond's stool. Mark, busy at the other end of the bar, pointed the offense out to Jerry Zirpolo, who promised to take care of it.

6

The drinks calmed Tracy and her father. After a few words with a well-dressed man, the bartender—Mark—sent the waitress over with a second round, on the house. Other people stopped by their table briefly, and now Carl pointed out things of interest both inside and on the golf course.

The bartender, Tracy thought. *Funny, he doesn't look like he should be tending bar.* But what did that have to do with anything now? She shook her head.

Johnnie Ray's "Cry" spun on the magic jukebox. Before that it had been "Sincerely," by the McGuire Sisters. Tracy gestured toward the glitzy contrivance. "Be back in a minute," she told her father, and walked over to it. She ran down the list of song titles, wrinkled her nose, grimaced.

"That's about the same reaction I had when I started here. But I had to do a great cover-up to get the job."

Mark stood behind her. "You won't find Aerosmith in there," he continued. "The Eagles are missing, so's AC/DC. Would you believe, not even Neil Diamond, Streisand or the Beatles?"

"You're kidding," Tracy said.

"God's truth, *emmis*, as Jul . . . As an old friend used to say."

"You have to listen to this *all day*?"

He nodded. "If you punch up 'Mule Train'—it's C-7—you get to watch me trash the jukebox and the lounge."

"Now *that's* bad!" Tracy smiled. "Hey, I hope you didn't think I was rude or anything before."

"No, course not; with what you must be going through now?"

"Well, thanks."

"I like both your folks, but your mother is some lady. She cracks everyone up! And she makes people feel like they're part of the family."

"Yeah, that's Mom all right. Thanks for the kind words."

"I just hope whatever it is . . ."

Tracy's eyes met his again. "She's . . . dying, Mark."

"Shit, no," he said softly.

"We wouldn't have left her side for a minute . . . except that . . ."

Her eyes glistened. He touched her arm tentatively. "I understand. Damn, I'm really sorry. I know this sounds trite, but if there's anything I can do to help you or your family, please call me here at the lounge."

"That's kind of you."

What was happening? Tracy wondered. Why was she opening up to a perfect stranger? That wasn't her way. But this Mark Bradley seemed like a nice person, and he did care about her mother . . .

. . . and she really believed his offer was as sincere as it sounded.

Tracy had always considered herself a good judge of character. But five years after Don Russell she still questioned her abilities.

Johnnie Ray's emotional fit ended; Perry Como's "Papa Loves Mambo" came on.

"Looks like the lounge is temporarily spared a trashing," Tracy said.

"What—? Oh, yeah."

He doesn't look like he should be tending bar. "I know what we ought to do." She had a devilish glint in her eye.

"What's that?"

"We switch a couple of the records. Somebody punches D-4 expecting Bing Crosby, but they get Iron Butterfly; 'Ina-Gada-Davida.' That ought to palpitate a few patrons!"

Mark couldn't help grinning. "Great idea. I'll have to try it. Meanwhile, all those patrons at the bar *will* have palpitations if I don't get behind it and serve them something." His expression turned solemn again. "You really are like your mother, you know? Take care of yourself, Tracy. I'll see you around."

She nodded. "I hope so." Then he was gone.

Her father had left the table. Preoccupied with Mark, Tracy had not noticed it until she started back. Looking around, she saw Carl Singer enter from the lobby.

"What is it?" she asked. "Did Muriel call?"

"No, *I* called Muriel," he replied. "Just wanted to check in. Muriel said she's still asleep, but she's rolling around, kind of restless. It's what she's been doing lately right before she wakes up."

"Let's go back," Tracy said.

At 5:14, as the Arroyo Lounge continued to fill with patrons, Tracy managed to catch Mark's eye for a moment . . .

(No, he really doesn't look like he should be tending bar.)

. . . before following her father out into the desert heat.

7

Bert Findley brought Joey home two minutes before Carl and Tracy arrived. Vivian was awake, sitting up, three pillows wedged between her back and the headboard. Although they had seen her less than an hour before, Tracy and her father thought she had deteriorated considerably.

Because of this, Carl was surprised to discover she "wasn't being herself again."

"The candles," she uttered, her eyes wide.

"Viv, what is it?" Carl asked.

"The candles, the candles," she repeated.

"She's been saying that since she woke up," Muriel told them.

"So bright, the flames from the candles are so bright." One hand trembled.

"Viv, it's me, it's Carl."

"Too bright, too bright!" Her other hand trembled, then the rest of her frail body.

"Vivian, please!" Muriel exclaimed.

"The candles! Too bright!"

Her bed shook, as though the earth had shifted beneath it. Her eyes were opened wide, in fear, it seemed. Carl's hard glance told Bert to take Joey out of the bedroom. The others closed around Vivian, holding her arms gently but firmly to keep her from hurting herself.

"The candles!" she cried. *"Too bright! The candles! Have to . . . blow them out!"*

"Oh no, Mom!" Tracy sobbed.

"TOO . . . BRIGHT . . ."

The trembling stopped; the anguish on her face eased. They helped her down, until she lay supine.

"Dear God, Viv," Carl said softly.

Quieter now, she uttered, "'This day I am going the way of all the earth.'"

"Mom!" Tracy cried.

The eyelids fluttered; she looked at them, smiled. "I love . . . you all." The voice was little more than a whisper. "It's over, and now she'll be at peace."

The lines of pain were gone. Still smiling, Vivian Singer closed her eyes.

CHAPTER FIVE

Downhill Grade

1

Jerry Zirpolo was a stocky man of medium height with a thinning halo of once-black hair, now peppered with gray. His age was, roughly, somewhere between forty and fifty-five. He wore a tie behind the bar, and most other times also, because he was from Long Branch, New Jersey, which was backeast (one word, that was how he said it), and backeast you wore a tie whether you were going to a hockey game or a porno movie. He always helped out at the Arroyo Lounge, because he'd begun his career tending bar and still enjoyed the hands-on experience. Jerry was a great guy to have on your side; he could be a sonofabitch when provoked.

In seven weeks, Mark had done nothing to provoke his boss. Jerry liked his bartender, and more importantly, he liked that the customers liked his bartender.

Jerry knew that Jack Redmond had not made his usual appearance. After all, he'd been serving him for years. Sometimes Jack would be away for weeks at a time, off to Arizona or New Mexico researching a new book, or L.A. to work on a movie. But he usually mentioned it to Jerry, or someone else at the lounge, before he left.

At 6:13 Thursday evening, there was a lull in activity. Mark stood at the end of the bar, near Jack's empty stool, absently polishing glasses as he glanced at the clock. Jerry joined him.

"Kind of strange, old Jack not being here," he said.

Mark looked at him. "I asked some of the customers, but no one knew anything."

"I didn't hear nothing either. Small town like this, with all these old folks, you usually get news updates and gossip by the hour."

"Jerry, can I—?"

"Go ahead and call him, Marco. I'll hold down the fort. Use my office."

"Thanks."

Mark went in back and dialed the number. After the third ring Jack's voice came on with a brief message: *"Rosie and me are out, wait for the beep and say your piece."* Mark said a few words, hoping they were screening their calls. But no one picked up.

Jerry had a few emergency numbers displayed on his phone. One was for the Valley Clinic. Mark hesitated a moment, then dialed.

"Yes, Mr. Redmond was admitted this afternoon," a woman told him. "His condition is listed as stable. I can connect you with his room if you'd like."

As the nurse transferred his call, Mark felt relief wash through him. Rosie Shannon answered the phone.

"Nice of you to call, Mark," she said. "We finally got the old curmudgeon asleep after a lot of bitching and moaning."

"Is he all right?" Mark asked.

"The pains were occurring more frequently all day. But I still just about had to put a six-gun to his head to get him here. Doc Hoberg's going to start a bunch of tests tomorrow."

"I'd like to see him. How late are visiting hours?"

"Screw the visiting hours. You come when you can, I'll make sure you get in. But he might still be out cold."

"That's all right."

Mark returned to the bar and told Jerry the news. "Yeah, afraid it was something like that," Jerry said. "No sense getting attached to anyone in a burg like this. All of 'em go soon anyway . . . But ya know, Jack Redmond's a tough old bird. If anyone's gonna be around forever, it's him."

Mark had a break coming at seven. He'd worked through enough of them in the past. He thought about asking Jerry for extra time to make a quick run to the hospital.

Two large parties came in from the central hall. Rita Vasquez began running herself ragged between the bar and the Cottonwood Room. Even with Jerry's help, Mark could barely keep up with the orders.

2

At ten minutes past nine, with only a few patrons scattered through the lounge, Jerry told Mark to get lost. Mark pedaled down to the Valley Clinic. There was no breeze, and the night was too new to have cooled things off. It was still over eighty degrees.

Rosie had said that Jack was in room 211. An elderly security guard in the lobby pointed him to the elevators, hardly looking up from his Tony Hillerman mystery. But Jodie Arnold, beginning her shift earlier tonight, was a more formidable barrier.

"I'm sorry, but visiting hours were over at eight-thirty," she told him. "You just can't—"

Rosie hurried down the empty hallway, the soles of her Reeboks squeaking on the tile floor. "Sit on it, dear," she said. "He's family."

The nurse fumed; Rosie took Mark by the arm and hustled him off. "Thanks for the rescue," he said.

"Don't mention it. I've had enough bureaucratic bulldurham for one day. Jack woke up a while ago, and I told him you'd probably be coming. He's been fighting sleep since then."

The writer's bed was tilted slightly, his head propped by two pillows. He smiled weakly when he saw Mark.

"Thanks for coming, boy," he said.

"Wouldn't have missed it. Sorry, but I came over so fast, I didn't bring you anything."

"Like what? *Flowers?* Hell, the only things I want are a couple cold San Miguels and a pack of smokes, none of which they allow in here."

"Damn right," Rosie muttered.

"How are you feeling?" Mark asked.

"Not likely to make the next club dance, but otherwise, OK. They'll do tests tomorrow, probably kick my butt out the day after."

"Glad to hear it."

Jack's wry look softened. "I'm sorry, boy; Christ, I really am."

"Nothing to be sorry about. You didn't plan this."

"Still want to talk? No second thoughts?"

"None; but the first thing is for you to get well. Then, after I *let* you beat me at Probe a few times . . ."

They bantered for another minute. Rosie, who had stayed out of it, watched Jack's eyelids sagging. The sleeping pills were at work.

"He needs to rest now," she said.

"I'll stop back tomorrow," Mark told the writer.

"And don't forget the goddamn San Miguels this time!"

Rosie went out into the hall with Mark. A pallid Dr. Wayne Hoberg had just checked in at the nurse's station and now walked toward them. The man moved with tired steps, Mark noticed.

"Jesus, Wayne, you look like shit," Rosie said bluntly.

"Thanks," he replied. "I've lost two patients—two friends—in the last twenty-four hours. Not that it's the first time. Hardly. But you don't ever get used to it."

"Who died?" Rosie asked, subdued.

"Ida Maxwell, late last night. And Vivian Singer."

"Damn, I didn't know about Vivian," Rosie said. "I'm sorry."

"Anyway, let me go look in on your fella." He started off.

"I'll be right there." Rosie saw that the news had disturbed Mark. "You knew Vivian, huh?"

Mark nodded. "She was a neat lady."

"Want some advice, Mark? Go to San Diego, or Laguna Beach or Venice; find a job in one of those beach communities, where the median age is less than half what it is in Smoke Tree. Then you won't have to deal with this every damn day."

"Goodnight, Rosie. Thanks."

Mark ignored the cold glare of Jodie Arnold as he waited for the elevator. All in all, it had been a totally depressing day.

He thought of Tracy Russell.

An *almost* totally depressing day.

3

The stupid creature seemed to only have two things on its small mind: *finding* food, and keeping itself from *becoming* food.

It had tried to resist—though feebly—the force that had driven it from its burrow during the day, the terrible hot day, which was not its time. It could cope with the dangers of night, but in the daylight hours those dangers were different, not as familiar.

The entity called Bruno . . .

He knew his name now; it was one of the things he remembered. Bruno, you idiot-child, your baby sister is already smarter than you'll ever be. Bruno, in time you'll be punished by God for tearing the wings off that bird, but your father will punish you sooner. Bruno, in the name of the Lord, what did you try to do to that woman . . .

. . . had made the creature go out, because Bruno wanted to see his new place of being in the light of day, not in darkness with many-eyed monsters roaring and the stars mocking him with their coy winks.

Bruno had made the kangaroo rat go toward the place of buildings and lights. This was not the place he had known . . .

A name had come to him, or part of a name: San Fra . . . It was all he could remember.

. . . no, not the San Fra place, because the buildings were different, and there were no big hills under them, and he had never seen these monster-things in San Fra, not ever!

The monster-things from the night before; it had to be them, because they roared the same. There were eyes in back and front, although their angry glow was gone. And inside the monster-things—*actually inside them*—were creatures with two arms and two legs, like . . .

Himself.

No, like he had . . . once been.

Prisoners of the monster-things, food for them, he thought.

Then, a kit fox had leaped out from behind a clump of brittle-bush, and he had let the instincts of the kangaroo rat take it out of danger. Its sudden, sharp changes of direction had confused the fox, had left it skidding in the sand as it tried to stay close on the rodent's paintbrush tail. Finally, after sliding into a buckhorn cholla and yelping in pain, the fox had scampered off, and the kangaroo rat took temporary refuge in the burrow of one of its own kind.

Again moving toward the place of buildings, Bruno had seen another puzzling thing. Along the edge of the black ribbon with the yellow stripes . . .

Road?

. . . a man stood and waved at the passing monster-things. Soon, one of them stopped in front of the . . .

thing like he had been

. . . man, who opened a (*Door? Mouth?*) and climbed inside.

Climbed inside.

The monster-thing ran off on its black round legs . . .

Wheels.

They were wheels, like on the carriages and coaches that clattered along the hilly streets of . . . San Fra.

Things in which people rode around.

Bruno understood that now, and they no longer frightened him . . . not so much, anyway. He urged the kangaroo rat closer to the place of buildings, but now felt the creature's growing terror. It was fighting him; it did not want to go there.

He was not sure he wanted to go there either.

He allowed the creature's instincts to take over. The kangaroo rat immediately began bounding back toward its own burrow. (How could it know the right one, Bruno wondered, in the scrub-and-sand sameness of this place?)

But it was nearly all the way there when a red-tailed hawk dove out of a nearly cloudless sky, intercepting it amid clumps of creosote. Talons raked at its furry body, nearly finding the mark. Another inch and . . .

Bruno

... the kangaroo rat would have been carried off, quickly dying after struggling weakly. But it darted away, and the hawk had to veer off to avoid colliding with a towering ocotillo. Before it could dive again, the rodent found its burrow.

Stupid creature! Bruno thought. Stupid, weak, helpless creature! So weary now that it needed to sleep again. Weak, useless creature! He hated it, wished he could tear it apart ...

... with his hands.

Hands.

4

The boy sat on the front step of the house on Oasis Drive, reading a paperback. Mark left his Schwinn in the driveway and started up the walk. Mark recognized the book: *A Princess of Mars*, by Edgar Rice Burroughs. Not a later edition that would cost a kid an arm and a leg, but the old Ballantine one with the Bob Abbet cover art and a fifty-cent price. It looked in mint condition, and the boy handled it accordingly.

"Hiya," Joey Russell said.

"Hey. Isn't it a little warm for you out here?"

"Nah. I kind of like it, sometimes."

Mark indicated the book. "John Carter meet up with Dejah Thoris yet?"

"Yeah, but I'm not sure she likes him so much. You read this, huh?"

"That and all the others; long time ago. I'm Mark Bradley."

"I'm Joey Russell." They shook hands. "You know my grandparents?"

"Uh-huh."

The boy's face suddenly clouded. "My grandma died yesterday."

"Yeah, I know; I'm sorry. That's why I came by, to pay my respects."

"Just ring. Other people are in there. That's kinda why I'm out here."

"I know what you mean."

"Hey, can I check out your bike?"

"Yeah, go ahead. You take care of that book. It's special."

Joey nodded. "Grandpa's got old copies of *every* Burroughs. He says the same thing."

Tracy had hardly slept the night before. When she opened the front door and saw the man standing on the step, she became acutely aware of her red eyes, her drawn, pale face. She wore old Levis and an oversized chambray shirt.

"When I croak some day," Vivian Singer had once said, "don't nobody go walking around in *widow's weeds* or undertaker suits. Make like it's a party and come as you are. Just barbecue my bones and sprinkle what's left over the eighteenth fairway!"

It took Tracy a second for recognition to register. "Oh, hi," she said. "Thought I heard voices out here."

"I was talking to Joey," Mark told her. "Nice kid."

"Thanks."

"I wanted to say how sorry I am about your mother."

Tracy nodded. "She was hurting so much toward the end, so . . .

now she'll be at peace

. . . maybe it was better that it happened so fast. It was thoughtful of you to stop by. Why don't you come inside? I know Dad would want to see you."

Tracy led Mark into the living room. Carl Singer was there, the Findleys, and a few other people Mark knew from the lounge, though not by name.

Vivian Singer's body was being cremated that day. Even though the Singers had never been religious people, there was a brief service planned for nine-thirty the next morning at the Episcopal Church of the Desert. Mark told Tracy and Carl he would be there.

Muriel brought Mark a glass of lemonade. He stayed for ten minutes. But it was already past ten-thirty, time to head for the Arroyo Lounge and hang out the *Open For Business* sign.

Tracy was glad Mark had stopped by.

When she opened the door, Joey was back on the step. He had moved the Schwinn up on the walk.

"Whose is that?" Tracy asked her son.

"It's mine," Mark said. "Only wheels I have right now."

"Hey Mom," Joey said, "why don't you go riding with him sometime?"

Tracy wasn't sure if she wanted to clobber her son or hug him. "I . . . have a mountain bike also. Maybe when things have settled down, you can show me the desert."

Mark nodded. "Maybe I can. See you tomorrow."

Tracy watched Mark ride down Oasis Drive. *What's with you, girl?* she admonished herself. *Your mother died yesterday; the greatest lady on the planet is gone, and you're . . .*

Weeping may endure for a night, but joy cometh in the morning.

Joey was looking up at her, a smile on his face. Tracy cast a mock snarl at her son and went inside.

5

Before going on to the Singer house that morning, Mark stopped at the Valley Clinic. Jack was out of his room, having tests done, but he'd found Rosie in the coffee shop.

"I left at eleven," she told Mark, "but they said he had a pretty good night. Didn't look half-bad this morning. I thought he was being optimistic, but maybe he *will* get out of here tomorrow."

On Fridays, activity in the Arroyo Lounge increased; nothing like when the snowbirds were in town, but busy enough. Families arrived for the weekend to visit parents and grandparents. The Smoke Tree Country Club's rental *casitas* went for a nominal amount at this time of year. So did rooms at La Casa del Sol, a resort hotel that offered live-jazz-at-poolside every Friday and Saturday night until after Labor Day. Others came to Anza-Borrego to camp, hike the canyons, ride their mountain bikes along washes and primitive trails, or their ATVs on the dunes farther south. Those who knew how to meet the desert on its own terms always had a memorable experience.

Some time between three-thirty and four, Mark took an

extended lunch hour and returned to the Valley Clinic. Jerry Zirpolo let Mark borrow his Mercedes 300E, not only to save time, but because the temperature on the digital thermometer outside the door of the pro shop read one hundred and ten degrees. Even though the hospital was only a couple of minutes away, the air conditioner in Jerry's car could flash-freeze passengers in a matter of seconds.

Jodie Arnold was off that day. Jenny Fitzpatrick, the nurse on duty, had something approaching a personality. She smiled at Mark as he passed her station. Mark wondered what she would be like after visiting hours.

Jack was awake but looked exhausted. All those tests, Mark figured. Rosie, sitting at the bedside, smiled at Mark, but not with her usual conviction. It took Jack a couple of seconds to notice someone else was in the room.

"Hello, boy," he said weakly. "Hey, I don't see 'em."

"See what?"

"The San Miguels you were going to bring. I expected a six-pack at least."

Mark smiled. "They exploded on the way over. All that good beer floating down Las Palmas Road . . . How're you doing, Jack?"

"They poked and prodded me all day. I gave 'em hell the whole time. Probably hate me now. One of 'em will give me cyanide instead of a sleeping pill tonight, or inject acid into my IV tube."

"It's when he *stops* giving them hell that we worry," Rosie said.

"You on a break from the lounge?"

"Uh-huh."

"Can you spare some time?"

"A little."

Jack looked at Rosie. "Be a good kid and get it, OK?"

Rosie started to say something, but instead shrugged and walked over to the closet. She brought out the Probe game. Jack motioned for Mark to take her chair.

"One game," Jack said, "*mano a mano*, no activity cards. Winner rules the galaxy."

Mark sat down. "Jack, are you sure you want—?"

The writer looked at him. For an instant Mark thought his wan face was almost childlike in its entreaty.

(Please oh please Mommy don't turn off the night light because if you do the thing in my closet will . . .)

"Please, Mark, just this one game."

Mark nodded. "You got it."

It was the seventh game of the World Series; the Stanley Cup. Overtime in the Super Bowl. Mark's *ornithosis*, blanks at both ends, against Jack's *roquelaure*, no blanks. In the end, as Mark fumed about wrongly guessing a blank and losing fifty points, Jack filled in the few letters remaining on his opponent's tray.

"What'd you say yesterday, about *letting* me win?" Jack said. "Smart-assed kid."

"So as ruler of the galaxy, what's you first move?"

"I might zap all the assholes on this planet. But that would only leave you and me and Rosie, and what would the three of us do for the rest of our natural lives? So instead, my first move will be to throw your butt out and get some sleep. Christ, I'm beat!"

The energy of the game had drained him. He could barely keep his eyes open. Mark stood and put a hand on Jack's arm.

"I'll see you tomorrow," he said. "You owe me a rematch."

"At my place, I hope . . ."

His eyes shut; he breathed heavily. Mark started folding the game racks.

"I'll clean that up," Rosie said.

She walked him out. "What is it, Rosie?" Mark asked. "Did they find anything today?"

"Tests are still inconclusive. Christ, poor Wayne Hoberg looks like *he* should be in one of these beds. But he's concerned, and he mentioned the possibility of bypass surgery."

"I was afraid of that. But if it helps . . ."

Rosie smiled at him. "He likes you, Mark. Hardly anyone else has come by, or even called. Just the wire services, and that's because some goddamn local stringer put the word out. Thanks for being his friend."

She hugged him and went back inside. Mark walked to the elevators, ignoring the even bigger smile flashed at him by Jenny Fitzpatrick.

6

Scott Millard was finished with California.

Whatever little good had happened to him in three years out here had been overshadowed by everything else. Now, he was on his way back to Shaker Heights, Ohio, which he figured may take a while, considering he had a grand total of three dollars and a few coins in the pockets of his jeans.

Home to Shaker Heights, hoping Rhea Millstein would have him back. But then, could a mother refuse her only son?

For the first nineteen years of his life he had been Scott Millstein, son of Howard Millstein, a small, bookish man of limited personal vision, and Rhea Millstein, a big-boned woman six inches taller than her husband in her stocking feet, the unquestioned ruler of the roost. She had put Howard into his grave before Scott was twelve. Scott had been a frail boy, always the shortest in his class. Even now, with prospects of additional growth long past, he had to stretch to claim he was 5'7".

So Rhea had fed him . . . well. Wouldn't want anyone to think her little Scott was a *faygela*. Instead, he had been short and chubby, her *butterball*. She called him that—proudly.

Scott the butterball, short and chubby—the cross he bore all through grade school, and Hebrew school, and high school.

When Scott took an interest in dancing, Rhea was fit to be tied. *Oy*, only *faygelas* did that!

Scott not only enjoyed dancing, he was good at it. He lost fifty pounds in the year prior to the Great Escape, when he bought a one-way ticket and rode the Trailways bus west in the general direction of California, never once looking back at Shaker Heights.

California! Rhea Millstein had exclaimed. *Everyone* out there is either a *faygela* or a junkie!

Scott had arrived in Los Angeles with a lot of hope and the little bit of money he had managed to withdraw from his account under Rhea's nose (it was in her name also). He had shared a shabby Reseda apartment with, at various times, Brian, Jay, Emilio, Tom, and a couple of guys named Robert.

One of the Roberts had been an especially good friend.

Are you hearing this, Rhea, your little butterball really is a faygela.

His dancing had been good enough to get him second and third callbacks from auditions. He had filled in for a couple of weeks on a stage musical, did a few local commercials, one national (the dancing bubbles of a toilet bowl cleaner; a lot of people probably saw it). But never The Break.

The endless parties had done him in, and the drugs. Marijuana, crack, PCP, meth, crank; there was little on the menu that Scott passed by. They were his sustenance.

They were what finally put him on the street.

No work, no money . . . no friends. Scott had become a Homeless Person. But being a Homeless Person was much better than being Gay. Folks were still turned off by Gays, but Homeless Persons had Comic Relief and Phil Collins and even presidents on their side. Yeah, what a life. Another day in paradise.

When he had gone two days with no more food than a couple of stale rolls and some wilted salad he had begged for at the rear door of a restaurant, Scott Millard made the decision to go back to Ohio. His dancer's body, once lithe and sturdy, now weighed in at one-thirteen.

Still, he left in a roundabout way. The other Robert had moved down to Oceanside and had once invited Scott there. So Scott had walked/hitched south, hoping to prolong (or even postpone) the return to Rhea. But Robert no longer lived at the address Scott had.

On the street again, this time the streets of Oceanside, he thought about going on to San Diego, thirty-odd miles farther south. But during the first night he was accosted by three drunken Marines, who tried to take his money, then kicked the shit out of him when they found he didn't have any.

In the morning Scott Millard's thumb was pointed eastward.

Tough getting a ride when you looked as bad as he did. Some guy in a dusty pickup, on his way to Dudley's Bakery in Santa Ysabel, let him ride in back. Santa Ysabel was up in the mountains, not exactly on the beaten path. What the hell, Scott thought, it was east.

But in the rural back country of San Diego County, no one

else stopped to pick up the disheveled young man toting the torn blue backpack. On the advice of the guy in the pickup he headed north on State Route 79. "Hardly any hills that way," he'd said, "and you want to work yourself up to I-10 anyway."

The guy had given him five bucks, some of which he'd spent in Santa Ysabel for food. No one picked him up on the lightly traveled road. Eight miles later he turned right (east again) on S2. A sign read: *Anza-Borrego Park Headquarters, 23 Miles*. "All downhill on the Montezuma Grade," the driver had said, "then flat as a pancake for a whole long way."

As he walked along, still shunned by motorists, Scott figured things could be worse. He hadn't done drugs in over a month now. Before leaving L.A. he'd had a blood test at a free clinic. *Yeah, Rhea, I may be a faygela, but I don't have AIDS.* Whenever he reached Ohio, he could make a clean start.

Scott was exhausted. The high desert was nearly as hot as the valley floor. Other than some water in a plastic milk container and half a loaf of Dudley's sheepherder bread, Scott had nothing else. At least he had that.

Late Friday night, Scott left the shoulder of the road and curled up in a field. He had always been a positive thinker, despite Rhea, and despite the California Experience. Today he had taken a big step, so it had been a good day.

Tomorrow would be even better.

CHAPTER SIX

Hands

1

Deputy Steve Cornwell climbed behind the wheel of one of the department's two black-and-white Chevy Blazers, his destination Rainbow Tree Farm. Before pulling away he noticed someone walking down Las Palmas Road. That cutie-pie barman, he thought. Same guy all the old farts seem to cotton to at the lounge, him always talking to them real friendly-like.

Hell, hardly anyone ever sat down and chatted with him. Maybe it was their good old-fashioned respect for his uniform, he figured. He wouldn't for a minute have considered his Neanderthal intellect as cause for the turnoff, no sir.

Nah, the guy didn't belong in Smoke Tree; that annoyed Steve Cornwell all to hell. Mark Bradley, his name was. He'd wanted to run a make on it, but the Chief told him not to waste his time.

Damn cutie-pie. And where the hell was his hot shit bicycle this time?

Cornwell made a u-turn and paralleled Bradley. Rainbow Tree Farm was in the other direction. He'd done this a few times before, when Bradley had been on the bike. Glancing to his left, the guy noticed him. Cornwell grinned and touched the brim of his Resistol hat. The cutie-pie nodded and looked ahead.

The Church of the Desert, which looked to be Bradley's destination, stood nearby. Bradley angled across a scrubby sand lot to the parking area, freshly oiled last month. A teal blue Toyota Cressida with a Missouri license plate had just pulled in. Cornwell knew Mr. Singer and figured the woman and boy were kin, owing that the old lady had just died. The woman: fine-looking, he thought, after a double take. Bradley shook hands with the man and boy; after a few words, he and the woman hugged.

Damn cutie-pie. Cornwell pulled away in a squeal of rubber. One day he'd find out what the hell he was doing in Smoke Tree.

2

Mark had left the Schwinn in his apartment. Somehow, riding a mountain bike up to the door of a church for a funeral service seemed inappropriate. Besides, the Church of the Desert was only a quarter-mile from Ironwood Terrace.

The service was brief. Rev. Claude Mather remembered Vivian from volunteer work she'd done, and had some kind things to say about her.

The ashes would be sprinkled on the golf course late that night by a chartered plane. "Don't want to shake up the old folks in the daytime," Vivian had said. None of the guests needed to be on hand for that.

Afterward, in the parking lot, Tracy told Mark they would receive visitors all weekend. "I'll stop by tomorrow morning," Mark said.

"Can we drop you anywhere?" Carl asked.

Mark shook his head. "I live close. Have to get to the club. We open earlier on Saturdays."

"Yeah, I know," Carl said. "I'll tell you, if the parade of people goes on all day, you may see us over there later."

Mark was looking at Tracy when he said, "I'll be glad to see you."

Saturday *was* busy, and to make it worse Eugene Price, who worked on Mark's rare days off and at some peak hours, phoned in sick. Mark and Jerry pushed themselves to the limits in keeping everyone happy.

The magic jukebox played almost non-stop. "Mule Train" came on at least once an hour. Mark ignored it.

Tracy and her father stopped at the lounge around six-thirty. The tables were full, and people stood two-deep at the bar. Mark saw them, but they turned and left before he could help them find a quieter spot. He couldn't blame them for wanting to get away from people.

Mark's first breather came after eight. He phoned the Valley Clinic. No, Jack Redmond had not been discharged. Mark hadn't figured that would happen. He rang the room; no answer. Concerned, he had Rosie Shannon paged.

Rosie had been crying; Mark could tell from her voice. "Jack had a massive heart attack early this afternoon," she said.

"Jesus, no!"

"Wayne Hoberg and Chris Goodrow did a triple bypass; just finished a little while ago. They've got him in the coronary care unit now. But . . ."

"What?"

"Doc says the damage was too great. He's not going to make it."

3

The guy in the pickup who had given Scott Millard a ride yesterday hadn't said anything about a turn-off for Anza-Borrego. Or maybe he had, and Scott didn't remember; that wouldn't have surprised him, he sucked with directions. Anyway, there it was, not ten minutes after Scott started off again in the . . .

Morning?

He'd chosen, at random, a comfortable spot amid some California lilacs. His sleep had been dark, dreamless, his fatigue keeping him immersed longer. The sun was high when he awoke. Hell, as far as he knew, he'd slept past noon. He'd traded his cheap digital watch a week ago for a meal.

Scott was now on County Road S22, which didn't mean a thing to him. Cars, campers, and pickups with shells passed intermittently. Sometimes he didn't even bother to look, just wagged his thumb. He was honked twice, sworn at once, mostly ignored.

Then, at the edge of a no-horse town called Ranchita, a pimply kid in a rusty old Pinto was crazy enough to give him a ride. He even offered Scott a small Kit-Kat bar.

"Hell, they was eight for a buck over at the AM/PM," the kid said, shouting to be heard over Soundgarden blaring from two Bose speakers, undoubtedly worth more than the vehicle itself. "Got three bucks' worth. Take another if you want, man."

They rode down the spiraling Montezuma Grade, Scott oblivious to the hazy sweep of the Borrego Valley as he managed to nod off, even with the loud music. A disturbing thought intruded on his lethargy: Ohio was a long way off, and he wasn't going to make it there on an occasional Kit-Kat bar and the rest of his Dudley's bread.

No, can't think that way! he admonished himself. Just get to the interstate and everything will be fine. Some long-haul trucker who hated boredom would take him most of the way. Four, five days, and Rhea Millstein would again set eyes upon her beloved son.

Gevalt, *what happened to my little butterball?*

The kid let Scott off at the eastern edge of Borrego Springs, the first town at the base of the grade. "You stay on S22 till you come to Highway 86," he said. "Take 86 north a bit and bang, you're in Indio, and you can't miss I-10."

Right, piece of cake, Scott thought.

"Someone'll pick you up," the kid added. "Shit, folks don't like to see no one walkin' along when it's a hundred-ten friggin' degrees."

Six eastbound cars roared past during the first half-hour. To the drivers, Scott might as well have been another roadside ocotillo plant.

He found brief shelter from the sun in a restroom at a campsite, where he refilled his plastic bottle and ate some more bread. Pulling off his tattered T-shirt he soaked it thoroughly and wrapped it around his head, then took a disapproving look at the wild man in a mirror.

An endless hour later, still walking, Scott wasn't sure if he'd even stuck his thumb out for a while.

He could see buildings ahead, another town. A sign off the road, not that far ahead, blurred, until he stood a few feet from it. *Welcome to Smoke Tree*, it said. He wasn't impressed.

Had to be a store there, Scott thought; buy something to eat. No, it was better to hang onto the few dollars for a while. Maybe at a restaurant, and he could beg some food. Wouldn't be the first time. *Feed the Homeless Person, do your soul good.* Christ, he wished he didn't look so crazy.

The sun was down enough for the shadow of the sign to be cast over a large rock, a yard back from the asphalt. Scott sat down, only now acknowledging the crushing weariness he'd been denying all day. He took a couple of swigs from the bottle. The water was warm, but it didn't matter. He decided against more bread, which his raw throat was finding harder to swallow.

He first noticed the animal standing (yeah, it stood on its hind legs) next to a barrel cactus, eight feet away. A mouse, he guessed as his eyes focused upon the creature. It emerged from the shade of the cactus, came another couple of feet closer, reared again; its eyes never left the man.

Scott didn't know exactly what kind of animal this was, nor did he care. All he knew was that it was a rodent, and his recent experiences with rodents, in run-down shelters and squalid back-alleys, were not pleasant.

"Get out of here, you filthy thing," he muttered, his voice sounding like two pieces of sandpaper being rubbed together. He waved the back of his hand at the creature half-heartedly.

The creature did not scurry off but came closer. Then it leaned far over to the right, like a sailboat yawing in an unexpected gust. Its entire body stretched out thinly; the short front paws scrabbled at the air.

What the hell's wrong with it? Scott wondered. *Maybe it's got rabies or something . . .*

He clutched at his head as something distended inside his brain. The pain was intense, but brief. He thought: *What happened? I . . .*

Another thought, not his: *Mine now.*

What? I don't under—

There was darkness, the warm embrace of ...

Sleep?

... into which Scott plummeted.

4

Bruno willed the body to stand; it obeyed, but shakily. Not used to it, that was all. But he would learn quickly, just as he had with ...

... the stupid creature.

The kangaroo rat still twisted, although its convulsions eased. Bruno's tentative steps toward it were those of a small child who had just discovered what an incredible ability it possessed. The creature regained its equilibrium, but before it could bolt away a shoe came down on its paintbrush tail, pinning it to the sand.

While the animal struggled, Bruno looked down at his new body through the man's eyes. Stretching out his arms, he studied the ...

Hands.

He had hands, like before, and his body shuddered at the thought, because he had done wonderful things with his hands, and would again.

Bending over, he caught the kangaroo rat. The thing nipped him, but he paid this no mind as, thrusting both thumbs into the soft underbelly, he tore it in two, noting how nearly exact the halves were.

He threw the spurting remains down to the sand, where some other creature would soon feed upon them.

Something troubled Bruno ... something he couldn't remember. It had just happened, and it had ...

... frightened him.

The fear he had felt running away from the blackness, only worse, so much worse. It had been brief, but so strong.

What was it?

Still, it eluded him. But no matter, because it was gone, and

maybe it would not be back. And he had other things to do, because
he was a man again, and he had . . .

Hands

The place of buildings was near. He could go there now, because
he looked like those who rode in the monster-things, and he would
not be noticed as he learned about his new world.

This body needed nourishment; he could tell that. Walking
tentatively, he started toward Smoke Tree.

5

Deputy Steve Cornwell emerged from Roger's Barber Shop,
where Roger Penrose had given the lawman his usual bi-monthly
buzz cut. As he climbed into his Blazer, he noticed the drifter on
the other side of Carrizo St. Cornwell thought: *Jesus, paint one of
them Nazi crosses on his forehead and you'd swear to God it was Charlie
fucking Manson!* An elderly couple in front of Nutz n' Boltz Hardware
& Sundries had given the dirt-bag a wide berth, and were now tut-
tutting from behind.

Cornwell shrugged, snapped the Resistol hat down over his
newly mown head and drove across the road, getting out of the Blazer
and intercepting the drifter in front of the Smoke Tree branch of
Wells Fargo Bank.

"Something I can do for you?" the deputy asked.

The drifter stopped, stared wild-eyed at Cornwell. "Need
nourish . . ." he began.

"Come again?"

Bruno probed the memory of his host. "I . . . want to buy some
food."

"Yeah? You got any money, boy?"

The dirt-bag thought again, then dug in his pocket, extracting
some bills and change. He held them out in an open palm. "Money."

Cornwell laughed. "Yeah, you're loaded. Get yourself a nice
dinner out at the country club." The smile faded. "Now listen, boy,
these old folks around here get edgy when your kind wanders in. That's
what I get paid for, keeping them from getting edgy, you understand?

So why don't you keep walking to the other end of town, which is just past that block there, you see? And I'm gonna stand here to make sure you get well past it, and this way there won't be no trouble. You follow that?"

The drifter pointed past Cornwell, who was six inches taller and outweighed him by nearly a hundred pounds, in the direction of Rusty's Market, between the bank and the police station. "I want to buy food."

He started toward the store. Cornwell, furious, grabbed his arm. *Goddamn fucked-up junkie.*

"Listen, boy, I told you—"

Turning, the drifter pulled out of the deputy's grip. "I want to buy food," he said again, dully.

This time Cornwell placed his bulk between the dirt-bag and the store, thrusting a finger in the man's face. His smell nearly caused the deputy to gag.

"You sorry bastard!" he exclaimed. "You're about this close to me hauling your ass in! Now you get out of here!"

Sorry bastard.

Bastard.

Around your neck . . . poor bastard.

One hand batted the finger away; the other clutched at the deputy's throat, slim fingers digging into the flesh. Cornwell stared, wide-eyed, into the face of the other; into what—for a moment—he thought was the face of Death itself.

Yeah, maybe this was old Charlie fucking Manson, got himself sprung from the California State Prison at Corcoran.

But the grip was weak, and Cornwell, recovering from the surprise, knocked the arm away, nearly breaking it. Enraged, he pushed aside the matted beard and returned the injustice, his meaty hand encircling the thin neck.

"Stupid little fuck!" he cried, lifting Scott's rag-doll body a foot off the ground. "Now I'll run your ass in for sure!"

He struck the man twice, and would have again, but a small, curious group was gathering. The drifter moaned, barely conscious as Cornwell dragged him to the station.

Chief Donald Upton peered over his old metal desk at the red-faced deputy. "Whatcha got, Steve?" he asked.

"Sumbitch dopehead drifter!" the deputy exclaimed. "Tried to choke me!"

Upton came around and looked at the limp, moaning heap on the floor, where Cornwell had dumped him. "Must've been a bitch for you to subdue."

Cornwell scowled. "It's the truth, Chief, and there were witnesses—!"

"All right. Throw him in the tank, and don't forget to log whatever's in his backpack. I'll have a talk with him, soon as he's *feeling better*."

There were two empty eight-by-ten cells in the back room. Cornwell opened the one farthest from the door. He was carrying the guy's body by the belt, as one would tote a gym bag. The cell contained three narrow cots. Cornwell held the prisoner over one, hesitated, glanced at the door; the sheriff was still up front.

Cornwell slammed the body against a brick wall and dropped it on the cot. Charlie fucking Manson was no longer moaning. He locked the cell and left.

6

Dr. Wayne Hoberg was tired in every possible way a human being could be tired. It had been a lousy day; scratch that, it had been a lousy week. Times like this, he wished he'd chosen pediatrics instead of geriatrics; would lose a lot fewer patients that way.

That might've been why, on the way to his car in the Valley Clinic parking lot early Saturday evening, he was less than thrilled to see Dexter Jones.

Oh, he liked Old Dex all right, as much as anyone in Smoke Tree liked the eccentric coot. Heck, he'd been his doctor forever. But just recently—the past year or so, Doc Hoberg figured—he must have bumped into Old Dex a million times; here, mostly, but at the club too, downtown . . . The inevitable jawing took time, and with Hoberg's responsibilities, he usually had little of that to spare.

"Hiya, Doc," the prospector called. He leaned against his jeep, which he'd parked next to Hoberg's maroon Lexus.

Hoberg nodded. "Dex. Good to see you. Everything OK?"

"Yep, fit as a fiddle." He tapped his chest then squinted his one eye. "But you don't look so great yourself."

The doctor scowled. "Thanks for reminding me. Actually, I was on my way home to get a few hours' sleep."

"Yeah, well don't let me stop you. I know you just lost a couple; hope that lets up for a while."

Hoberg shook his head sadly. "You didn't hear, then. I figured it was all over town."

"Just got in from my diggings. On Bighorn Creek, down toward the sink, I found this vein, see, and it might be . . . Heard what, Doc?"

"It's Jack Redmond, Dex. His heart. Chris Goodrow and me went in, but there wasn't much we could do. So much blasted damage! If that stubborn fool would've come to see me for a checkup a year ago . . . Sorry, Dex, I know you were friends."

"Then . . . he's gone?"

"No, but he doesn't have long. Rosie's with him now. I'm coming back after I get some sleep."

"Yeah, sure, Doc, didn't mean to hold you up."

Hoberg drove off. Old Dex glanced at the clinic, shook his head. *Damn . . . Jack Redmond; poor Jack.*

Old Dex had been lying; he didn't feel fit as a fiddle. Felt like hell, actually; had for a while. Real tired. It had been a busy week, and now it seemed like it still wasn't over.

Poor Jack, he thought again and drove away from the Valley Clinic.

CHAPTER SEVEN

The Outside Time

1

His last three hours at the Arroyo Lounge were the longest ones Mark had ever spent there. Even after eleven, patrons still called for drinks and shoved quarters into the magic jukebox. But finally Jerry Zirpolo, himself overworked, told Mark to go. He would close up.

Mark reached the Valley Clinic six minutes later; too fast on a bike in the dark, even though he knew every bump and pothole on Las Palmas Road. The security guard directed him to the coronary care unit, first floor. The charge nurse, in the mold of Jodie Arnold, issued a stern challenge to this blatant trespasser, but relented when Mark said he was Jack Redmond's nephew.

Two other patients occupied the ten-bed unit. Jack's curtained cubicle was near the back wall. Mark saw defibrillators, tourniquets, respiratory equipment, and crash carts loaded with everything needed for emergency treatment. Dr. Wayne Hoberg ran a well-prepared CCU; but then, in a town like this, it was a necessity.

Mark peered around the curtain. Tubes and wires seemed to

grow from Jack's frail body. Rosie Shannon, looking haggard, sat by him.

"Sorry I couldn't get here sooner," Mark said.

"It's all right; he's been asleep most of the time. The pain would be too much otherwise. Doc wanted him to at least be comfortable."

Mark sat down next to Rosie, and they were silent for a while. Despite the painkillers, Jack's face still appeared to be twisted with hurt. Occasionally he would emit a soft moan, and once he spoke a few meaningless words, perhaps responding to a dream.

Then, near midnight, his eyelids fluttered open. He stared at the acoustical ceiling tiles, disoriented.

"Ro . . . sie?" he said in a whisper.

"I'm right here, Jack." She stood.

"Rosie!"

She leaned over the bed, looked into his face. "Here, right here, babe. It's OK. Mark's with us too."

"Mark's here?" He seemed more coherent. "Let me . . . see him."

They traded places. Jack said, "Hey boy, what do you think? Do I look like . . . the back of a frigging computer terminal, or what? The only place they . . . don't have a tube or wire stuck is up my ass . . ."

"Jerry wanted me to tell you something," Mark whispered. "He said nobody's going to sit on your barstool, not ever."

"Damn right no one's . . . gonna sit there!" He winced. "You tell your sonofabitch boss I'll . . . be back to warm it up, real soon." A broad grin cracked through the pain.

"What's so funny?" Mark asked.

"I whipped your butt in that . . . last game of Probe, didn't I?"

The Last Game of Probe. The Final Showdown; End of the Trail; the Last Roundup.

"You sure did, Jack."

"Mark?"

"Yeah?"

Mark could barely hear him and leaned closer. "I saw Boot Hill . . . in my dreams I saw Boot Hill, and . . . lots of friends waiting there. It wasn't . . . so bad."

Sleep reclaimed him. Mark again sat down by Rosie, who sobbed softly. Her vigil continued; his began.

2

At 1:47 a.m., officially Sunday morning, Jack Redmond's eyes snapped open. The floor-length curtain, pulled around two sides of the bed, fluttered for a few moments, as though caught in an errant breeze. Rosie, who had been nodding, looked up, startled. Mark jumped to his feet.

"What the devil—!" she exclaimed.

Coldness assaulted them, first chilling, then numbing. Jack's bed shook; IV stands rattled, as did a washbasin and a half-filled water glass on the night table. Steadying himself, Mark grabbed the terrified woman's hand.

"Jack!" Rosie cried, wanting to reach him but unable to lift herself from the chair, which also shook.

It ended abruptly, but left them unnerved. There was another sound, something like . . . a jet of gas escaping from a broken valve, though that wasn't exactly it, Mark thought.

The hissing faded.

Jack sat up in his bed.

He looked around, smiled. "The music, nice music," he whispered.

The coronary care unit was graveyard still. Mark said, "Jack, what is it?"

There was confusion on his face now. "The flames . . ."

Rosie stood. "Jack?"

He was trembling. *"The flames . . . the flames . . . !"*

"Jack, stop it!" Rosie cried.

He reached for the glass on the night table, pulling out an IV tube. His eyes grew wider. He flung the water wildly, some falling to the floor, most reaching the back wall, under the blood pressure monitor and oxygen valves, where it trickled down. Mark wondered how he managed to hold onto the glass.

Now he was smiling again. He looked at Rosie and Mark.

"The flames are out," he said softly.

The glass fell from his fingers.

Jack Redmond lay down again, closed his eyes . . .

. . . and died.

3

For a moment, upon awakening, he remembered nothing, and was frightened.

A dim bulb lit the cell. *Cell.* Using Scott Millard's eyes, Bruno looked down at the puny body. Why had he chosen *this*? He would not make that mistake again. The man in the uniform could have killed him . . .

The man in the uniform, who had hit him and dragged him and thrown him against a wall.

This cell could not hold him, nor could this body. Fully aware now, he only had to move along . . .

Then, he remembered what had frightened him earlier. It was the moment, the brief passage from the stupid creature to the ragged man, when he was *OUTSIDE*. Not part of anything, he had felt like screaming but had gone inside quickly, and it was over.

SCREAMING TERRIBLE OUTSIDE TIME.

No, he could not just leave, not face that again, until . . .

He urged the ragged man up on shaky legs, to the bars of the cell. Weak hands circled two of them and shook. Not sturdy at all, not like those in San Fra, when he had been unable to escape, though he had tried.

Chief Upton jolted awake when he felt the vibrations on the wall alongside his cot. *Christ, 4:45 in the morning.* It had been a quiet Saturday night; he'd sent Steve Cornwell home at 1:30. If not for the "prisoner," he would have locked up the station and had his calls forwarded to his home. Why his deputy strong-armed every damn derelict . . .

Upton opened the door to the back room and switched on a bank of lights. "All right," he said peevishly, "you can stop shaking . . ."

The drifter was staring at him with those crazy eyes. Upton stopped a couple of yards away; anxiety seized him.

"What the hell . . ."

Bruno leaped from the body.

Scott Millard crumpled to the floor of the cell.

Screaming now . . . screaming . . . can't help it . . . OUTSIDE . . .

The sheriff clutched at his head as the pain struck him. "Jesus!" he cried.

Must get inside . . . can't stay . . . out . . .

Upton fell to his knees, moaning like a wounded beast.

The barrier was solid, like a stone wall, and he sensed pain as he dashed himself against it. *Let . . . me . . . in . . .*

"*No!*"

LET . . . ME . . .

"*STOP!*"

Too strong . . . too strong . . . can't get inside . . . can't . . .

Bruno retreated into the cell then out a barred window into the pre-dawn coolness. A shrill keening went on and on, echoing in the room. Eventually it faded into silence.

4

Chief Upton lowered his hands and stood, shaky. He glanced around. The kid sat up in his cell.

"What're you looking at?" the cop asked.

"You . . . tell me. What am I doing in here?"

"You don't know?"

Scott shook his head. "I was walking along the road . . . in the daytime. That's the last thing I remember till I . . . woke up now."

"We didn't find no drugs in your bag, but are you on something?"

"No sir, I swear I'm not."

"You don't remember assaulting my deputy?"

His bemused look assured the chief otherwise. "No sir."

Upton rubbed his head. "Yeah, well . . . you hungry?"

"Very."

"I'll see what we got around." He unlocked the cell. "First, you go use those facilities, grab a shower. I'll leave your bag at the door; noticed some . . . cleaner clothes in there."

Scott stepped out of the cell. "Thanks." He looked at the cop. Curiosity had replaced the wild look in his eyes. "Sir?"

"Yeah?"

"What happened before?"

Upton shrugged, turned. "Go take your shower, son."

Still wondering about that himself, Upton checked the small refrigerator they kept in the office. Cornwell used it more than he did. Most of a club sandwich was wrapped in wax paper. There were apples, and half a six-pack of A&W root beer. In the deputy's desk was a bag of Chips Ahoy, only a few missing.

Scott Millard looked and smelled a whole lot better when he appeared fifteen minutes later. He ate nearly everything the sheriff gave him, except for one apple and some of the cookies, which went into the backpack. Upton asked him questions during the meal, and he answered them honestly.

A little screwed up, the sheriff thought, *but not a bad kid.*

"Tell you what, I'll drive you to the end of the Seaway," he said. "It'll get you that much closer to the interstate."

"That's nice of you, sir. Thanks."

Before Scott finished, a call came in to the office: Mrs. Crawley hearing sounds outside her bedroom window, a burglar, maybe. Almost never was, Upton knew; but he had to check it out.

"You can wait for me here," he told Scott.

"No thanks, I wouldn't want to be sitting around if your deputy came in. I'll start walking."

"Good point. He's not scheduled for a while, but you never know." Upton smiled. "If he didn't shoot you for breaking out, he might do it for eating his stuff. Yeah, go ahead; it's cool out there now. If I get done fast, I'll drive by and pick you up." He thought a moment, then reached in a back pocket, pulled out his wallet. "In case I get stuck, maybe this'll help." He handed Scott a twenty.

Scott smiled through his still-damp beard. "Thanks, sir, thanks for everything."

They went outside. Upton drove off quickly, not bothering to turn on his light-bar or siren.

5

The early morning was actually *too* cool for wearing only a tee-shirt, but after the last couple of days, Scott couldn't complain. Tell the truth, it felt good. The ache of hunger was gone—for now—and there was food in his bag, and twenty-three bucks could take someone like him a long way. His optimism soared. *Rhea, your little butterball is on the way home!*

The desert promised a thundering dawn of incredible hues. Not that the thought of the sun climbing overhead filled Scott with any great anticipation; still, it would be an awesome sight, and owing to the fact that it was unavoidable, it might as well be enjoyed.

Half a mile past Smoke Tree, in the pre-dawn light, Scott saw the coyote. It was twenty yards ahead on the other side of the road, a couple of feet back from the asphalt. Standing on all fours, motionless, it watched him.

Scott slowed but did not stop. *All right*, he thought, *what do I know about coyotes, besides the fact they're no damn good at catching roadrunners?* He knew they were scavengers, ate anything dead or dying, as well as small animals, rodents and such. When he'd lived in the San Fernando Valley, there had been trouble with coyotes coming out of the canyons and foothills into new tract developments, scrounging through garbage cans, killing cats and small dogs, occasionally attacking an infant or toddler left alone in a backyard. But on the whole they were timid creatures, fearful of man.

OK, so why wasn't it running from this man? he wondered. He was only ten yards away now.

Desert coyotes were small animals, seldom more than twenty-five pounds. Their mountain cousins could weigh more than twice that. The one across the Seaway could have been either; it was at least thirty-five, forty pounds. In general, the breed had a natural emaciated look; but in the case of this one, that image belied its sleekness and strength.

Five yards away Scott called, "Go on, Wylie, beat it." The animal did not move. Scott flailed his arms. "Fuck off!"

He bent down to pick up a piece of granite.

The animal bolted across the road.

When he stood, the coyote leaped and struck him in the chest. He fell backward, against a tall barrel cactus. He screamed as the deadly spines ripped into the back of his head.

His scream became a gurgling froth of blood as the coyote tore out his throat.

Pulling him away from the cactus, the animal shook him, as a terrier does a rat, then dropped the limp body to the sand.

The coyote must not have made a kill in a while; it was hungry. Three yards back from the Borrego-Salton Seaway it fed on Scott Millard, nee Millstein.

6

Like Chief Upton had figured, the call amounted to nothing; some animal poking around, that was all. These old folks could get awful spooked, especially ones like Mrs. Crawley, who was new to the desert. It had taken him some time to calm her down.

Forty minutes had passed since he'd left the station. The kid might've gotten picked up by now, although with the light traffic, and the way he looked, it was unlikely. A mile and a half, two tops, and he'd find him.

With the sun in his face on the Seaway, Upton nearly passed by the bloody mound on his right. The animals caught his attention: five or six turkey vultures hovering overhead, sometimes dropping down and scolding three small, scrawny coyotes, all that stood between themselves and a grand feast.

It took Donald Upton another moment to realize what they were feeding upon.

"Jesus H. Christ!"

He drew his service revolver and fired a shot, which echoed loudly in the surrounding stillness. The coyotes slunk off; the birds rose higher but continued to circle.

Upton walked reluctantly toward the mound.

It was the kid, no doubt about that. He still wore the blue backpack. One side of his face had been mostly eaten away, leaving him with half a death's-head. His left arm had been chewed down to the bone; there were bite marks everywhere else. A broken chunk of the barrel cactus was lodged in the back of his head.

Upton remembered thinking, *Kid don't have much meat on him,* before he staggered off to puke in the sand.

7

The ringing phone jarred Steve Cornwell awake at 6:12. He'd only gotten a few hours' sleep and had downed a couple of beers before turning in.

"Wha' the fuck—" he muttered into the receiver.

"It's me. Wake up, I need you!" It was the chief's trouble voice, which he seldom heard.

"Yeah, what is it?"

"I'm on the Seaway, just east of town. Got a body, real fresh one. You call Porter, then get out here, now!"

Christ, a body! Some asshole camper wandered across the road and got splattered by a truck!

"On my way, Chief."

Yesterday's clothes still lay on the floor. *What the hell,* he thought, pulling them on. He splashed water on his face, brushed his teeth then called Dr. Ronald Porter, who doubled as coroner in Smoke Tree. Woke *him* up too. *Big fucking deal.*

Three minutes later Cornwell stood in the driveway of his small, one-bedroom bungalow. His place was on Palo Verde Drive, in the Red Hill section of town, the neighborhood of nearly everyone else that didn't live in the Estates.

He was fumbling with his keys, still shaking off the last vestiges of sleep, when the furry streak hit him in the face. Toppling backward, he struck the concrete with enough force to knock most men unconscious. He tried to fight it off, because—while he had not yet seen his attacker—he knew his death was close at hand.

Powerful jaws closed on his throat as he tried, without success, to draw his revolver.

8

The coyote savaged the dead man's face for a few seconds; then, aware of being within the place of buildings, it ran off, blood dripping from its jaws and leaving a spotted trail. The street being at the edge of the desert quickly allowed it to reach the low dunes, where it turned and looked back.

Bruno was pleased with the strength and swiftness of his host. After feeding upon the ragged man he had run to the place of buildings, and with great speed had soon found what he wanted, the monster-thing with the words that said *Smoke Tree Police Department*. He had waited, and before long the man in the uniform had appeared.

Bastard.

It had been good to kill again, to see them bleed, and die. Not the same, of course, as killing with his . . .

Hands.

No, nothing was like that. It would come again; one day, it would come.

But the outside time, the *screaming terrible outside time* before he had come upon his new body!

Not again, not for a long while.

He was *inside*, and he had killed again, and for now it was all right.

Turning, he set off swiftly, circumventing the Estates and running north, toward the maze of canyons in the mountains.

C H A P T E R   E I G H T

Wrong And Right

1

Chief Donald Upton's first assumption had been that Scott Millard was hit by a vehicle on the Borrego-Salton Seaway, knocked far to the side of the road then fallen upon by scavengers.

But with the discovery of Steve Cornwell's body, that thinking changed. A neighbor had found Cornwell within minutes of the attack. No scavengers had yet been drawn to it. Clearly, some animal had been responsible. An elderly woman across the street came forward to say that, glancing out her window earlier, she had seen something running into the desert. A coyote, she was pretty sure; yeah, God's truth, a coyote. Seen enough of those around here.

If so, it was crazy. Upton could marginally accept a starved or rabid animal attacking the slightly built drifter out in the desert. But big Steve Cornwell, in a residential neighborhood, after sunrise? No way.

Steve Cornwell. Scott Millard. Cornwell had arrested the boy, had roughed him up. But then, Scott hadn't been Scott, had he? Because this morning, in the cell . . .

Crazy goddamn thinking, Upton decided. Not enough sleep, and now the loss of his deputy. Yeah, most folks didn't like Steve Cornwell; but the boy was OK at his job, and he'd worked for Upton nearly four years now.

Upton called in Mike Barber, his part-time deputy, advising him that he was working full time until further notice. County boys from the substation in Borrego Springs, and a few other towns, drove over to Smoke Tree. If some killer animal was loose within the town limits, Upton needed all the help he could get.

Rangers from the Anza-Borrego State Park headquarters also appeared. They were skeptical about the reports of a coyote being responsible for what had happened. No, they couldn't dispute the fact that an animal had killed the deputy, and more than likely the other man. But a coyote? Maybe a dog that had wandered away from a campground, pit bull or Rottweiler or something, but not a coyote.

In any case, Upton's job was not only to track down the animal and kill it, but to avoid the panic that such an operation could cause in a community of nervous senior citizens.

2

Mark Alderson was biking up Las Palmas Road at 9:15 on Sunday morning when a deputy in a green-and-white county sheriff's car pulled up alongside and motioned for him to stop.

County cop, he thought as fear spread in him. He'd seen them passing by on the Seaway, but never out this way. They had finally caught up to him; the nearly two months of peace he'd known were over.

The past thirteen hours—since he'd learned about Jack Redmond—had already been a nightmare for Mark. The flatline on the EKG monitor had brought the staff and their crash cart, and they had tried—fortunately without success—to bring the writer back to a brief life of pain and helplessness. Later, Mark had driven the distraught Rosie home then biked to his apartment. It was past 3:30 when he finally crawled into bed. Even then, his few hours of sleep had been shattered by frightening images from his past, superimposed over the strange happenings at Jack's bedside.

And now, this.

He had staggered out of bed thirty minutes ago, barely enough time to shower. The lounge opened at ten on Sunday, and he'd first wanted to stop at the Singer house. Now, as he imagined himself in handcuffs on an eastbound plane, he realized what disturbed him the most was the possibility of never seeing Tracy Russell again.

The deputy did not get out of the car, but rolled down the window on the passenger side. "Morning," he called.

Mark nodded. "Hi."

"You hear what's going on in town?"

It suddenly occurred to Mark that this had nothing to do with him. "Sorry, I just got up not long ago."

The lawman offered a concise account of the killings, the minimum details meant to create the maximum effect.

"Riding around like that," the deputy concluded, "kind of leaves you vulnerable."

Mark pointed in the direction of the country club. "I work there. I'll be off the street quick. You think you'll find this animal soon?"

"I think we'd better."

The deputy drove off; Mark pedaled up Las Palmas Road for another three hundred yards, then turned onto the long, palm-lined Smoke Tree Road. The man in the security kiosk was on the phone, his back toward Mark as he passed.

People in the Estates had probably been warned already. Oasis Drive and the shorter cross streets were deserted, no one doing yard work, jogging or walking. Not unusual though, Mark figured, with the temperature already soaring.

Tracy met Mark at the door. "I'm glad to see you," she said. "I was worried about you riding over here."

"You heard, then?"

Tracy nodded. "The police were around earlier. God, that's scary! We'd been out on the patio, but we came inside."

As they sat down in the living room, Mark said, "You look better this morning."

"Thanks. I can't say the same for you. Are you all right?"

He told Tracy about Jack Redmond. "I'd heard that he lived here," she said. "You knew him well then?"

"I was . . . yeah, pretty well."

"I'm sorry, Mark."

Carl Singer passed from the kitchen on his way to one of the back rooms. Unshaven and haggard looking, he nodded at Mark but said nothing. Mark glanced at Tracy, who shook her head.

"Mom's death finally hit him last night . . . hard. I'm really worried about him."

"Will you be able to stay with him a while?"

"As long as he needs me . . . actually, that goes both ways."

"I understand. What about your job?"

"I'm a teacher, so I have the summer free."

"That's right, I remember your mother mentioning . . ."

Tracy squinted an eye at him. "My mother told you about me?"

You should meet my daughter, Mark. Maybe when she comes out here this summer . . .

Mark nodded sheepishly. "Yeah, I guess so."

"Well, Mr. Bradley, that makes me feel good. Mom was a very discerning person." She glanced at the window. "You know, it's weird . . ."

"What is?"

"Sometimes I think maybe her being gone hasn't hit me yet; that I should be walking around like Dad. Then I think, it *has* hit me, because I grieve for her so much, and I'm going to miss talking to her, and touching her. But you know, I still feel she's with me, Mark, inside me, and all around. Does that sound nuts?"

"Uh-uh, not at all."

"Have you ever heard of George Anderson?"

"The spiritual medium? Yeah."

"If he were to sit down in a room with me, he would be overwhelmed by Vivian Singer's presence. She would come through as clearly as music off a CD. And her message would be that she really hadn't died, that she would never die as long as Dad or Joey or me was still around. I really believe that."

"From what I knew of your mother, I think you're right."

Tracy shook her head and smiled. "And her last message from the other side would be to tell us how lousy we've all been eating without her doing the cooking!"

They both laughed, then Tracy cried. When it was over she asked Mark, "Are your parents still alive?"

"No, they're . . . they both passed away."

"I'm sorry."

"Accident, it was . . . an accident, a long time ago." He looked around. "I haven't seen Joey."

"He's in his room, with a friend," Tracy said.

"Another kid, in this town?" Mark was dubious.

"As a matter of fact, they've been quiet. Let's have a look."

Tracy knocked on Joey's door, then pushed it open. The boy, sitting on his bed, was dwarfed by Gary Masten. They were looking through albums of baseball cards.

"Hey," Joey called.

Gary looked up. "Mark, hi-ii!" he exclaimed, a crooked but warm smile lighting up his ruddy moon-face. He hurried to the door, his massive arms engulfing Mark. They pounded each other on the back.

Like so many with Down's syndrome, the back of Gary's head was flat. His eyelids appeared to be inflamed, while his prominent ears had extremely small lobes. His nose was flat, his neck short and broad. But his hands were large, fingers long and thick, though the pinkies were curved. His light brown, medium-length hair was stylish. He was dressed in jeans, a blue Padres tee-shirt and an enormous pair of tennis shoes.

"Well, I guess you two have already met," Tracy said.

Mark nodded. "On our bikes, riding along one of the washes. Gary's a great rider. We've done it a couple of times."

"Gary was working next door, at the Findleys, when the police came around," Joey said. "Mom thought it would be best if he stayed here till they catch the monster."

The big man nodded. "We called Harry. He knows I'm here. Harry will check on me . . . later." His words were spoken slowly, not slurred, but deliberate. He'd worked hard to control his once-raucous voice.

Mark knew he was talking about Harry Keller, his guardian. "I'm sure Harry's glad you're safe," he said.

"But they are wrong, Mark," Gary went on. "I know they are wrong."

"What are they wrong about?"

"They said a coyote hurt those people. I see coyotes all the time. I like coyotes. They are wrong."

"Well, let's hope they can—"

A siren wailed, close by. Then, gunshots, four or five, their echoes running together.

"What the hell . . ." Carl exclaimed from the hallway.

They hurried to the front window. Other people were out on Oasis Drive. Farther up the street Chief Donald Upton's Blazer, two county squad cars and a Land Rover from the State Park headquarters were spread out in a ragged semi-circle. Another green-and-white, light bar flashing, had just turned onto the street.

Bert Findley, on the sidewalk, waved to Carl and the others. They went outside.

"What's going on?" Tracy asked.

"They caught that coyote going through Bill Kasendorf's garbage can," Bert replied. "Shot it dead."

"How do they know it's the right one?" Carl asked.

"It's got to be. No one's seen a coyote in the Estates for months now. Besides, I heard it went after one of the deputies."

"If I was cornered," Mark said, "I'd go after someone too."

The lawmen had lowered their weapons, apparently satisfied it was over. Two park rangers carried the carcass out and slipped it into a plastic sack. The coyote's head leaned sharply, as though the neck had been broken; its tongue lolled pathetically. Later, it would weigh in at a fraction under twenty-four pounds, better-than-average size for a desert coyote.

Carl shook his head. "It looks so damn small."

"A wild animal that's starved or crazy can do some bad things," Bert said.

While the activity continued, Mark glanced at his watch. "I'd better get to work. The whole town might need a drink now that this is over."

Tracy looked at him. "Mark?"

"Yeah?"

"What about that ride we were going to take?"

He smiled. "How about Tuesday?"

"Tuesday's good."

"I'm supposed to have a day off tomorrow, but if I know Eugene Price and his ailments, I'll be working then too. That's OK, I guess. Jack's funeral is tomorrow morning, if Rosie Shannon gets all the arrangements done today. And around here, you don't want to ride in the afternoon."

"I wouldn't think so," Tracy said. "Early Tuesday?"

"Very early. Can you handle it?"

She stuck her tongue out. "I'll be ready and waiting impatiently by the time you get here."

All the official vehicles, save for Chief Upton's Blazer, had gone. The crowd in front of the Kasendorfs' house was dispersing.

"Come on, Gary, it's over," Bert Findley said. "We can get back to work now."

Before starting off after Bert, Gary Masten turned to Tracy and Mark. "They are wrong," he said again.

3

The whole town did *not* descend upon the Arroyo Lounge. Business was steady, but never overwhelming, nothing Mark and Jerry couldn't handle. Toward the end of the afternoon, with the weekenders on their way home, it finally slowed down.

During a break, Mark called Rosie Shannon. Yes, she was holding up; a sister had arrived from Los Angeles to stay with her. Funeral arrangements had been made for Monday. Mark gave Rosie the phone number of Mrs. Jenks, his landlady, in case she needed him for anything beforehand.

Mark would indeed be working on Monday. Eugene Price

called Jerry to say he was doing better, but the doctor had suggested another day of rest. He'd be in Tuesday, for sure. Jerry, who was going to the funeral, decided not to open the lounge until afterward, out of respect for Jack. Mark needn't worry about getting to work late.

Amid talk about golf swings, and the Padres game in progress that afternoon on television, much of the subdued lounge conversation centered upon the violent deaths of the two men. And while the majority agreed that the matter was done, there remained an undercurrent of doubt.

They are wrong.

Mark offered no opinion, although he was asked more than once.

Tracy did not stop by the club on Sunday. Her father had fallen even deeper into his depression, enough to make her consider calling Dr. Hoberg and seeking his advice. But in the middle of the afternoon Carl sat down next to his daughter, a stack of old photo albums in his arms. He began to talk as he flipped through the pages, hardly pausing for breath, not wanting to stop. Joey joined them, and they talked, and laughed, and cried, and ate peanut butter-and-jelly sandwiches as they played games long past the boy's bedtime.

When she went to bed that night, Tracy knew her father was going to be all right.

4

Jack Redmond, for all his fame, had been a lonely man.

Aside from Mark and Jerry, Dexter Jones and Doc Hoberg, only a handful of Smoke Tree's residents attended the services at the Church of the Desert. Rosie came on the arms of her sister and a nephew. Tim Brady represented Hollywood. Older than Jack, Tim in his heyday had played Jed Stockton in three movies, and on the Dragoon television series for two years. Jack's New York publishing house, which had earned a dollar or two during their forty-year association, was represented by a telegram. Understandable, since all the old-liners had beaten Jack to Boot Hill, and no single editor had been able to work on more than two books with the irascible writer in the past decade.

Interment was in the Eternal Hills Cemetery, at the end of Las Palmas Road—now a graded path—south of town. Rev. Mather, who hardly knew Jack, continued the theme he had begun in church, of how much pleasure Jack Redmond brought to people with his God-given gift for storytelling. But he made it brief, because the midday temperature was one hundred and nine degrees.

5

Mark and Jerry had driven to the club from the cemetery. Jerry promised Mark a ride home after closing.

Later that evening, Jerry would swear this was the slowest day in the history of the Arroyo Lounge. Mark was inclined to agree. Even some of the regular foursomes were absent. And he could only polish the glasses and fill up the bowls of hamster food so often.

When Tracy stopped in at 7:20 there were five other patrons scattered through the lounge, two of them sitting at the bar. Mark waved her to the stool at one end; not the last stool. Jerry had made good on his promise, roping off Jack Redmond's corner. A sign reading Jack's Place would soon hang there above newspaper clippings, photos of Jack and Jerry, of Jack and other Smoke Tree luminaries. Rosie Shannon would donate some of Jack's memorabilia for the corner.

"Seven & Seven, right?" Mark asked.

Tracy shook her head. "I needed it last week, but actually, I have one of those about as often as the Cubs win the World Series. A beer is fine."

"San Miguel?"

"San what?"

Mark smiled. "I forgot, you St. Louis people only know one beer. You go around humming that tune all day with visions of Clydesdales prancing through your head."

Tracy wrinkled her nose. *God, she was cute when she did that.* "OK, wise guy, let's try your San whatever."

Mark brought her a bottle and poured it. "How's your dad?" he asked.

"Much better. He found a way to start healing himself, and I'm darn proud of him. I left him and Joey playing Trivial Pursuit, arguing over an answer on one of the cards that Dad swears is wrong."

"I'm glad to hear it. Are we still on for tomorrow?"

"Absolutely. I ride at least three times a week back home, and I've really missed it. By the way, this is good beer, even without the horses."

They talked about bicycling for a while. Mark poured her a second San Miguel. While he was off taking care of another patron, Tracy studied Jack Redmond's corner.

"Your boss must've liked him a lot," she said, when Mark returned.

"Those two had some knockdown-dragout debates; stubborn men, both of them. But Jerry was one of Jack's biggest fans. He had Jack autograph every book in his collection. Over a hundred titles, not counting multiple copies."

Tracy was impressed. "All those novels; he had a full life."

Mark thought about the few people at the funeral. "Yeah, full."

Jerry came over while they were talking. He nodded at Tracy. "Hey, Marco, looks like you found something to keep you busy. It is so dead tonight, I mean, D-E-D." He glanced at his watch. "Why don't you take off early? You deserve it after this week. I'll probably shut down at nine."

"Thanks, but you're driving me home, remember?"

"Christ, I forgot. Sorry."

"I can take you home," Tracy said.

Jerry winked at Mark. "Sounds like a plan to me."

"You sure it's OK?" Mark asked Tracy.

"Of course. I wasn't going to stay much longer anyway."

Mark took off his apron. "Thanks again, Jerry."

"Six days in a row, with hardly any backup?" Jerry put a hand on his shoulder. "Thank *you*, Marco. Hey, I know you're scheduled for the Fourth of July on Wednesday, but if I think Eugene is up to it, I'm gonna have him work so you can take it off. I'll leave a message with your landlady."

"That's great."

The sun was beyond the western mountains as they walked to Tracy's car, the sky an incredible canvas of iridescent hues. It had already *cooled down* to the low nineties, and would drop another twenty degrees before the next sunrise. This was one of the desert's finest moments.

"I'd totally forgotten it was almost the Fourth of July," Tracy said.

"That's understandable," Mark replied. "Anyway, if you want a parade or something, Smoke Tree's not the place. They'll shoot some fireworks off on the golf course; that's about it."

"Sounds fine. Joey will like that."

They drove down to Las Palmas Road. Turning, Tracy indicated the large *Smoke Tree Estates* sign. "Maybe you can answer my son's burning question," she said. "Mine too."

"I'll try."

"*What* is a smoke tree?"

Mark smiled. "It's easier to show you than explain it. Can you last till tomorrow?"

She wrinkled her nose again. "Well, if I have to . . ."

They passed one county green-and-white on the way. Chief Upton had requested the help, being undermanned. Most of the furor over the previous day's deaths had subsided, but the lawmen were still alert. The coyote they'd killed in the Estates had not been rabid, subsequent tests proved, and that bothered Upton.

Tracy drove into the nearly empty parking lot of Ironwood Terrace. "Is it always as quiet as this?" she asked.

"No, quieter." Mark looked at her. "Uh, my place isn't any big deal, but I did clean it the other day. If you want to stop up . . ."

Tracy gripped the wheel. "Thanks, but I . . . better get back, see if Dad needs to be rescued from Joey. Maybe—"

"It's OK," Mark interrupted. "I appreciate the ride."

He extended a hand. Tracy shook it, held it a moment, leaned over and kissed him on the cheek.

They said good night. Mark, smiling broadly, climbed the steps to his apartment as Tracy drove off.

CHAPTER NINE

Desert Trails

1

The coyote had been given its head through the canyons, a place that would have confused—even defeated—the most experienced hiker. This maze of arroyos and steep-walled passes, choked with granite boulders that had been varnished by the desert, was its habitat.

Since yesterday it had made two kills—a ground squirrel and a cactus mouse—had fed on the carcass of a jackrabbit after frightening off some turkey vultures, and had eaten amply of seeds and flowers, which were a staple part of its diet. Others of its kind—smaller, mostly—had approached, hoping it would hunt with them, as was their way. Together, they might even bring down a bighorn sheep, one of the grandest prizes. Then, they had stopped and stared at their brother, and had sensed what they could not see. Terrified, they had fled.

More stupid creatures, Bruno thought.

The others were not as stupid, the ones called . . .

Man. Like he had once been.

Like he would be again.

But not the man he was watching now, not inside that!

Its belly full, the coyote had crawled into a niche high on a rocky slope during the heat of the day. It had fallen asleep, and later, upon awakening, had seen the man on the canyon floor, by the water, where earlier it had drank. The man kneeled down, doing . . . something, a thing he should have known, but could not remember, except that it had something to do with the San Fra place, something important.

Those fragments, those half-memories, they tormented him.

It was an old man, thin, weak-looking, of no value to him, even if the passage through the screaming terrible outside time was brief. What would he use that body for, except perhaps to die inside it?

No value at all . . .

But he was *here*, in this creature's place, alone. If he were to die, he would not be found for a long time, not before the animals and shrieking birds had picked off his flesh and torn out his organs and left behind only the bones. Bones that would bleach dry when the sun was over the canyon.

The coyote extracted itself from the place where it had spent the day.

2

Dexter Jones had come late to his diggings.

Recently, he'd been staying in bed long past sunrise. That had never been his way. But he was old now, and the night work was taking its toll. Tired, so damn tired. He had to give it a rest for a spell, leave it alone.

But he couldn't; he knew that.

Through the years this small leg of Bighorn Creek, where it curved around a jagged granite outcropping about ninety yards in from the mouth of Madhouse Canyon, had continually surprised him with its yield. Nothing much more than some "color," sometimes a fingernail-sized flake; but steady, reliable, not like the rest of the creek. He'd always suspected the Mother Lode was nearby, the Big One, but so far it had remained hidden.

Did he really want to find it? he wondered. What would he do then? So if he had looked at all (he wasn't even sure he had), it was half-heartedly.

Darkness was filling the canyon, even though the sun would not be down for a while. Old Dex looked at the "color" in a Ziploc bag one more time. Not much; but at home he would add it to what was already inside a big old coffee tin. He had a couple of those, the full one so heavy he could hardly lift it. Some day he would have it assayed, and cash it in. Some day . . . For now, it was time to go. He put the plastic bag, along with his old iron wash pan, a small shovel and pick ax, into a canvas rucksack, the same one he had worn while marching across Europe a long time ago.

Halfway to the mouth of the canyon, he saw the coyote on the west slope. A big one, he could tell, even across the distance. Old Dex only had one eye, but it was a damn good eye. The sight of the creature caused him no alarm; saw 'em all the time, he did. They passed as near as five yards from where he worked. And he liked the scrawny things, too; respected 'em for surviving out in a place like this.

Removing his battered sombrero, Old Dex waved it with a flourish and bowed deeply. *Ha, he probably figures I'm crazy. Well, he ain't far from wrong.*

When Old Dex turned, the coyote started down the slope. Twenty yards farther along, the prospector looked back.

The animal stood by Bighorn Creek, still staring impassively at the man. It had narrowed, by half, the distance between them.

"Well, drink up, boy," Old Dex said. "Don't let me stop you. I was just leavin' anyway."

Ahead, the canyon walls veered away sharply. Loosely piled stones and a sharp drop-off presented a final obstacle to exiting the canyon. Old Dex concentrated on his footing. Though he'd done this hundreds of times, he'd also stumbled often enough to have learned caution.

Now the familiar walls of what had been Concordia Sanitarium were in sight.

The coyote stood above Old Dex, atop a boulder.

Old Dex grinned. "Damn, boy, but you got your mind set

on somethin'. You tryin' to follow me home, is that it? Chrissakes, wouldn't that be the craziest thing! Go on, beat it. Find yourself a nice mama coyote and bed her down."

He laughed and continued walking.

The coyote leaped from the boulder, landing lightly, a few loose stones shifting under its paws. This time Old Dex turned completely around.

They were two yards apart.

Until now the creature's eyes had been intent on the man. Now, looking past him, they fell upon the adobe ruins.

Blackness. A silent blackness that was less than nothing.

Inside his host, Bruno shrieked.

The coyote leaned over on its side, as though paralyzed, its paws scrabbling helplessly in the stones.

"Damn thing must be hurt," Old Dex said.

Move away from here. Move away. The screaming terrible outside time was less awful than this place. Move away, before . . .

The creature regained its feet and, yelping, bolted into the canyon. Old Dex could see it running along the creek briefly; but the tributary twisted away, and the animal was gone.

"Damnedest thing," Old Dex muttered. He shrugged, turned and walked the remaining distance to the ruins. The sun had just gone down.

3

Halfway up Las Palmas Road on the way to the Estates, Mark nearly turned back.

Why was he doing this? Was it just a friendly bike ride with someone who shared a similar interest? Or was it more than that?

And if it was more, why pursue it? With the reality of his past, and the non-reality of his future, how could he even *think* of becoming involved? Of involving her?

No, not fair.

Still . . .

You should meet my daughter, Mark.

He wanted to see her; he wanted it very much. For the first time since it had all begun (*Was it six months now? Seven?*), something else mattered.

Fifteen minutes before sunrise, Mark began pedaling faster.

4

Tracy had been outside for a while, thinking. OK, she was going on a bike ride—one of her passions—with a nice guy who happened to be one of the few people she'd met in a week who wasn't more than twice her age. He lived here, and she lived 1500 miles away; he was a bartender, and . . .

No, not a bartender. That was what he was doing now, but that was not what he was; it was not *who* he was.

So why here, in a place like this? Almost as if he was . . .

. . . *hiding out.*

Or running away, or . . . what?

So many questions.

Did she want to know the answers?

Yes, because she liked Mark Bradley. And even if she questioned her own judgment, there was still Mom. Her mother had never been one to offer up her daughter to every eligible male with whom she had a conversation. Not by a longshot, and especially not after the nightmare of Don Russell. Since then, Tracy had done little more than casual dating, and not much of that. She and Vivian had spoken about it many times, Tracy saying that, some day, she might be more open to a relationship. Mom had always been supportive.

But Vivian Singer had liked Mark Bradley and had spoken to him about her daughter.

Tracy crossed her arms against the pre-dawn chill and looked around. "You wanted me to know something, didn't you, Mom?" she said and smiled as a breeze fluttered across her face.

Mark rode up Oasis Drive a minute later. Tracy made a show of glancing impatiently at her watch.

"Thought you'd keep me waiting all morning," she said. "Did you sleep through your alarm?"

Mark glanced at the sky, barely lightening, and shrugged. "Sorree." He indicated her bike. "Iron Horse. That's a nice one."

"It's old and it's been ridden hard, but I take care of it. You ready?"

Tracy wore a faded blue, hooded sweatshirt, black Cannondale bike pants that ended above the knees, and an old pair of tennis shoes that bore the chain mark scars of previous campaigns. Even without makeup she looked great, Mark thought as he watched her slip on a yellow Bell helmet.

"Let's do it," he said.

They coasted down to Las Palmas Road, headed south briefly, turned east on Cahuilla Lane, past the Valley Clinic. Cahuilla Lane seemed to go nowhere. Further development of the Red Hill section, across Las Palmas Road, had been delayed some years ago. While utilities, cable and phone lines, sewage and the like were all in, only four scattered houses had been built.

The last house, and most isolated, belonged to Harry Keller, Mark informed Tracy. Harry was a kindly man who, for eleven years, had taken care of Gary Masten. Back then, the eight-year-old retarded boy had been found wandering the streets of downtown Los Angeles. A miserably scrawled note in his pocket read, *I can't take care of boy no more. He is Gary Masten. Please someone help him.* No trace of his parents, of anyone knowing him, was ever found.

So, Mark explained, Harry Keller had become his guardian. Harry had just retired from teaching and was about to lose his mind. The boy gave his life new meaning. Tutoring him at home, Harry quickly became aware of Gary's capabilities. They moved to Smoke Tree to live in Harry's investment when Gary was twelve, and his education continued. When the boy was old enough, Harry found him all the part-time jobs he could handle. At seventy-three he wanted Gary to be as independent as possible. After all, Harry wasn't going to be around forever.

As fond as Mark was of Gary, he was glad the boy did not see him ride past that morning. He and Tracy circumvented the reflective barrier at the end of Cahuilla Lane and were immediately upon a narrow, firmly packed deer trail that twisted in and out amid the brittle-bush, creosote, and clumps of different cholla cactus, but mostly took them farther east. Mark, who knew every inch of the trail, pedaled swiftly. Tracy stayed with him, seldom more than a yard behind.

Soon the path veered south-southeast, and continued that way. Towering ocotillo was everywhere; so were thick barrel cacti, bare-branched chuparosa and foul-smelling cheesebush. Tracy's eyes darted between the flora and the path ahead, which had narrowed even more.

They emerged from the foliage about twenty yards from the shoulder of the Seaway. Pedaling with reckless abandon, Mark angled across the asphalt and rode the other shoulder in the direction of the rising sun.

Another half-mile east a nameless, graded dirt road turned off S22 to the south. It was barely wide enough for one car, but allowed plenty of room for Tracy and Mark to pedal side by side.

"Well, how do you like it so far, eating dust and all?" Mark asked.

"It's great, but you're crazy, you know!"

"Thank you, I try. Don't worry, after the initial burst of energy I usually slow down. We turn here."

"That was qui—" she began, but he had already taken off on another trail, one so narrow she hadn't even noticed it. For another five minutes they weaved through more of the same flora, plus burroweed, indigo bush and tall agave. Once, a terrified jackrabbit bounded high to get out of their way.

When Mark finally braked to a stop, Tracy nearly rode up his back. They were at the edge of a broad indentation in the desert floor . . . shallow, but wide.

"This is Indianhead Wash," he told her, "and yonder lies the answer to your question."

Tracy had removed her dusty wrap-around sunglasses but was still brushing sand off her face. "What question?"

"*That* is a smoke tree."

The spiny tree, growing in the middle of the wash, stood

between fifteen and twenty feet high. Its color was an odd gray-green, lending it a ghostly, ethereal quality. From where Tracy stood, it looked like a broad puff of smoke.

"That's *really* weird," she said, impressed.

"See those little purple buds? Unlike many desert plants, this one blooms in the summer. When . . . if we come back next week, they'll be even brighter."

Past the first tree, others grew all within the depression, though not in the middle. "And they only grow in the wash?" Tracy asked.

"Sometimes along the edge, but mostly in."

"You like the desert, don't you?"

"It's OK." He shrugged. "Since it's where I am now, I make the most of it."

"You kind of strike me more as a beach person."

He hesitated. "I've been that, too."

"Oh yeah? Where?"

"Huntington Beach, San Diego." He pointed down the wash. "Come on, this is the fun part."

He sped off on the dusty floor, Tracy following. They weaved between the smoke trees, ironwoods—trees so dense they nearly sank into the sand—and broad palo verdes, avoiding the low cheeshbush and burroweed. This was definitely *not* Missouri, Tracy thought.

The wash continued toward a range of mountains farther south. They slowed, conceding to the early morning heat. Tracy had pulled off her sweatshirt not long after the sun had risen.

Eventually they left the wash for an old, seldom-used jeep trail, part of which, Tracy noticed incredulously, had been paved. They made small talk as they rode. Tracy realized something then: however reluctant Mark Bradley was about discussing his past, she was reticent over sharing details of her life with—and after—Don Russell. So, who was any more mysterious?

But she spoke freely of her childhood in the Midwest, her parents. She'd once aspired to acting but had not been talented or attractive enough (that revelation drew a disbelieving scowl from Mark) to pursue it. So she taught it instead, content with some occasional community theater work. She also painted, not well (her assessment), but enough to teach the fundamentals to others with more talent.

She also spoke about Joey, without a doubt her favorite subject. Sure, being a single mother was not the easiest thing in the world, and as neat as Joey was, he'd had his share of "kid moments" in his nine-plus years. Still, she couldn't imagine her world without him.

This man, this Mark Bradley: he was, she thought, what she could imagine her son becoming. Bright, sensitive, well spoken; boyishly good-looking too, certainly that. He hadn't said a great deal. But she felt good with this man; she felt . . . *right*.

And it scared her, oh God, it did. Because Don Russell, too, had once felt so right.

Yet here, in the midst of this chance encounter in the desert, Tracy sensed herself succumbing to feelings dormant for so long. If she had been scared before, now she felt downright petrified.

They went in and out of box canyons, sometimes pedaling far back, occasionally meeting dead-ends after the first turn. Tracy would have been hopelessly lost, but Mark never once had to ponder the way.

They stopped at mid-morning in the shade of some fan palms within the mouth of a canyon. Tracy had borrowed Joey's water bottle, in addition to her own; it was hardly enough. Mark had three bottles on his bike, and a large canteen in the backpack he had worn. He'd also brought granola bars and cookies.

"You tired?" Mark asked.

Tracy nodded. "Getting there."

"We'll be working our way back to town from here on. Actually, we got a break in the weather."

"We did?"

"It's a little cooler today; shouldn't go any higher than a hundred-six."

"Brrr."

They started back on a maze of trails that Mark followed easily. Soon they reached the graded Las Palmas Road, intersecting it near the Eternal Hills Cemetery and Rainbow Tree Farm.

"What are you and your family doing this afternoon?" Mark asked as they neared downtown.

"They were stone cold asleep when I left, so I have no idea."

"There's a double feature playing in Borrego Springs. Why don't we all go?"

"They have a movie house out here?"

Mark smiled. "Believe it or not."

"I don't know about Dad, but Joey will love it. What time?"

"Pick me up at one-thirty?"

They stopped near Carrizo Street. "I'll ride up to the Estates with you," Mark said.

"Don't be silly, you live right here. I know the way."

"You sure?"

"Yeah."

They looked at each other awkwardly. Then, Tracy leaned over, and they tried to kiss, but banged helmets instead, and laughed as they took them off.

The kiss was brief, but said, in part, some of what they were holding back. Tracy's hand touched his cheek as they separated.

"Thanks for the morning," she said.

"It was . . . my pleasure."

5

It had killed and killed all night, indiscriminately, stopping only once to feed, an instinctive act, barely remembered. A bloody trail of its nocturnal prey—kangaroo rats, a roadrunner, pocket mice, even a tiny kit fox—had been left for the turkey vultures and other scavengers across miles of sand.

Now, in the daytime, it was far from its habitat, to the northwest, in canyons where it had hunted before, though only for survival. It was weary, and on its own might have found a cave or other niche in which to curl up, away from the fiery day. But it was impelled to go on, to continue the hunt, even while many of the creatures it sought were themselves at rest.

It was impelled to kill.

6

Bobby Eklund liked the desert almost as much as he disliked people.

He disliked having to put up with their bullshit day after day. His service manager was the worst. Bobby worked as a mechanic at an auto dealership in Escondido, and that sonofabitch did nothing but give him shit. Other mechanics did too; customers . . . and those goddamn salesmen, they were the biggest assholes of all. And it didn't stop after work, no sir. That hag of a landlady, the inconsiderate tenants in his apartment building that took his parking spot and made noise outside his bedroom window and always bitched about his trailer . . .

Christ, he hated all of them!

That's why Bobby liked the desert, because he could get up when he wanted, not when someone revved his motorcycle at five a.m. He could look around at sandstone and scrub and granite and know there wasn't a goddamn soul within miles.

He sat in a beach chair under an awning on the side of his Winnebago, sucking on his second beer of the day. A Dwight Yoakum cassette played on his boom box; not loud, like he usually played it, because Pam was still asleep inside, and any damn noise bothered her. Dumb broad. Yeah, she was good-looking, had big tits, and she could really turn on in bed. But to her, a trip to the desert meant a weekend in Vegas or Palm Springs. This was the second time he'd brought her out here, probably the last. There was always Patti in Customer Service. So what if she was a little chubby? She was nice, and she liked him, and from what one of the other guys said, she could get it on pretty good herself.

It was the fifth time Bobby had camped in this particular spot, which a park map told him was called Rattlesnake Canyon. He had discovered it over a year ago, by accident. First, he'd turned off the main road east of Borrego Springs, onto one of those paved streets that seemed to go nowhere. Paved street had become graded road, then jeep trail for a couple of miles before dropping into a wash. Bumpy as hell for a mile or so (Pam bitched about that). Then, a narrow path along a ridge, and a sharp turn into the canyon. Not something most people would do in a trailer; not something anyone would do when there was rain, or even a threat of it. But Bobby Eklund had found it, and in all this time he'd never seen a clue that another soul had been out this way.

OK, so he'd compromised, just to get Pam to come along. A few days here, then they drive up to Palm Springs for the weekend. Let Pam get her kicks shopping elbow-to-elbow with all the other damn tourists. He'd probably just stay in the trailer.

Even bleary-eyed, Bobby could see the coyote against the backdrop of yellow and reddish-brown rocks, about thirty yards away. Bobby didn't like coyotes much; for that matter, he wasn't too fond of anything with fur or feathers. He'd always believed in something his daddy used to say: "If it's got four legs or two wings, it's prob'ly worth shootin'." Bobby thought his daddy was a heck of a guy.

The coyote stood motionless, staring at him. Bobby put down his beer and got up slowly. "You stay right there, fucker," he muttered to himself. "Got a little surprise for you."

He went inside the Winnebago and felt under the cot for his .30-.30. Pam Stallings heard him and rolled over.

"What're you doing?" she asked.

Bobby held up the rifle. "A little huntin' is all."

Pam buried her head in the pillow. "Oh Christ, you gonna shoot that thing?"

"Yeah; just shut up, OK?"

When he went back outside, the coyote was no longer where he had seen it. He looked around the slopes.

"All right, where in hell did—?"

There was a scrabbling sound from on top of the trailer. Bobby looked up.

The .30-.30 flew from his hands as the coyote knocked him to the ground.

Pam heard the scream and climbed groggily out of bed. She walked to the door, dressed only in a pair of red bikini panties Bobby had bought for her.

"What was that—?" she began.

Death's eyes glared up at her. The coyote's jaws dripped the blood it had let free from Bobby Eklund's throat.

Pam took a step back, stumbled. The coyote fell upon her inside the trailer, killing her quickly, savaging her body for over a minute, until the energy of its rage had diminished.

The coyote started back into the desert.

CHAPTER TEN

Dedication

1

Mark Alderson was almost ready at 1:20 when he heard a loud knock. Joey Russell stood grinning in the doorway.

"Mom's keeping the car cool," the boy said.

"Good idea. Come in a second."

Joey looked around the modestly furnished apartment. "Cool place."

Mark grimaced. "If you like early motel. It's OK."

"Hey, thanks for asking me to go along with you guys."

"Sure. Is your grandfather coming?"

"Nah, he's gonna spend the afternoon with the Findleys."

Mark had a cheap CD player, which he'd bought with his first paycheck from the country club; nothing he'd feel bad about losing if he had to leave in a hurry. Joey eyed two short stacks of CDs in front of it.

"Hey, Mom and me have most of these," he said. "You like the old stuff too."

"Yeah."

"We got the Led Zeppelin, we got the U-2 and Fleetwood Mac's *Rumors*. Don't have Chicago's hits from the eighties, but we got the last two before it. And oh yeah, we got *Sergeant Pepper* and all the Beatles stuff."

Mark smiled. "You guys have good taste. Come on, I'm ready."

Tracy had been about to turn off her engine when Mark and Joey appeared. As Mark had predicted, the temperature was one hundred and five, and would only go up another degree or two. It was still hot enough.

Joey claimed the back seat. Mark climbed in next to Tracy. Dylan's "It Ain't Me, Babe" played softly on the tape deck. Tracy sped off, concerned her engine was going to overheat.

"That was great this morning," Tracy said as they drove the seven miles of the Seaway toward 'downtown' Borrego Springs. "I hope we can do it again."

Mark nodded. "We will, but not tomorrow. I have to work."

"No!" Tracy exclaimed. "Only one day off? That's not fair. Don't you think your boss is taking advantage of you?"

"Not really, he just got used to me always being available. I preferred it that way, till . . . The good news is, I'll probably get off at three or so. The other good news is, Jerry's hiring another bartender part-time. Eugene's having too many health problems to be counted on anymore."

"Glad to hear you might have some relief. Anyway, I wouldn't have been able to ride in the morning. The Findleys' son and his family are driving over from San Diego for the holiday. They'll be here later this afternoon. I knew George Findley from back home. We're entertaining them tonight, and we have more plans tomorrow."

The Center Theatre in Borrego Springs stood nestled at the rear of a u-shaped cluster of stores along Palm Canyon Drive. They saw a Jackie Chan chop-'em-up, which Joey loved, and a romantic comedy that he thought was OK, except for all the kissing stuff.

Afterward they browsed through stores at The Mall, across the street, then had Mexican food at a family-owned restaurant that, Tracy admitted, beat anything they had in Missouri. Joey ate five tacos by himself, a feat that impressed Mark.

"This kid has one of those metabolisms," Tracy said, "that pudgy women on endless diets would kill for! Makes you sick."

Mark rumpled the boy's hair; Joey grinned, a runnel of salsa escaping down his chin. *He likes this man too*, Tracy thought. In his short life the poor kid had gotten the shit-end-of-the-stick in the Father & Son Game. Aside from his grandfather, there'd been no other male role models. Past reactions to the infrequent guys in his mother's life had ranged from indifference to downright hostility. But . . .

He likes this man.

It was all beginning to make Tracy's head swim.

They dropped Mark off at his apartment a few minutes past six. Joey stayed in the car as Tracy walked to the door with him, hardly aware that she had taken his hand.

"Today was . . . one of the nicest days I've had in a long time," she said. "Thanks for everything, and especially for taking Joey to the movies."

"I really like that kid," Mark said.

Tracy turned, faced him, took his other hand. "I really like you, Mark Bradley."

"Likewise, lady."

They kissed, this time longer. Mark's face was crimson when they separated. Tracy supposed she didn't look any less like a schoolgirl.

"Will your visitors be here *all* day tomorrow?" Mark asked.

"No; in fact, they're starting back in the afternoon."

"Then we can do something after I get off."

"Sure; what?"

"I don't know; I'll call you from work."

Mark stood on the landing and watched them drive off. Joey had moved to the front seat and was grinning as he gave Mark the thumbs-up sign. Tracy shoved her son's head down playfully.

2

Rosie Shannon called Mark on Mrs. Jenks's phone early

Wednesday morning, asking him to stop by the house at his convenience. The Arroyo Lounge was opening at ten on the Fourth. Mark said he would come by before then.

The nephew had left the previous day, but the sister was still there. She led Mark into Jack Redmond's study, where Rosie was busy on the computer. They hugged, and Rosie took him out on the patio.

"How are you doing?" Mark asked.

She shrugged. "OK, I guess, except I miss the old buzzard like hell. I'm keeping busy. Dead or not, the publisher wants Jack's new book delivered by the end of the month."

"I thought he hadn't finished it."

"The first draft was done; the rest is manual labor, fill-in-the-blanks, that sort of thing. Tell you a secret, Mark: I've done most of the final drafts on his last three books. But I need to get away for a while. I'm driving back with my sister tomorrow and finishing it in L.A."

Mark nodded. "I understand."

Rosie had brought a file folder out with her. Fingering it she said, "Before he died, Jack told me something. He wanted the dedication in his last book to be for you."

Mark looked at her, stunned. "I don't know what to say . . ."

"There's a catch, though. He said Mark *Bradley* would absolutely not do; you'll have to write out the correct name yourself so they'd spell it properly."

She handed him the folder. The words on a single sheet of paper read, *To Mark _____, best damn Probe player I ever knew.*

Rosie gave Mark a pen. He hesitated.

"The book won't be published till January," she said. "Whatever it is, Mark, it'll be over by then."

I hope you're right, Mark thought, *because a million or more people will see it in the hardcover edition.*

He wrote out A-L-D-E-R-S-O-N and handed it back to Rosie, who did not even look at the name.

"I wish I could thank him," Mark said.

"You just did." She gestured across the valley. "Do you believe this weather?"

The Fourth had begun as a rare July day, cool and overcast, a few thunderheads sitting over the Santa Rosa Mountains to the north. While that threat was diminishing, the clouds remained. Without the sun it would be twenty degrees cooler than yesterday.

"Let's enjoy it while we can." He looked at his watch. "Time for work."

Rosie walked him to the door. "You know you're welcome to stay here while I'm gone."

Mark looked around the luxurious house; it was tempting. Then, he saw the tabloid headlines: *Fugitive Found Living In Dead Writer's Home.*

He kissed her cheek. "Thanks, but I'm fine."

3

Tracy was glad to take Mark's call at noon. "We're barbecuing steaks," she said. "Wow, I wish it was over."

"Why?" Mark asked.

"George Findley's sort of . . . different from the person I remember over twenty years ago. He's OK, I guess. But Jill, his wife . . ."

"Yeah?"

"I've always taught Joey not to say anything about anyone, if it wasn't complimentary . . ."

"I think you've made the point."

"But Mark," she blurted, "the woman is an obnoxious bitch!"

They both laughed, and Mark said, "I'll rescue you at about three-fifteen."

"Great. Are we riding?"

"This kind of weather presents us with a rare opportunity. Will you settle for a long hike?"

"Yeah, I'd love it!"

"I'll even have you back in time for fireworks."

"Not to worry," Tracy assured him. "Harry Keller is bringing Gary over. Dad and Harry are old baseball buddies. They're going to watch a game, catch the fireworks after. So, we don't have to hurry. You want me to make sandwiches or something?"

"Sure; and bring a bathing suit too."

"A *bathing suit*? Where exactly are we hiking?"

"It's a . . . special place. Trust me."

"You're trusted."

4

It was closer to three-thirty when Mark pedaled up Oasis Drive. He had already changed at the club. Tracy, in jeans, hiking boots and a denim railroad shirt, looked like an L.L. Bean centerfold. Mark was glad she'd put on long pants; catclaw thorns did nasty things to exposed flesh.

Mark left his Schwinn in the garage, securing Joey's solemn vow to guard it with his life. The boy, on his own bike, followed Tracy and Mark until they left the street where it dead-ended past Verbena Road. He waved and did a wheelie back to the house. Tracy tried not to watch.

Here, bordering Smoke Tree Estates with its opulent homes and lush green fairways, was the raw desert. The contrast of these two adjoining worlds never ceased to amaze Mark. Stepping into Mortero Hill's wilderness backyard, Tracy's reaction was the same.

Passing between the scrub and cactus for a short distance, they joined the winding Bighorn Creek, which circumvented the Estates to the west. Here, it meandered less for a quarter-mile or so. Its steady flow surprised Tracy.

Farther north they passed an odd-looking complex. Mark had been waiting for Tracy's reaction, certain she would wrinkle her nose. He was not disappointed.

"Is that the city dump or something?" she asked.

Mark laughed. "That, my dear, is the mansion of our town eccentric."

Actually, Dexter Jones's residence was a rather conventional ranch-style home that might not have warranted a second look if not for the motley assortment of red bricks, adobe, stucco, and three kinds of wood from which it had been built. The eye-opener (eyesore, most agreed) was everything *around* the house, including a stack of nested camper shells, an ancient Airstream trailer, three partly-rusted pickup trucks on blocks, a fourteen-and-a-half-foot Sears aluminum boat, an assortment of engines, and a twelve-foot contrivance called a long tom, used well over a century ago during the valley's gold rush. Old Dex had unearthed it near the creek. Beyond the residence was the remains of an outhouse, half-moon and all. Tracy did a double take at that.

"I only know him a little, but he's a friendly old guy," Mark said. "You'd enjoy meeting him."

Tracy shook her head. "Another time. I *have* to find out why I'm wearing a bathing suit under my clothes on a hike in the middle of the desert!"

They passed the house and walked another hundred yards. Stopping suddenly, Mark hugged Tracy, an awkward feat with both wearing backpacks. She smiled at him.

"What was that for?"

"I want you to do something for me today."

"What?"

"Tell me about Tracy Russell."

She nodded. "I will, on one condition: you tell me about Mark Bradley."

"I can't."

"Why not?"

Mark took a deep breath. "Because Mark Bradley doesn't exist. But I *will* tell you about Mark Alderson."

5

Old Dex saw the two young folks walk past his cabin along Bighorn Creek.

He recognized one, the bartender fella from the country club. Nice kid. The woman was new. Hell, it was good the boy found *anyone* in this burg under seventy, so more power to him! And that was a fine-looking female, even if he was staring at her from far-off with one good eye.

Usually he would have waved down the rare soul passing by,

but not today. He'd been sprawled on his couch when he saw them out the window, but hadn't moved. The television was on: Oprah. He loved Oprah, usually taped her to watch later, since he was mostly at his diggings when she came on. But today he'd worked Bighorn Creek down near the sink for less than two hours before coming home; now, watching Oprah, he hardly knew what anyone was saying.

Old Dex was tired, more damn tired than ever before, especially since all the crazy stuff had started. Part of it, he figured, was just plain getting old. The body says, *Hey, I done enough for you, and now I don't feel like doing no more, so just piss off.* Old folks' curse. If it ain't your heart or your kidneys or your eyesight letting you down or the cancer eating some part of your insides or your arteries hardening up, then it's likely your brain going to seed.

And if he didn't have all that to worry about, he also had to deal with *them*. Lately, most of them had begun to understand better than before, and they were more demanding, less patient, and the confrontations had been—at times—more exhausting than the work itself.

Hell, what could he do? All he ever wanted was to help. They knew that; the ones who could understand, they knew. And he would keep on helping . . .

Just as long as he could.

But they had to back off, let things happen like they were supposed to. That was the way it had been; that was the way it still had to be. Some stuff couldn't be rushed.

He would go there tonight and tell 'em that. Then, he might not show up for a day or two or three, unless there was a good reason. If he didn't have to deal with it every day, maybe he wouldn't be so damn tired, and he could go right on helping them . . .

. . . until it was over.

Hell, Old Dex felt better already.

He went to the kitchen, poured a glass of milk, made a sandwich, and resumed his affair with Oprah.

Past Lives

1

"You're kidding. An insane asylum?"

"Unless the PR person who wrote the Smoke Tree Estates information brochure made up his own history, that's what this was."

"But way out in the desert? I mean, how did people even get here back then?"

Tracy stared up at a well-preserved, four-foot-long section of Concordia Sanitarium's outer wall. The top was at eye level, its foundation well below the sand, which had built up on the surface. Much of the main building had fallen in upon itself, leaving precarious mounds of rubble in some places, twisted formations in others, where runnels of melted adobe had entwined, then hardened. These shapes, along with the awareness of what the ruins had been, heightened the eeriness of the place.

"Stagecoach trails ran through here," Mark told her. "One, I think, was not too far away. As for putting an asylum in this place, that probably made sense for its time. They couldn't treat the mentally ill effectively, so they hid them instead."

They walked across an area that had been the courtyard. A small cairn of stones and splintered wood marked the location of an old well.

"What happened to this place?" Tracy asked.

"I don't know. The brochure didn't say."

Tracy suddenly froze, looked around. "What's that?"

Mark was puzzled for a moment, then smiled. He pointed toward the mouth of the canyon. "It's the wind cutting through there. Sounds weird, huh?"

They went on to Madhouse Canyon. Before coming to the ruins, Tracy had begun talking about her life with Don Russell. The diversion now behind them, she continued her story.

Despite a happy and reasonably sane childhood, Tracy had abandoned all common sense when, at the age of seventeen, she had fallen hopelessly in love with Don Russell. He was a year older and had just transferred to Tracy's high school, where girls were already fighting for his attention. Tracy Singer, "Flat-chested and plain as vanilla," considered herself lucky to attract the tall, handsome boy.

Motherless since birth, Don grew up with an abusive father and an endless succession of his slatternly girlfriends. He became a survivor, relying on a sharp wit and a glib tongue. Mostly, his interests involved wagering on sporting events, everything from local high school basketball games to the Super Bowl. Every school seemed to have one kid like Don Russell; you wanted to make a bet or buy a pool ticket, you went to him. Some of his connections on the outside were, to say the least, unsavory.

But Tracy overlooked his foibles, because she was in love, and was also of the naïve opinion that gambling was a harmless diversion. Even Vivian and Carl Singer, despite their reservations about the boy, had to admit he treated their daughter well. They were married when Tracy was twenty-one; Joey was born three years later.

Early in their marriage, things were promising. Don disassociated himself from his gambler friends and became a "working stiff," while Tracy finished college. His first job, which Carl helped him find, lasted nearly two years—until he was fired for organizing baseball pools.

Afterward, things went to hell. Don could hold no job longer than four months. His "old problem" returned with a vengeance. No longer content to organize pools, he wagered on everything, and Tracy sank right along with him, waiting for the "big score."

By the time Vivian Singer intervened, struggling to bring her daughter to her senses, household money no longer existed; the savings account had dwindled to pocket change. Tracy finally confronted her husband, but Don was able to turn on the charm and soothe her. He had always been good at making her believe things would be better, because it was what she *wanted* to believe.

It was after Joey was born that Tracy stopped loving Don Russell. He was not abusive to Joey—not in a physical way. But he took little part in the child's care, and only played with him when he was "good." Even when the boy was older, he seemed disinterested in being a father. Still, Tracy endured, against her parents' urging, maybe because she felt sorry for him, or because divorce was "just not something the Singers did."

Then, with emotional and financial pressures peaking, Don Russell went on a weekend binge. On Monday morning the only thing that belonged to Tracy was her son.

She saw Don one more time after that, four months later, long enough to have him sign the divorce papers. She refrained from having him arrested, but swore that, if he ever tried to see her or Joey again, she would do exactly that. Predictably, it was the last time she ever spoke to Don Russell.

2

Initially they followed Bighorn Creek into Madhouse Canyon, but abandoned it when the catclaws became a dangerous obstacle. They traversed the east slope, not particularly steep yet, and were able, briefly, to walk side by side.

"An experience like that could sour a person on relationships for life," Mark said.

"I felt that way for a long time, even though I was so much

like him in those first few years. Scary ... Mom was the one who said it'd be different; not everyone was like Don Russell, she told me, so why make the rest of your life miserable because of him?" She shook her head. "Mom knew it wouldn't work with Don, all the way back to when I was in high school. But she never said 'I told you so,' not once in all the years after ... Are we going up *there*?"

The canyon walls had pinched together; Bighorn Creek was barely visible through dense brush below. The ridge they were on had narrowed; debris made the footing treacherous.

"You have to work," he said, "but it's passable."

She walked behind him. The walls drew in more tightly. At times they dropped down and utilized the creek bed, which was nearly dry in places where it was wide. But a steep incline, or an abundance of catclaws, always forced them back to one of the slopes.

Soon it seemed they were doing more climbing and boulder hopping than hiking. A brief but rugged stretch required half an hour to negotiate. Mark had been concerned about this part; but Tracy was enjoying herself and did not complain. And, Mark admitted to himself grudgingly, she could out-climb him.

Patches of green eventually broke the sameness of stone, scrub and cactus up ahead. Cottonwoods and sycamores grew on the barren slopes, often in small clusters, occasionally a lone sentinel. They rested briefly in one grove, not for the shade, because the sun had stayed hidden all this time. Once, Mark saw darker clouds and was concerned about a sudden rainstorm, which left the canyon at risk of flash flooding. But it passed quickly.

Fan palms began to appear higher up, which delighted Tracy. To a Midwesterner, a palm tree personified everything tropical and exotic. Like the cottonwoods and sycamores, some stood alone; but higher up there were dense clusters.

"This is a good sign," Mark said. "It means we're almost there."

"Glad to hear it," Tracy replied, panting animatedly.

Negotiating the west slope high above Bighorn Creek, they had been listening to its trickling flow. Now, the sound of running water grew louder. They climbed past the largest cluster of palms yet. Mark led Tracy into a narrow, steep-walled grotto.

"Wow!" Tracy exclaimed.

A twenty-five foot waterfall cascaded down the rock wall, which was blanketed with wet moss and delicate maidenhair ferns, the latter a rarity in the desert. Passing into a hidden channel between the rocks, the run-off poured into the creek below. Little sunlight reached this place, no matter how hot the day.

"It's called Moonlight Falls," Mark said.

"So this is why we wore bathing suits."

"Nope."

"It's not?"

"Moonlight Falls is not exactly an overrun tourist attraction, but folks do find their way up here occasionally. My place is not in any of the guidebooks. It's only five more minutes from here. Can you handle that?"

"Oh, I think so."

"Five *rugged* minutes."

"I'm still trusting, so lead on."

Rugged was an understated misnomer. Farther in, where the grotto ended, they scaled a wall by utilizing a series of precarious hand and footholds. Above, on a ledge that was hardly a ledge at all, they inched along for another fifteen feet. The facing was split by a defile, so narrow it was necessary to pass through sideways with their backpacks off.

The defile curved sharply, then widened. Looking back at Tracy, Mark waved his hand. "Welcome to Alderson Hot Springs," he said.

The frothing mineral spring occupied a craterlike depression about five feet in diameter. Bubbles popped occasionally; there was a distinct sulfurous smell, not unpleasant. Laying down her backpack, Tracy smiled broadly at Mark.

"Go ahead, feel it," Mark said.

She put a hand in, withdrew it instinctively, then felt it again. Not boiling hot, but quite warm, over one hundred degrees. "How deep does it go?" she asked.

"Way down under the mountain. A splinter of an earthquake fault is what causes the upswelling. You feel around with your foot, you'll find a small, bottomless hole in the middle. There are ledges to sit on."

She began unbuttoning her shirt. "What are you waiting for?"

Tracy had worn her blue and black, one-piece bathing suit. Mark's was in his backpack. He pulled it out and disappeared into the defile. When he returned, Tracy was in the hot spring, water up to her chin.

"Get in here, quick," she said impatiently. "You owe me a story, mister, and I can't wait to collect."

3

After the long climb up Madhouse Canyon, the hot spring soothed their tired muscles. This water, containing sulfates, iodine, chloride, and parts of two dozen other minerals, was therapeutic. Through the centuries it was claimed that mineral springs could cure everything from rheumatism to arthritis to "constitutional taints." Sitting there for the first five minutes, Tracy could believe it. Only Mark's description of his beginnings tempered her pleasure.

"I'm not so naïve to think everyone had parents as neat as mine," she said. "But I'll never understand why people even bother having children, if they can't commit themselves to the child's needs and development."

"Even so," Mark said, "plenty of other kids in similar circumstances did better than me. Get put in a good foster home, or better still, get adopted. Hell, I was only two when my mother died. You would've thought *somebody* would want a two-year-old. But it never happened.

"For the next fifteen years I spent my time between an orphanage on Long Island, and a bunch of foster homes. The orphanage was OK; a handful of overworked, underpaid people trying to take care of hundreds of kids . . . But they fed you, gave you a bed in a dorm, sent you to school. If you started young enough, and didn't watch television or read books so you wouldn't know what it was like to get a story at night or to be tucked in, it was all right.

"The foster homes, that was something else. At best, you hoped they would be indifferent. They collected their stipend, fed you, gave you things to do around the house. But the ones I kept getting . . . You wonder how trained social workers could be fooled by these people. Verbal abuse was the least of it. In one home I had to work whenever I wasn't at school; hardly time to get homework done. And in another," he shuddered, ". . . the man was a drunk; beat the crap out of me sometimes, but never left a mark where anyone could see it."

Tracy shook her head. "How did you get out of that one?"

"I was eleven, wiry, stronger than I looked. He was so drunk one day while he was hitting me that he could hardly see. I grabbed a kitchen fork and stuck it in his neck. He bled like crazy; screamed his head off. His wife finished the beating, and they sent me back to the orphanage. My punishment was a month in the Blue Room—that's what they called the isolation cell. Two meals a day, no visitors, no play time. If it hadn't been for my books . . .

"I finally ran away from the whole damn thing when I was seventeen. Lived on the streets for a while, did what I needed to survive.

"It was after lots of scrounging, washing dishes, that I met Tony Vincent. He was twenty-two, and dressed fine, and I thought he was cool. Tony shared his big apartment with five other kids, two of them girls, all my age or younger. So I moved in.

"Before long I realized that you might as well have called Tony *Fagin*. The kids living there—all runaways—would do anything for him; me too. And even though he was small-time, Tony was involved in everything bad.

"So that was how it went, for the next three years. Crazy as it sounds, it was the first real family I ever had. New kids came and went, but me, Tony, and three others went the distance. I was a punk, Tracy, a goddamn punk. We stole for him, made drops, whatever. The girls worked the streets.

"Then, Tony got into bigger stuff, with guys from South America. His new 'business associates' gave us the creeps. And he was sticking his neck way out with the law, too. He already had a record, enough to keep him in the slam for a long time if he went before a judge again.

"When he finally screwed up, Tony asked me to take the fall

for him. And I did."

"Oh Mark, *no!*" Tracy exclaimed.

"I served six years, half the damn sentence. Would've been a lot more if it hadn't been my first time. You know, I'm not really sorry for those years. I figured it was payback for all the stuff I never got caught doing.

"But I didn't feel that way then. I hated the world for screwing me and couldn't wait to get even.

"I cooled it at first, especially after learning Tony was doing time for something small. The rest of the gang had scattered. So I settled in at a halfway house, went through the motions of looking for a job, did what they expected.

"It was right after I got out that I met Julius Mandell, my parole officer. He looked like a sweet little old guy, but could he be a hard-nosed sonofabitch. Our first meetings were bad; I was a real hard-ass. But he must've seen something in me that no one else had, because he kept on my case, and before long, well, he got through.

"I suppose it was when we started talking about books. Julius loved to read too—he owned lots of Jack Redmond's stuff—and it didn't take much to get me going. A fifteen-minute session would go an hour. Pretty soon I couldn't wait to go to his office, or see him show up at the halfway house.

"We got to talking about lots of other things. Julius helped me find me a job; nothing much, loading dock work, but it was a paycheck. I got my own place, a tiny loft room, mice and all . . . but it was *mine!* The first piece of furniture was a bookcase Julius had made in his workshop, filled with about a hundred paperbacks he'd bought at secondhand stores.

"Two months later, Julius brought me to his house, out on Long Island. It was Passover, and he and his wife were having a *seder*. I didn't have a clue what that was, but it was great. Anna treated me like family from the moment I walked in the door. I must've gained five pounds that night.

"Afterward, I *was* like part of the family. I got a better job, took a nicer apartment out near their house. They encouraged me to get my high school diploma, and I did. I enrolled in some general business courses at a community college; not that I had a clue where I was going, but it was a start. And the Mandells couldn't have been any prouder if I'd been their own son.

"Fifteen months after taking my case, Julius retired. He was already past mandatory retirement age, but had sneaked some extra time, because it was what he loved to do. My new parole officer was a drone, but it didn't matter, because I was one of his easiest cases.

"My relationship with the Mandells was great; they became the parents I never had. I couldn't forget my past, but they helped me to deal with it. Anna had been a social worker before her retirement, and her insight was incredible.

"I was still going to school, taking a number of courses in literature. That was something I really liked; I even thought about teaching some day. Then, I remembered all those kids still going into foster homes to begin their nightmares, because no one gave a rat's ass, or had no clue how to weed out the bad ones. Maybe, I decided, there was something I could do about it. Anna couldn't have been any more supportive. And the more I thought about it, the more I knew it was what I wanted.

"By this time I had another job, delivering bottled water on a good route. For me, the money was great. I also got to talk to people every day, something I'd never been much good at before. So, here I was, two years and a few months out of jail, still on parole, and doing OK. I remember thinking back then how it seemed to bug John Fowler, my parole officer, that I wasn't some kind of big problem.

"Things went to shit after that, Tracy. One night, Tony Vincent showed up at my door. He'd just been released, and managed to find me. It was weird, because he was so far removed from my new life that it took me a moment to recognize him. Still, the man had been like a brother. So I let him stay a couple of nights, which was all he wanted. I gave him some money, and he left. All that time he never said a word about the years I spent in the slam for him.

"I don't know how stupid I could've been to think it was over. Tony was back a couple of months later, up to his usual crap. Drugs, mostly. He'd even managed to recruit some of the old gang. He wanted me back in, said something about my route job being great for distribution. I told him to stay out of my life, that I was straight and liked it that way.

"At first his persistence was sort of casual. But after a while he became indignant, brought up the past, told me how much I owed him. *I owed him!* He would come to my apartment, flag me down on the street; once, he was waiting for me on campus.

"One night, after I'd refused Tony again in front of my apartment building, there was a knock on the door. It was John Fowler. He had this gleam in his eye, I swear. He'd seen me with Tony Vincent, no doubt of it. He shoved a finger in my face, said 'Watch it, asshole,' and left; wouldn't hear me out. He even wrote me up. Julius tried to intervene, but it didn't do any good.

"That was the week before he found out about Anna. She hadn't been feeling well; tired, mostly. They did tests, found pancreatic cancer spreading like crazy. So much for the piece of land they owned in Florida and the cottage they were going to build on it."

Mark paused for a moment, looked away. Tracy placed a trembling hand on his arm.

"Julius...was devastated," he finally continued. "They'd been together over forty years, no children or anything. I never thought two people could love each other as much as Julius and Anna.

"After that, Julius grew more distant. I swear that, inch by inch, he was dying along with her. One time I tried to talk to him about my problems, but he didn't even hear me.

"The next time Tony showed up, I . . . told him I'd do whatever the hell he wanted—*one time*—if he would get out of my life for good."

Tracy put both hands to her mouth, but said nothing.

"He agreed. Said they needed a safe house to store some shit... cocaine, a big shipment due in the following week. It only needed to stay there a couple of days, then it'd be gone and he'd never bother me again. I warned him about Fowler keeping an eye on me, but he said I shouldn't worry about that."

"They *killed* him?" Tracy exclaimed.

Mark shook his head. "On the day the stuff came I went to Fowler's office on some bullshit pretext, then 'let' him tail me as I took in a whole lot of bookstores. I know they would have done him if they'd seen him near my place."

"Then you saved his life."

"For whatever that's worth. The DEA was all over my place the next morning. I was on my route when Jim Epps, one of our old gang, found me and told me what had gone down. They'd gotten Fowler involved too, and he wanted my ass, big-time.

"So that's it, Tracy. I'd done another stupid goddamn thing and I would've been back in a cell for a real long time. And that wasn't going to happen. No one was going to help me; not Julius, not anyone."

"So you ran." Tears streamed down Tracy's face.

Mark nodded. "The rest of it doesn't matter. A couple of days in one place, a week in another. Almost two months in Smoke Tree; that's a record. But as soon as I think it's closing in on me again . . ."

"You can't keep running, Mark!" she cried. "There's got to be—!"

"Tracy, I don't want to talk about it anymore, OK? I'll take you back to town, and I won't bother you again. You don't need to be involved in this."

She put an arm around his neck, kissed him. "I didn't know Mark Bradley too well, but I liked him. Now I know Mark Alderson, and I like *him* even more. You're a decent man, Mark. You don't want to talk about it now, fine; but I already *am* involved, and I'll do whatever I can to help you."

Mark started to say something, but she kissed him again, crushing his lips to hers, probing tentatively with her tongue, then more insistently. They separated, and Tracy stood.

"I believe we're improperly dressed for a hot tub, don't you?" she said.

She peeled off the bathing suit and tossed it aside. As she stood there, hands at her sides, Mark drank in the sweet smoothness of her well-shaped body, the small but nicely proportioned breasts. Her nipples were rock-hard; beads of water from the pool clung to the dark mound between her legs.

Mark stood, took off his suit, catching it briefly on his growing manhood, making Tracy laugh. He cupped her breasts gently, leaned over, kissed each one in turn. Tracy tossed her hair back, a little frightened, mostly thrilled as he explored her body . . . for so long now uncharted territory. She lifted his head in both hands, kissed his face a thousand times as she entwined her legs around him. Mark returned her kisses, her soft gasps of joy exciting him more. Clinging urgently to each other, they sank into the hot spring.

4

The coyote had come to its hidden niche, in the hills high above the Bad-Tasting Water place, yesterday afternoon, and had not moved since. It was tired, so tired from all the killing, all the running; nor could it understand what had happened. So it had slept, and it felt better now, and started thinking about feeding its hunger . . .

Until the thing inside, which had also slept, began to stir. And suddenly the man-creatures at the Bad-Tasting Water place, which the coyote had paid little mind to, were of interest.

The animal knew that, soon, there would be killing again.

More memories had returned to Bruno after the woman in the . . .

Big monster-thing.

. . . trailer. A *woman*. It had something to do with the San Fra place; the San Fran . . .

San Francisco.

In San Francisco there had been a woman, and she had laughed at him because he looked so odd and talked so slowly, and she had called him names. And he couldn't say very well what he felt . . .

What he desired.

. . . but he had tried anyway, and it had started the trouble, because the woman, who did the *Thing* with other men every night, had laughed even harder at him when he'd wanted to do the *Thing* with her. And then his family had found out, and they started telling him, telling Bruno, what a bad person he was for wanting to do the *Thing*, and he had screamed inside, like he'd screamed a thousand times before, and he'd looked at his hands, and . . .

The woman in San Francisco.
The woman in the trailer.

The woman . . .

Below, in the bubbling pool, with the man. Standing, pulling off her clothes, naked. Touching, kissing, clutching, in the water again . . .

The woman in San Francisco.

Sitting on the edge of the pool, legs spread apart, head tossed back, the man's face in . . .

The woman in the trailer.

Laying supine on the sandstone floor, feet dangling above the cloudy pool, the man on top of her, fingers intertwined, two bodies moving, moving together, and the sounds, the sounds . . .

The woman.

The sounds growing louder, and the woman twisting her head from side to side, and the two bodies thrashing, and again the sounds . . .

He wanted the woman.

. . . rising uncontrolled, echoing off rock facings (*oh mark oh mark*), meaningless sounds . . .

But he couldn't have the woman because he was an animal.

. . . that forced the creature from its niche, and with a final look at the woman's face . . .

(*oh mark oh mark*)

. . . it fled, confused and angry, farther back into the canyon.

CHAPTER TWELVE

Flames

1

They sat quietly in the hot spring, and it felt warm and good, and they wanted to stay in it forever with their spent bodies pressed tightly together. Tracy's eyes had been closed as she lay with her head on Mark's chest. She opened them and saw him looking up at the small patch of sky visible between the granite facings.

"Penny for your thoughts," she said.

"Huh . . . what'd you say?"

"I advised you of a one-cent tender offer to be apprised of your current whereabouts."

He smiled. "Can't do much with a penny."

"All right, a dime then. You seemed to be up past those cliffs."

"I was back in Jack Redmond's room. It was so weird that night . . . when he died."

"Tell me about it."

"You'll think I'm crazy . . ."

"I won't think you're crazy. Mark, please tell me."

Her voice was firm, eyes intense. Mark detailed the writer's last few minutes. It was evident that Tracy would not scoff at his story.

She was silent for a while after he finished. Then, in a voice choked with emotion, she talked about the odd behavior of Vivian Singer. Now it was Mark's turn to look astonished.

Afterward Tracy said, "I hadn't even thought that much about it, until you told me about Jack Redmond. My dad figured she was turning senile, getting Alzheimer's or something, and I went along with that. But nobody just gets that way overnight, do they?"

"Before your Mom, have you ever had anyone die in front of you?"

"No, never."

"Me neither. So who's to say what happens at that moment?" He shook his head. "I'm not sure we'll ever find out—oh damn!"

"What?"

Mark dug in the pile of clothes on the sandstone floor and found his watch. "I'd forgotten about the time."

Tracy grinned. "Couldn't imagine why."

"Yeah, well, we have about forty minutes of daylight left to get out of the canyon."

"Isn't that enough? I mean, it's all downhill, right?"

"It's quicker than climbing up, but it's still hard. And after an hour in here, check how willing your body is to move."

Tracy tried—unsuccessfully—to lift herself out of the hot spring. It was as though the mineral water had drawn out all of her tension and stress, leaving her helpless.

"I see what you mean," she groaned. "Wow, I didn't know you could get *this* relaxed."

Mark eased his body to the rim and pulled her up. Standing on the sandstone floor, their bodies dripping, they kissed again, briefly. Their fingertips touched as Tracy backed away.

"Tracy, I—" Mark began.

She silenced him gently. "We'll have *lots* of time to talk."

2

They dressed quickly and retraced their path out of Madhouse

Canyon. Tracy looked up at the sky and wondered if Mark had been wrong; it appeared as though night would fall at any moment. No, it was the daylong overcast that still lingered.

Nor had Mark been wrong about the descent. It was quicker, but required care, as well as a few detours when the way was suddenly too steep, or choked with brush. Mark fell once, bruising a hip. A nasty clump of hidden catclaws scratched Tracy's arm, drawing blood. Despite her protests, they stopped so that Mark could clean and bandage the worst of it. From experience, he'd been prepared.

The gray haze made their footing more tentative as, nearing the lower part of the canyon, they angled toward Bighorn Creek. Mark had brought along a Maglight, and they used it to avoid some of the worst obstacles. Once, a cottontail cut across the beam, startling them.

Night had fallen totally by the time they reached the mouth of Madhouse Canyon.

A gloomy night, clouds obliterated a moon only days away from fullness, as well as the net of stars normally thrown across the desert landscape. The only rift in the blackness—faint, at best—was from the distant lights of Smoke Tree.

"We made it!" Tracy exclaimed, pumping her arms like a jubilant child.

"Out of *there*, anyway," Mark said. "Let's rest a minute."

A wind knifing through the canyon sent them farther away from the mouth, to the sheltered side of a boulder. Their sudden appearance frightened a foraging kangaroo rat, which bounded off. They stretched out gratefully.

"You hungry?" Tracy asked.

"Yeah. Any sandwiches left?"

"Uh-uh, we ate the last of them up there. I have some granola bars."

"Me too. Not exciting, but better than nothing."

"If you can hold off till we get home, there's this big roast in the fridge that Muriel made for us. Plenty left, if Dad and Joey haven't devoured it."

"Sounds great. OK, we'll— Did you see that?"

He pointed toward the adobe ruins, dim shadows fifty yards distant. Tracy stared at them, but saw nothing.

"What was it?" she asked.

"It's gone now; only saw it for a moment. A light of some kind. We should have a look."

"Maybe it's none of our business. Besides, that place kind of gave me the creeps."

"We have to pass by. I doubt if it's anything. You can wait by the creek."

They rejoined Bighorn Creek and followed it to where the runoff had flowed underground to the well. When Mark cut across the sand to the walls, Tracy followed.

"I'd rather be with you," she said.

He took her hand. "You're really spooked, aren't you?"

She shrugged. "Guess so. Maybe it was talking about Mom, and Jack Redmond; I don't know . . ."

Mark smiled. "Let's go back. We don't have to—"

"Hey, who's out there?"

The voice startled them. Mark turned and shone his flashlight beam on a narrow crack in the nearest section of the adobe wall. The lanky figure passing through the crack shielded his eyes against the glare.

"It's Dexter Jones," Mark told Tracy, lowering the light.

"Who—oh, it's you." Old Dex flipped away a cigarette he'd recently lit. "Saw you walkin' earlier, but I figured you was long gone from here by now. Well, come closer."

"Dex, this is Tracy Russell," Mark said. "Tracy, meet Dexter Jones."

Tracy shook his thin, bony hand. "Nice to meet you, Mr. Jones."

The prospector winked (or blinked; it was hard to tell with one eye). "My friends call me Ole Dex, and we just became friends. My, you *are* a pretty one!"

"Thank you."

Old Dex glanced at his watch. "Crissakes, I gotta get back!"

Mark looked at him. "Dex, what are you doing out here?"

"Nothin', just . . . stuff. Ya know."

"You can't be looking for gold at night, not in there."

"Well yeah; no, it's . . ."

"Mark, why don't we let it be?" Tracy said.

"I gotta go," the prospector said again. "It's time . . ."

"Time for what?" Mark was persistent. "Dex, are you OK? You look tired. Is there anything we can do to help?"

"No, I gotta—!" He stopped at the wall, looked at Mark and Tracy, walked back toward them. "You wanna help?"

"Sure, if we can," Mark said. Tracy thought a moment, then nodded.

His back was bent and he looked wan; Mark was sure of that now. "You'll think I'm a crazy ole fool if I tell you."

Tracy and Mark exchanged knowing glances. "Right now there's not much you can say to make *that* happen," Tracy said.

Dexter Jones put a hand to his chin and pondered that for a moment. Finally he said, "Well shoot, it's what I'd been hopin' for a long time, so . . ." He looked at his watch again. "Maybe seein' it'll make it easier. Come on, young'ns, this way."

He turned, and the rift took him. Tracy and Mark followed Old Dex into the ruins of Concordia Sanitarium.

3

The wind that swirled amid the fragmented adobe walls, though nothing compared to what whistled through the canyon, was disturbing enough under the circumstances. Tracy and Mark stayed close behind Old Dex. Although he carried a flashlight in his back pocket, he ignored it as he deftly traversed the clearly familiar ground. He led them deeper into the ruins, where rubble lay strewn heavily. Even here the old man seemed to find easy passage.

Tracy suddenly felt cold.

Despite the overcast day and the coming night, the temperature was in the upper seventies. And they had been working hard enough not to notice any chill. Tracy glanced at Mark and knew he felt it too. His face mirrored confusion; hers, something more. She squeezed his hand tightly.

"Over there now," Old Dex said. "Not the most comfortable place, but it's where we have to be."

The area, once inside the main building, had been cleared for a few yards around. Old Dex sat on a narrow, bench-like adobe formation, motioning Tracy and Mark to a wider one opposite him.

"Why here?" Tracy asked.

"It was about two years ago when I first sat out here at night," Old Dex explained. "I felt it right off, like you're feelin' it now. Took some gettin' used to, it did. And you might as well know, it gets a who-ole lot colder when they come."

"When *who* comes?" Mark said.

"The people who died here."

"The people who . . ." Tracy shook her head.

"Didn't I tell ya you'd think I was nuts?"

"I didn't say that. I . . . just don't understand."

"Didja know this place was once a looney bin?"

"An insane asylum. We knew that, but not much else," Mark said.

"Back in the 1870s Concordia Sanitarium had this godawful fire. Everyone inside, I mean *everyone*, was killed. With staff and inmates that was, oh, mebbe sixty folks."

"And those are the people who—?" Mark began.

"Hey, ya feel that?" Old Dex exclaimed.

The cold was biting. Tracy pulled free of Mark and encircled her trembling body with both arms. They looked around, saw nothing. Then . . .

An ice-white mist appeared, wavering, a few yards away: the hoar-frosted breath of a giant in some arctic wilderness, suspended in the bitter cold long after it had been exhaled. Its first discernible shape was that of the pipes on a calliope, with their varied heights, the tallest rising six to seven feet above the rubble-strewn surface. The height of these pipes changed as they moved, pistonlike, up and down, up and down, but slowly, more like breathing than anything mechanical.

The translucent mass of hoar-frost was four feet across, then six, eight. It continued to grow, the ends curving, becoming a semicircle, the pipes still moving up and down . . .

"Scared witless I was, first time it happened," Old Dex said, his voice rising above the shrillness of the wind. "But trust me, ain't a thing to worry about."

The ends of the icy mist continued to stretch, moving closer, closer. Mark, watching the portal shrink, wanted to grab Tracy and run from the restricting place but could not move.

The ends touched; the circle completed.

"Helluva lot bigger back then," Old Dex went on. "Actually had to get up and move closer to see what it was all about."

Tracy and Mark pressed tightly against each other on the adobe bench as the ethereal mass spun hypnotically around them. For an insane moment Mark thought of the old-time music from the Balboa Park carousel in San Diego, where he had spent a few days earlier that spring before moving on. He quickly shook the sounds from his head.

A tendril of the frost-wall splintered off and floated toward them.

"Now don't you worry," Old Dex told them again, his voice soothing. "When they do this, it means—"

Tracy gasped when she saw the face in the frost-wall.

Nothing more than two eyes at first . . . *two eyes staring at her*, she was sure of it. As she watched, transfixed, the face became more distinct, although it was still impossible to tell whether it was a man or a woman.

A second tendril flaked off from the hoar-frosted mass.

There was another face, and a third, and the upper parts of bodies took shape, and the faces were clearer, though the expressions were vague. Mark noticed that their hands, while close together, were not linked.

The first tendril inched closer to them.

"These are the people who . . . died here?" Mark asked.

Old Dex nodded. "Yep."

Tracy gestured with a shaking hand. "What are they doing?"

"Not sure; prob'ly whatever they were doin' on the day . . ."

The first tendril took shape suddenly: a young, round-faced man, obese, laying on his side, blank eyes staring up at Mark as he lolled his tongue, drew it in like a reptile and grinned, his body rolling around like a child's top near the terminus of its spin.

The frost-wall became a circle of people, mostly old, their features drifting in and out of clarity.

"But why are they still here?" Tracy asked.

"I wondered the same thing myself. But for the longest time I couldn't figure it out. So I just sat here with 'em, 'cause after you stop bein' scared it gets sort of OK."

The second tendril became a girl, no more than a teen. A pretty girl, Tracy saw, looking at her cascading locks of hair, but so troubled, so . . . She knelt a yard from Tracy, wide eyes staring, lips moving in an unheard plea. Tracy's heart ached for the girl. She held out a hand; the child reached for it.

"Tracy, no!" Mark exclaimed.

"It's OK," Old Dex assured him.

Fingers brushed for an instant; not a chill, as Tracy had expected, but a rush of warmth through her body for that all-too-brief moment.

The girl smiled.

The tendril re-formed into ice-smoke, then drifted away rapidly beyond the wall.

"Ya see, that's what it's like," Old Dex continued. "So I felt good about bein' with the poor devils, because what I finally figured out was they were trapped here and couldn't get on to someplace better, on account of the awful way they died. Later on I found out I was right."

"How did you know that for sure?" Tracy asked.

"Because they told me."

"They *talk* to you?" Mark exclaimed.

"One of them does. His name's Jacob. And it's not really talkin', more like . . . feelin'. I dunno. Didn't start till about a year ago. Never more than a word or two here and there, but over time I put a lot of it together.

"Jacob said the same thing I had guessed, that they all just wanted to pass on over, get away from this place, find some peace. But they don't know how to leave or nothin'. So I come up with some ideas, and I throw 'em out, and Jacob, he tells me if I'm on to somethin' or not, which most of the time I ain't. Then I sort of hit on it . . ."

The misty caucus-race moved faster, stepping over the obese man, whose grin was gone as he flailed his arms and legs.

"Jesus, you led them into the bodies of people who were dying!" Mark exclaimed.

"Yeah, that's it, how'd you guess?" Old Dex said, surprised. "Ya see, when they go inside—"

"Oh my God!" Tracy cried, raising her hands to her face. *"You mean . . . one of these things was inside my mother?"*

"Your mother?"

"Vivian Singer," Mark said. "And I was with Jack Redmond last weekend, when he died."

The prospector stared at them, stunned. "Crissakes, I'm sorry; shoot, I *really* am! If I'da known, then I wouldn'ta told you like this, but—"

"My mother died with one of them inside her!" Tracy shrieked, as Mark held her. *"YOU MONSTER!"*

The heads of those in the caucus-race turned from side to side, agitated.

"I know what it sounds like," Old Dex said, "but if you'd just listen to me . . ."

"You'd better talk," Mark snapped, still holding Tracy.

"OK," he went on, "so I figured that in this townful of old folks, where it seemed like someone died every other day or so, it would be easy. Yeah, I felt the same way you did, back then. But in the first place, the person was dyin' anyway, and second, I learned they was actually *glad* to be doin' good by takin' along one of these tortured souls and freein' 'em from this. Now that's the God's truth."

"Maybe they wouldn't have died as quickly without one of them inside!" Tracy exclaimed.

Old Dex shook his head. "Nope, every one of them died when it was their time. Now, let me tell you something. I hardly knew your ma, and I sure wasn't around on her last couple of days, right?"

"So?"

"First off, the spirit has to be inside *before* that person dies. Sometimes, like with Jack, it happens close to the right time. But with your ma, it was different. I overheard Doc Hoberg sayin' how bad it was, that she prob'ly only had a day or two. Actually, she went longer. OK, here's what I couldn't know. There was times when you and your dad thought your ma was . . . *different*, right?"

Tracy sobbed, unable to respond. "Yeah, that's true," Mark said.

"When she was like that, whoever was inside her was takin' away a lot of her pain. Crissakes, they already hurt so much, a little more don't matter."

Tracy looked up. "That's . . . right."

"And when she passed on," Old Dex continued, "she went real peaceful. She knew she was helpin' someone, and it made her feel good."

Now she'll *be at peace.*

Tracy nodded but again could not speak. Mark said, "Jack died the same way."

The prospector shrugged. "I know it sounds kinda . . . obscene, I guess. But it's not hurtin' any of the townsfolk, and as for these poor souls . . . hell, look what it's been like for way over a century."

The caucus-race whirled frantically now. Something . . .

Flames?

. . . rose from the sand, consuming them, and their faces were twisted in agony, but they danced their mindless dance, and the obese man, laying atop the . . .

Flames?

. . . continued to writhe as the whole spectral scene wavered tenuously.

"Make it stop!" Tracy cried.

The circle closing, eyes pleading, hands reaching through the . . .

Flames?

A tendril of frost erupting through the wall, taking form: the young girl, haunted eyes wide, engulfed by . . .

Flames, yes they were flames for sure.

. . . trying to stand, grasping with bent fingers, the flesh of her body peeling away, rivulets of white frost running down, her face dissolving, a lipless mouth formed in a silent scream . . .

"Make it stop!"

Gone, the images gone, and the ruins of Concordia Sanitarium still, except for the occasional breath of the wind between the crumbling adobe.

Tracy sobbed in Mark's arms. Dexter Jones looked at them sadly.

"All I ever wanted to do was help," he said. "Since I started doin' it, about half of 'em have gone over peaceful-like. But there's still so much work to be done, and . . ."

"And what?" Mark asked.

Old Dex shrugged. "I ain't young, ya know, and doin' this beats the heck out of you. Lately I been . . . run down, I guess. Doc Hoberg says it ain't nothin' he can find, told me to stop workin' so hard at my diggings, quit smokin', that sorta thing. But I'm afraid, boy; afraid *I'll* be takin' one of 'em with me real soon, which will leave the rest behind forever."

"Can't . . . you just . . . slow down?" Tracy gasped.

"That's probably what I should do; but it could also be the worst thing, if I really *don't* have much time left. Actually, I was gonna try and get that through to Jacob tonight. Ya see, ever since I started this, I've been here every night. Early on, only a few of 'em—staff people, not inmates—understood what was goin' on. Jacob chose to stay behind and help, but the others all went first," he hesitated, ". . . except for one."

"Who's that?" Mark asked.

Old Dex shook his head. "It ain't important yet. Thing is, they all sorta understand now, and they're impatient, because they want it to happen quicker. I have to spend time just talkin' 'em down; Christ knows what they might do . . ."

"Help, you said . . ." Tracy looked at him. "You want us to help you do this?"

"Yeah; I guess so." The man looked smaller, pathetic. "I can't do it much more, and the two of you know what's goin' on and all . . ."

Tracy turned away. "Mark, take me home now." She stood.

"Yeah, sure."

Old Dex walked with them across the ruins. "I didn't expect you'd give me an answer right off, but at least think about it. Crissakes,

I don't want to abandon them! If you wanna talk, I'm either at home or somewhere along the creek."

Tracy stopped, looked at him. "This was too much to handle, Mr.—Dex. I need to think, talk to Mark. Maybe we'll see you again."

The old man nodded. "That's all I can ask for. Thanks."

They walked to Bighorn Creek. Old Dex stayed back, even though he would be returning the same way to his place. Right now, they needed to be alone.

CHAPTER THIRTEEN

New Blood

1

The glow of Smoke Tree appeared bright against the tar-black desert sky.

Tracy and Mark, lost in their own thoughts, said little. But near the edge of the Estates, Tracy looked up at him.

"Was that real, or did you slip me drugs out there?" she asked.

Mark shrugged. "Even after seeing what we just did, I might not've believed it . . . except for what happened to Jack and your mother. Jesus, Tracy."

"It *does* sound obscene. Like a violation of someone's soul. But I can't forget two things: the peace and warmth coming from Mom a few seconds before she died, and . . . and the desperation in that girl's face when . . . the flames . . . *oh Mark!*"

He held her again, until the sobbing had eased. "You want to help him," he said. It was not a question.

"Yes."

"Me too. But you're forgetting something. You weren't planning to stay in Smoke Tree forever, and as for me, well . . ."

"Let's talk about it tomorrow. I can't handle any more tonight."
He kissed her. "Agreed."

As they approached the Estates a sudden explosion shattered the silence and brought them to a stop. Ahead, the sky came to life in a profusion of variegated streaks, a dawn wildflower blooming in time-lapse photography. More bursts followed.

"Fourth of July fireworks," Mark muttered.

"We really *have* been in another world."

The fireworks continued as they walked down Oasis Drive, exploding over the fairways of the Smoke Tree Country Club. Not the most impressive display either had ever seen, but effective enough. Residents of the Mortero Hill section, those who had not driven or walked over to the golf course, sat on lawn chairs in front of their houses, oohing and aahing as they had done on countless Fourths past.

The driveway of the Singer house looked like the bleachers at a tennis match. Carl sat in a row with Joey and Gary Masten. Bert and Muriel Findley, and the gnomelike Harry Keller, were in front. Gary's guardian, Tracy thought, possessed what doubtless qualified as the world's kindliest face.

Joey was content to wave when he saw his mother and Mark coming down the street. But Gary, briefly ignoring the light show, jumped from his chair and ran to meet them, hugging Tracy and pounding Mark on the back.

"Good grief, the two of you look like you've been through the wars!" Carl exclaimed.

He wore a smile; Tracy hadn't seen him do much of that in the past week. She was glad. His eyes seemed to say *I'm glad you're with this man, because your mother liked him.*

"I was afraid of that," Tracy replied.

"What'd you guys do?" Joey asked.

Tracy glanced at Mark, who shrugged. "Oh, nothing much exciting," he said. "Walked a lot."

"He-ey, look at that one!" Gary exclaimed, waving at the sky.

Tracy hugged the big boy again. "We're going to skip the pyrotechnics and grab a bite. There *is* some of that roast left, yes?"

They all looked at one another with expressions of guilt. Harry

Keller thrust out his hands, waiting to be shackled.

"So arrest me, I couldn't resist it," he said. "I ate the who-ole thing."

Muriel rolled her eyes. "He's only kidding. There's lots."

Tracy cut thin slabs of roast beef, heated them in the microwave oven and served them open-faced over sourdough bread, drenched in Muriel's thick mushroom gravy. They devoured them in the living room, the front curtains open so they could watch the end of the fireworks. The nation's birthday was toasted with cans of San Miguel beer.

"I seriously think," Tracy said, "this was one of the most . . . unforgettable days of my life."

"I'll second that, lady. We'll either sleep like death tonight, or we won't get a wink."

She yawned. "In my case it'll be the former. Did you say if you were working tomorrow?"

"Yeah, all day from eleven on. I'll be training the new guy. But get this: after tomorrow, *three* days off! And Jerry swore on his stupid jukebox—it was handier than a Bible—that he won't even *think* of calling me in."

Tracy kissed him. "Consider most of your free time accounted for, pal."

"Tough job, hanging out with the likes of you, but I guess someone's got to do it."

She swung a roundhouse a few inches over his head. They laughed like kids, then were silent as they finished the sandwiches. Mark finally said, "Do you want to see Dexter Jones in the morning?"

"Yeah. Is there a road out to his place?"

"A dirt trail, but it's drivable. Pick me up at nine."

She put a gentle hand on his face. "Mark, are we crazy?"

"As crazy as loons, but that's what it's all about."

The fireworks ended with a final impressive barrage. The Findleys folded up their chairs and went next door. Gary followed Carl and Joey inside so he could say goodbye to Tracy and Mark, then drove off with Harry Keller.

"Guess I'm outta here too," Mark said.

"Will you be at the club tomorrow?" Carl asked.

"Yes."

"I'll see you, then; I'm playing golf with the Findleys. Tracy too, if I can talk her into it."

"Never," Tracy whispered to Mark as she walked him out. "I hate that game."

They kissed long and deeply in the driveway, not caring if anyone on Oasis Drive saw. Tracy watched him ride off, waving even after he was gone from sight.

2

Bruno stared at the man through the coyote's keen eyes.

The animal hid in the shadows of the creosote at the edge of the Estates, where the man and woman had left the desert. Earlier, in its mad flight from the canyon, it had cut a path of destruction through jackrabbits and chuckwallas and other stupid creatures. It had given a wide berth to the Terrible Cracked-Stone place, which was far more frightening than the place of buildings and lights. Before long it had come to the creek.

Which was when the man and woman had walked by.

The woman.

Such limited awareness, compared to the four-legged thing. It had stalked them, coming within yards, close enough for the *screaming terrible outside time* to be brief if he entered the man, and he wanted to enter the man, the same man who'd already done the *Thing* with the woman, because *he* wanted the woman, almost as much as he wanted to kill . . .

But the man would be strong like the one in the uniform had been, and the screaming terrible outside time would be endless, because the animal would run away . . .

Still, he wanted the woman.

The uncertainty defeated him, for they had reached the . . .

Street.

. . . place of buildings and lights, where there were others, and it could not expose itself, so it had stopped at the edge, and watched, terrified of the fire and thunder in the sky, but not wanting to leave.

Now, the man had ridden away on the ...

Bicycle.

... wheel-thing, and the woman had stood for a while before going inside.

The coyote turned and fled back into the desert, though not before its wail broke the post-fireworks silence of Mortero Hill.

3

Thursday morning's fiery sunrise foretold an end to the one-day respite. Tracy came by at a few minutes before nine, as Mark returned from Rusty's Market. He put his things in the apartment, and they set out for Dexter Jones's place.

"Well, I was right," Tracy said. "Slept like a log."

"No dreams?" Mark asked.

"None. You?"

He shrugged. "There usually are; something I've lived with for a while. But I got some sleep, and I feel OK. Did you manage to beg out of the golf game today?"

"Yeah. I told Dad I wanted to spend the day with Joey, which is the truth. It's got to be dull for him around here. Back home he has plenty of friends, but there are no children in Smoke Tree, I mean *none*. His only friend is Gary Masten, which is fine, except Gary is working most of the time. Anyway, I'm taking him to the mall in Indio, buy him some new CDs, books, whatever."

"He'll like that ... and I'm sure seeing the inside of a mall won't break your heart."

Tracy stuck her tongue out as they neared the Valley Clinic. Mark indicated a jeep trail on the right, partially concealed by scrub. Tracy turned, and in seconds they were being jarred by a succession of potholes. She slowed the Cressida to a crawl.

"I thought you told me this was drivable," she said.

Mark shook his head. "I biked it a few weeks ago, and I don't remember it being this bad."

After forty yards of pounding, the road leveled. Four minutes later they pulled into the narrow drive leading to Dexter Jones's junk-strewn yard. The prospector was waiting at the door. His lean body, Mark thought, looked painfully bent.

"Sure glad you're here," he said as they walked up. "I got coffee on the stove; hundred-mile stuff. Come on in."

Old Dex's coffee was even stronger than that; Mark estimated at least *two* hundred miles to a mug. They sipped it in the wood-paneled den, a clean room despite the profusion of books, and decades worth of magazines Old Dex had never gotten around to throwing out.

"In the light of a new day," Tracy said, "I have trouble believing last night really happened."

Old Dex nodded. "I felt that way too, and not just the first time. But before long you can't let go of it." He looked at them hopefully. "Kin you folks help me?"

"Do you understand I'll only be in Smoke Tree a short while longer?" Tracy asked.

"Yep, kinda figured that. But any time at all is something." He turned to Mark. "Besides, you'll still be here, won't you?"

Mark looked at Tracy for a moment then said, "Yeah, I will. What do you want us to do?"

Old Dex had been leaning forward in his easy chair. Now, he shut his eyes for a few seconds and sat back. It was as though an immense weight had been lifted from him.

"For one thing," he said, "sit with them in the ruins, like we did last night. Then, guide them to wherever they'll be goin' when the time comes. That usually happens real late."

"Anything else?" Tracy asked.

"Nope, but it's enough. The sittin' and the guidin's been what's wore me out. The rest of it is just hangin' around the hospital, the club, other places in town, findin' out . . . ya know. I'll still do that. No one pays any mind to me, but young'ns like you snoopin' around might raise a few eyebrows."

Tracy leaned over and put a hand on the old man's arm. "I had a hard time accepting this, because of my mother. But the more I think about what you've done, your sacrifices, the more I believe you're one heck of a person, Mr. Dexter Jones. I'll be proud to help you."

"Me too," Mark said.

"Life took away one eye, gave me a bum leg. But on the whole it's been good to me, and I got no complaints. Movin' those poor souls along is a fine way of givin' something back. Why don't you come over about a half hour before sunset? We'll walk up to the ruins."

"I'll be here, but Mark will be at work," Tracy said.

The old man led them outside. They noticed how much straighter he stood.

"One other thing," he said. "I've never been shy about shootin' off my mouth. Folks know I love to talk. But I ain't ever said a word about this, no sir. Figured I'd either get committed or arrested. You understand?"

Mark nodded. "It stays between us. I . . . wouldn't want to get arrested either."

Before they were out of the drive Old Dex, whistling, began throwing his gear together for a few hours on Bighorn Creek, in search of the elusive second nugget.

4

Gary Masten worked on the Kasendorfs' front yard, farther up Oasis Drive. A few minutes earlier Joey's mom had stopped by to see if he wanted to go to Indio with them when he was done. But he had more work here, and then, after lunch, Harry would drive him down to Rainbow Tree Farm, to do work there too. Too bad. He liked Joey's mom, because she was so pretty and so nice to him, and he really liked Joey, who was now his best friend (after Harry Keller, of course). He sort of understood Joey would be leaving soon, and that made him feel sad.

The Kasendorfs' yard, an attractive one, was typical of the desert. A three-foot hedge of pyracantha extended along the length of the house. Dwarf Natal plum lined the brick walkway. The ground cover was sturdy Algerian ivy, which Gary had trimmed and watered. In a few places, Sprenger asparagus cascaded down over native rock. The sole tree, dead center, was a sweet acacia.

Gary did his job well. He liked yard work, and liked the results even more. And the Kasendorfs were real nice to him. They always paid him above the going rate; Mrs. Kasendorf served him all the lemonade he wanted, and she baked the best chocolate chip cookies in Smoke Tree.

Gary finished shortly before noon. He put the tools back in the garage then hosed off the driveway and sidewalk, leaving the front looking as neat as a pin, like Harry always told him. Mrs. Kasendorf offered him more cookies and lemonade, but he refused politely, saying it was lunchtime. Climbing on his big Nishiki Colorado mountain bike, Gary pedaled off.

5

The coyote should have been asleep inside a cool niche somewhere.

Its involuntary rampages had left it exhausted, and the desert's midday hour was not its favorite time. But it could not resist the thing within, which had urged it here, to the edge of the Estates, where it now lay in the minimal shade of a small creosote bush.

Bruno had wanted to see the woman again. The glimpse had been brief; first, when she'd come to the house in her monster-thing, next, when she left with the boy.

But before that, and after, something else had caught Bruno's interest. The man, the big shirtless man doing something in front of another building, closer to where the coyote lay. Bruno had seen the man before; last night, with all the others, but he'd paid him little mind. Now, he stared at the man's face and sensed there was something . . .

Something familiar.

. . . that warranted his further interest. He needed to be closer, but not here.

When the big man rode off, Bruno forced the coyote to its feet. But while the stupid creature's will could not resist, its weary body was helpless. It staggered along the sand while circumventing the Estates, Bruno raging over its weakness. By the time it came to the edge of Las Palmas Road, the big man was no longer in sight.

The coyote was panting hard, its heart thrumming. *Can't die, can't die, or else . . .*

Bruno relinquished his hold. Knowing it was free, the coyote stumbled toward the maze of northern canyons.

6

Harry Keller already had Gary's favorite lunch ready: two ham and Swiss cheese sandwiches on seeded rye, both pieces smeared with brown mustard; two oranges, each cut in eight wedges; a Classic Coke; and two Hostess cupcakes, the no-cholesterol chocolate ones.

"You're a pretty big guy," Harry always said, "so we've got to watch that cholesterol."

Not that Gary was too clear on the dangers of cholesterol, but it sounded like a bad thing, and besides, these cupcakes were good.

Before they left, Gary took a cold shower. At one-thirty, Harry dropped him off in front of Rainbow Tree Farm; he would return for him in four hours.

"Take it easy in there today," Harry said. "It's pretty darn hot."

He said that all the time, but it was OK. "Yeah, I sure will."

The farm, owned by Terry Cooper, encompassed two hundred and fifty acres, two-thirds of which were planted with trees hardy enough to withstand the torrid climate. Visitors were impressed with the numerous rows—some canopied—of palms, acacias, jacarandas, olives, and others. Counting Gary, who was his only part-timer, Cooper employed fifteen people among the field workers, drivers, and office personnel.

Jorge Montoya, Pedro Rodriguez, and Jaime Alvarez were field workers. Jorge had been there for years and spoke English well, making him the unofficial foreman of the Mexicans. Pedro could get by when he had to. But Jaime, who was Pedro's cousin, had recently arrived from Guadalajara and spoke no English at all. Still, he was a good-hearted man who said a great deal with his broad smile. Gary already liked Jaime almost as much as the others.

"Hey, *El Gigante!*" Jorge exclaimed when he saw Gary. "Ees 'bout time you show up for work."

Gary grinned. He liked these games, which had become routine. "Wh-what's the matter," he said slowly, "you guys can't get along without me?"

Jorge translated for the others, who laughed heartily, despite having heard it before.

Pedro assumed a boxer's stance. "We cut you down, *El Gigante*. We not 'fraid."

The tallest of the three Mexicans, Pedro stood nearly a foot shorter than Gary. It was a comical sight, these Davids and their Goliath, all ducking and feinting, the swarthy men throwing playful jabs that Gary warded off with his massive forearms. They went at it for a minute, laughing themselves silly, until Jorge decided that Señor Cooper, their boss, might catch them slacking off. Still laughing, they went back to work.

Four hours later, Harry Keller watched Gary wave goodbye to his co-workers and hurry to the car. Gary, although tired, smiled happily. He'd always been pretty happy, Harry thought, since they'd come here. Yes, he'd done a good thing bringing the boy to Smoke Tree; a real good thing.

Barriers

1

When Tracy and Joey got back at five-thirty, Carl Singer was sitting glumly in the living room. The boy went into his room to listen to a new CD; Tracy sat down next to her father.

"How did it go?" she asked.

"OK. We got nine holes in; but . . ." He sighed. "Damn, I missed her so much today! I can't hardly remember the last time I played without her."

Tracy took his hand. "I was afraid it would be hard for you. Sorry I wasn't there."

"No reason you should've been. I know golf's not your thing. Anyway, we're going to do it again on Saturday. I don't think your mother would approve of me moping around."

"You got that right."

"How'd you and Joey do?"

She gestured toward a bunch of shopping bags she'd left by the door. "Not bad."

"Great . . . uh, princess, can I ask you something?"

"Sure."

"This Mark Bradley, you like him, huh?"

She nodded. "Yeah, Dad, I do."

"Do you know much about him?"

"More than I can share right now; but I will."

"You know best, princess. Actually, I like the guy."

Tracy kissed his cheek. "Thanks. You've got every reason to be dubious after . . . you know. But I've never been this sure of anything before."

Carl was surprised. "That serious, huh?"

Tracy didn't hesitate. "Yeah, serious."

Dinner came quickly out of the microwave oven. After seven Carl and Joey settled in to watch a Padres game. The boy still had his earphones on and was rocking from side to side. Tracy told her father she was going for a walk and would return after dark.

Carl winked at her. "You wouldn't be headed toward the club, would you?"

She smiled. "You never know."

2

The day had hardly begun to cool off. With the sleeves of a heavy sweatshirt knotted around her waist, Tracy hurried up to the end of Oasis Drive. Soon she had found the creek, the way surprisingly familiar to her.

Dexter Jones waved from his porch. Despite the heat he was dressed in what Tracy swore was a London Fog raincoat. Add a wide-brimmed straw hat and he looked like one of those bank robbers from the Great Plains over a century ago. He joined her, and they continued slowly along the creek.

"I was out and around, doin' my thing." Old Dex gestured toward the ruins. "Not good news for those poor devils, but everything's quiet in town. Unless somethin' happens suddenlike, there won't be nobody passin' on over tonight."

"I'm not sure how to respond," Tracy said. "Either way . . ."

"Don't try. I made myself crazy with it for a long time."

"What will we do there?"

"I want Jacob to touch you, and your fella too, so he knows you both and can trust you when I don't come."

She looked at him. "Would you mind me saying I was scared?"

Old Dex laughed, which started a brief fit of wheezing. "I'd be darn surprised if you weren't!"

To Tracy the ruins appeared ominous in the twilight. It was deathly still, no wind cutting through the adobe monoliths or the nearby canyon. The rush of Bighorn Creek faded only seconds after they angled away from it.

They were within the outer wall, near the perimeter of the main building, when Old Dex stopped. He stared, transfixed, at a corner of the old sanitarium, twenty-five yards away. Tracy had taken a few more steps before realizing he'd fallen back.

"What is it?" she asked.

But he continued to stare, oblivious to her presence. Tracy looked also, seeing only the same mounds of rubble that were everywhere else.

"Dex, are you OK?"

He turned quickly, startling her. "Wha-? Oh yeah, fine. Just thought I saw a . . . coyote or somethin' over there."

"Aren't there always some around here?"

"Seems like they all the time avoid this place . . . like a poisoned water hole or something. Come on."

They continued to the same spot as the night before, Tracy still impressed how easily Old Dex stepped amid the mounds of crumbled rock. They sat down and waited. Tracy pulled on her sweatshirt, despite the absence of the night chill.

Darkness crept down the slopes of the eastern mountains. Somewhere, a wind arose, speaking to them in whispers.

Tracy knew they were there before the frost-wall was visible. *Oh damn*, she thought, *I wish Mark was here.* Hands linked on her lap, like a schoolgirl, she watched the circle form. All of it seemed to happen more quickly than on the previous night.

The first tendril to break free of the wall undulated toward them.

"Jacob," Old Dex whispered, extending a hand.

The wisp took form, and it was a man, taller than any of the pipe-like protuberances on the wall. A gaunt, angular face that stared curiously, the head cocked severely to one side, sometimes lolling, never pulling up straight.

"Jacob," Old Dex said again as the specter's bony fingers reached for him. "How're you doin', old friend?" He was silent for a few moments then said, "First thing, I want you to meet someone. I want you to meet *Tracy*. She's gonna help your people, Jacob. You understand? Tracy will help when I can't."

The wisp swayed. Old Dex withdrew his hand and glanced at Tracy. "Do the same thing," he said.

Only now Tracy realized she had squeezed her fingers bloodless. She extended a trembling hand. Jacob's fingers touched her's, seemingly passing through them. A microsecond of intense cold, then a surging warmth, like she had felt from the young girl.

"Hello, Jacob," Tracy said, her voice cracking.

What she felt, rather than heard, was a gentle puff of air, expelled with the softness of a lover's whisper. *Traa-ssss*, she thought it said.

"I'll help you, Jacob," she told the entity. "I'll do whatever I can."

The dark eyes seemed to be staring through her. *Traa-ssss,* it said again. *He-elp goo-ood doctorrrr.*

"What?" Tracy asked.

He-elp goo-ood doctorrrr, Traa-ssss.

"I don't—"

The specter threatened to waver into insubstantial mist. *He-elpgoo-oodoctorrrrgoo-oodoctorrrrrr.*

Old Dex pulled Tracy's hand away, replacing it with his own. "OK, old friend, calm down, will ya?"

Jacob's image re-formed. Tracy said, "He was telling me something, but . . . it made no sense!"

The prospector nodded. "Yep, that's the way it is a lot of the time. Jacob, listen to me. We can't take anyone over tonight, you hear? Not tonight."

Old Dex pulled his hand back, as though it had been burned. Jacob's features became indistinct, and again the image was a snaking mass of hoarfrost, an angry serpent that reared for a moment before rejoining the wall. The circle began to spin faster, pipes rising and falling.

"This part is the hardest," Old Dex said, "tellin' 'em what I just did."

As she watched the dizzying dance, Tracy did not see the second tendril break away. The young girl was at her feet, hand out, when Tracy turned suddenly. Her movement startled the spectral teen, who melded with the wall even more quickly than Jacob.

"Oh, *damn!*" Tracy exclaimed.

The caucus-race sped on.

When the flames began, Tracy buried her face in her hands. Old Dex took her arm.

"Come on, no reason to see this," he said.

They walked toward the agonized faces in the frost-wall. A wind from . . .

Somewhere.

. . . sounded like screams. Then, the wall was gone, and they hurried through the rubble to the courtyard, where they stopped.

"Oh, that went badly!" Tracy cried.

"Nah, you were fine," Old Dex assured her. "Better'n I was early on."

"But did you see them—!"

"Like I told you, they're frustrated when nothin' happens. They'll settle down after a spell, and'll be waitin' the next time. Will your fella be comin' tomorrow night?"

Tracy couldn't stop thinking about the young girl. "Yes."

"Good. Well, let's go; we're done for now."

They walked back along the creek; the old man kept falling behind. Tracy now had some idea of how his ghostly Samaritanism had drained him. She slowed down, matching his steps.

"Do you want me to walk you inside?" she asked, when they were near his place.

"Nope, I'm OK," he said with little conviction. "See ya

tomorrow."

Tracy walked back to the house, joining her father and Joey. The Padres were playing the Cardinals; her team. But she hardly noticed the action on the screen.

At nine-fifteen she drove over to the club. She'd dropped Mark off at work that morning, after they'd met with Dexter Jones, and had promised to pick him up.

"Saved!" he exclaimed. "Jerry told me to leave whenever, especially with Ray Clifton here. Looks like he's going to work out fine."

Mark introduced Tracy to Ray, the new bartender. They left the Arroyo Lounge a minute later. On the short drive back, Tracy detailed what had happened at the ruins.

"You still want to go through with it?" Mark asked.

For a moment, Tracy saw the young girl's face in her windshield. "Yes, I do."

They drove into the parking area of Ironwood Terrace. Tracy switched off the engine and turned to Mark.

"I don't feel like going home just yet," she said.

3

Early Friday morning Tracy, Mark and Joey biked Indianhead Wash and some of the trails southeast of town. If Mark had any concerns about the boy keeping up with them, they were quickly dispelled. Joey could outride them both and seemed tireless.

In the afternoon they went to Mortero Hill's community pool, one of four in the Estates. Mark received a few looks of surprise from residents, though most greeted him cordially. They sat under a broad umbrella, sipped lemonade and watched Joey do belly flops.

Later, Carl Singer announced that Saturday's round of golf had been canceled. A better plan had been hatched.

"The Cards still have three games left against the Padres," he said. "Harry Keller's up for it, and you know the kids are. Bert and Muriel said they'd go too. We'll leave soon, spend the weekend in the city, come back after the Sunday game. You two wanna go?"

Tracy had been a Cardinals fan forever. But there were things to be done here.

And time alone with Mark ...

"Thanks, Dad, but I'm not much in the mood for crowds. We'll hang around the pool all weekend."

Early that evening, Vivian Singer's daughter revealed her inherited culinary skills by cooking Mark the best dinner he could remember since Anna Mandell had fussed over him. Disdaining dessert, they made love in the coolness of Tracy's room. They would have been content to lie there forever; but the day was passing quickly.

Tracy remembered Dexter Jones's spoon-melting coffee and packed some leftovers for him, enough to last two meals. They walked out to his place. Old Dex, standing halfway up the drive, waved excitedly when he saw them.

"I just got back from the Valley Clinic." He shook his head sadly. "Poor Mr. Dowling, he was doin' so much better last week, but now he's taken a bad turn. Doc Hoberg says he won't last out the night."

"So we have work ahead of us," Mark said.

"More'n that. Seems like Pearl Newsome's slipped into a coma. She'd been improvin' too, Doc thought. But hell, the dear woman's eighty-five, she is. She may hang on a while, but she won't come out of it, he's sure."

"Two of them," Tracy said softly.

They walked to the ruins, arriving there a few minutes later than the previous night. This time Old Dex sat next to Mark, and when the frost-wall appeared, the prospector introduced him to Jacob. Tracy saw the puzzled look on Mark's face as he *listened* to the specter. But it was brief, because Jacob leaped quickly back to the old man.

"Yeah, you're anxious to find out," Old Dex said. "Well, old friend, you'll be glad to know that two of you will be passin' on tonight. You hear that? Two!"

The image flickered in what might have been jubilation. Separating from the old man, it wafted over to the slow-moving wall, becoming part of it.

"What happens now?" Mark asked.

"Jacob's lettin' the others know, choosin' the two that'll come. They have to be led out of the circle and away from this spot before the flames come."

"The girl; please, let one of them be the girl!" Tracy exclaimed.

Two misty tendrils drifted toward her. She extended a hand to the nearest one. Part of the frost took form; the girl's haunted eyes peered out from the whiteness.

Old Dex shrugged. "Yeah, I agree. Poor thing . . . But we ain't been able to make her go yet. I tried, Jacob did, but she's just too darn scared or somethin'."

"Let me," Tracy said.

The girl's image was complete now, except for a swirl of mist where her feet should have been. Her hand still outstretched, Tracy smiled. *Do it slowly, slowly; she's so easily frightened.*

"Come now," she said in a voice barely above a whisper. "You don't belong here; you don't need to suffer anymore. Come."

Their fingers touched; warmth filled Tracy, though now it alternated with brief pulses of icy cold: the girl's fear. Soon the warmth was all she felt. She stood slowly, aware of nothing else but the specter before her.

"That's right, you don't have to hurt ever again."

"Start leadin' her out of the circle," Old Dex said quietly. "Any direction, it don't matter."

Tracy took a tentative step to one side. The girl moved with her. A second, and a third.

"Yes, that's it," Tracy said.

But now she felt the cold returning as they neared the perimeter; she read the terror in the girl's face, and the pulsing chill displaced the warmth.

"No, no please don't, *please*—"

Bent white fingers were withdrawn; the girl became mist and was pulled back into the wall.

"No, *oh no!*" Tracy cried.

"I never came that close to gettin' her out," Old Dex said. "You did good."

"Yeah, good," Tracy muttered.

"OK, here's Jacob and the others."

Three tendrils appeared; Jacob had brought a man and a woman. The man, while not as tall as Jacob, was leaner, almost skeletal. Both appeared expressionless. They drifted close, stopped; Jacob backed away.

"Each of you take one," Old Dex said. "Hurry now. Whatever happens, don't stop till you're outside the circle."

Tracy reached for the man and started walking backward; Mark followed with the woman. They felt only warmth until they came to the frost wall, then hot-and-cold for the instant of passage. Tracy was on the other side first.

The spirit would not come through.

It was hung up, like snagged clothing. She was afraid of yanking it harder, afraid of losing it in there.

"Dex—!" she exclaimed.

"Pull as hard as you need to," his calming voice said. "Don't worry, they'll come through."

She did . . . nearly too hard, stumbling backward as the spirit broke through the frost wall, which wavered, then quickly re-formed. Mark did not hesitate with his charge.

Old Dex came through a moment later.

The caucus-race spun rapidly.

Tracy could see inside the circle, past the pipe-organ figures, where the flames were consuming the young girl. She cried out, turned away.

The images returned to their private purgatory, except for the pair that had been brought out. Their expressions remained blank.

"You can let go now," Old Dex said. "As long as they can see you, it's all right."

Tracy and Mark withdrew their hands. The spirits wavered, but remained as they had been.

"You oughta know that sometimes they fade out on you," Old Dex went on. "But don't worry, they'll still be around."

"Glad you told us," Mark said dryly.

"So now we just wait with them until it's time?" Tracy asked.

"Yep, unless you want to take them home. You leave 'em, they'll go back in there. They have to see you. This is one of the worst parts; so borin'."

"What time do we go?" Mark asked.

"Hospital's real quiet after eleven, when the shift changes. If you can hold out longer, that's even better."

Tracy and Mark sat down. When the old prospector lowered his body, they read the pain of the effort on his face.

"Why don't you go home?" Tracy said. "We can take care of the rest."

"You sure?"

"If you tell us what to do."

"Just get 'em near the hospital. This side of the main road's close enough. Follow the old trail past my place. Once you get 'em there, they seem to know what to do." He shrugged. "Maybe they get *drawn* in. After that, you're done."

The old man thanked them. Relieved, but still bent in fatigue, he started back for his place.

"Mark, did Jacob say anything to you when your fingers were touching?" Tracy asked.

"Yes, but nothing that made sense. Why?"

"The same thing happened to me. Dex didn't seem to think it was a big deal, but . . ."

"What?"

"I can't shake the feeling he's trying to tell us something important. That's crazy, huh?"

"No, not if you feel that way. We'll talk to Dex about it."

They settled in for the vigil. Tracy was tired. Mark told her to rest. She protested, but within five minutes was asleep, her head resting on Mark. The spirits watched them.

Mark thought, *So, dude, anything new or exciting happen to you recently? Well no, not much, but here I am, with a woman who I think I'm in love with, babysitting a couple of ghosts.*

Old Dex was right: the spirits winked in and out for the next few hours, sometimes individually, mostly together. It was disconcerting at first; but before long Mark hardly paid attention to their comings and goings.

When she awakened, Tracy was surprised to discover it was nearly 11:30. "Why didn't you get me up sooner?" she exclaimed.

"You were tired. Besides, I like watching you sleep."

She kissed him. "Well, shall we deliver— Where are they?"

Mark smiled. "Come on, folks, beam aboard."

The spirits appeared. "Beam aboard?" Tracy muttered.

They started out of the ruins. The spirits followed, bobbing, gliding, always about two yards behind. If they had any curiosity about their surroundings, it was not evident; their eyes remained on their guides.

Tracy had half-expected to see Dexter Jones in front of his house; but if the old man was watching the strange procession at all, it was from the darkness within.

The jeep trail led them to Las Palmas Road. Twenty yards away they heard a car, and waited. When it passed they moved ten yards closer, turned and paralleled the asphalt for another few seconds, until they could see the Valley Clinic across the way. They stopped and pointed, but the spirits already knew. They bobbed past and were soon over the street.

The woman turned, looked at Mark and Tracy; then, she and the skeletal man winked out.

"Mark, we did it!" Tracy exclaimed. "They're going to be free!"

Mark smiled wearily. "Let's head back."

Whoever was on duty in the security kiosk would have been curious about two people entering the Estates on foot at midnight. After following Las Palmas Road to the end, they went back into the desert, soon emerging on Oasis Drive. They jogged the last fifty yards to the house.

They showered together, spending more time in each other's arms than with the soap. Mark was first out of the bathroom, Tracy following a few minutes later.

When she reached the bedroom, Mark was asleep.

Tracy looked at him, smiled. "I love you, Mark Alderson," she said softly, and slid under the covers next to him.

CHAPTER FIFTEEN

Dungeon

1

Dexter Jones swore he was feeling a whole heck of a lot better. Tracy and Mark, concerned about the prospector, called him early Saturday morning. Yeah, he'd gotten a real good night's sleep, and nah, he wasn't going out looking for gold today, just staying put watching baseball, movies, whatever; likely stop by the clinic later. Speaking of which, he wondered how their "special delivery" had gone.

"It went well," Tracy told him.

"See, I told ya," Old Dex said. "Oh, and I called in before. Mr. Dowling passed on about two in the mornin'; poor Pearl Newsome's still hangin' in, but her condition is grave." His chuckle was without humor. "Always thought that was a helluva way to describe bein' one step from dead."

Smoke Tree's mid-morning temperature was one hundred and two degrees. That was fine, for they'd already decided this was a day to do nothing. Except for a couple of hours at the pool, they stayed inside the rest of the time. They listened to Don Henley and Linda Ronstadt, watched old musicals and Marx Brothers films from the

Singers' big collection. Mark liked this house; it was a house to be lived in. Whatever kind of place Tracy had, he knew it would be the same.

Sitting there, holding her, his heart ached to imagine that such joy could last.

They had made love upon awakening, and in the afternoon, they felt themselves succumbing again. Clothes had been tossed aside, and they had moved from the couch to the carpet, when Mark, pulling free from Tracy's urgent kisses, grinned at her.

"What's so funny?" she asked.

"I love you too, Tracy Russell."

"You *heard* me? Why you—!"

She assaulted him playfully, and they wrestled on the floor, but it was brief, because neither their emotions nor their desires could be denied any longer.

2

Old Dex did seem greatly improved, almost spry.

Tracy and Mark came up Bighorn Creek at 7:45. He waved from the porch and hurried to meet them.

"Pearl Newsome passed on about two hours ago," he said. "Went real peaceful, the nurse said."

"Do we have more work tonight?" Mark asked.

"Nope, it's quiet in town. This'll be a quick one."

"Maybe not," Tracy said.

Old Dex looked at her strangely. "What do you mean?"

"We'll tell you later," Mark said. "Come on, it's late."

Tracy insisted she would talk to Jacob by herself. Mark and Old Dex waited in the courtyard, near the rubble of the well. The prospector was curious about what the young people had on their minds; but Mark remained silent as he stared in the direction of the spectral caucus-race.

When Tracy emerged from the denser ruins, she was shaken. The *meeting* had gone longer than Old Dex thought it should, considering what little there was to be done.

"I held Jacob as long as I could," Tracy said, "trying to

understand what he was saying. He repeated it over and over, then became frustrated, and left."

"Were you able to tell what it was?" Mark asked.

"I think so, but it still makes no sense: *Help good doctor.*"

"I thought it was something like that." He faced Old Dex. "You haven't told us all there is about this place; you've been holding something back." It was not a question.

"You've spoken to Jacob for a long time now," Tracy added. "Surely you were curious about what troubled him so deeply."

Old Dex stared at his boots. "You two are sharper'n I figured. Guess I chose well." He looked up. "I wasn't tryin' to hold nothin' back. Whatever it is, I don't understand it too good, and it sort of scares me. And if it scared the both of you right off, you might not've wanted to give me a hand."

"*Help good doctor,*" Mark said. "You know what it means?"

"I have an idea. Follow me. It'll be easier to explain, after . . ."

"After what?" Tracy asked.

He did not respond, but led them back into the dense rubble, away from the place where the frost-wall appeared, toward Bighorn Creek. Tracy remembered him staring over here the other night. He seemed less sure of his footing.

"Just a second now," the prospector said, slowing. "It starts right around . . . *here!*"

They felt it too, sudden and overwhelming, a terrible anxiety, something burrowing in and out of their flesh, pulling itself along with small, needle-sharp talons. Mark groaned; Tracy clung to him; neither noticed that Old Dex had backed away. Their eyes darted about; they swatted at the air . . . at something they could not see.

"*What is it?*" Tracy cried.

They pulled free of the force. Tracy shuddered uncontrollably, despite the warm night. Mark put his jacket over her shoulders and glared at Old Dex.

"You could've warned us!"

"How do you describe *that* to someone?" the old man replied.

"Wh-what's here?" Tracy asked. "Is it . . . more of them?"

"Maybe; one, anyway."

"One?"

He led them farther away from the spot. "Let me tell you the whole thing, see if it makes any sense. Now, I said before I'd been seein' these poor souls for two years. Likely they been doin' the same thing a lot longer'n that. But old Jacob, now he didn't show up till about a year ago. My first guess was that he'd been trapped somewhere, prob'ly below, and only then found a way to join the others.

"When he started communicatin,' he kept sayin' the same thing you heard. Took me a while, it did; but I finally figured out who he was talkin' about."

"*Who* he was talking about?" Tracy asked.

"Uh-huh. Whatever is left in historical records of Concordia Sanitarium mentions the name of its founder, a Dr. Everett Cooke. It was reported that Dr. Cooke died in the fire back in 1878, but I'm sure of this: none of those I already helped to pass on over, or the ones still around, is him."

"So you think maybe he survived the fire?" Mark said.

"It's possible, but unlikely. My guess is, he and Jacob died in some other part of the Sanitarium. Jacob managed to break free after all that time, but Dr. Cooke's spirit is still trapped there, and he knows that."

"'Help good doctor,'" Tracy mused. "It would make sense."

"But why didn't Jacob go back for him?" Mark asked.

Old Dex shrugged. "Fear, ignorance, whatever. Prob'ly the same reason they can't break away without our help. Anyway, after that I started pokin' through the rest of the ruins, but there was nothin'. Jacob kept repeatin' his message, and it got frustratin'.

"Then, a few months ago, I knew this was the place, right where you were just standin'. It wasn't anything like that then, but it was strong enough. Someone cryin' out, you could sorta feel it. Had to be Dr. Cooke, I figured."

"Did you try and do anything?" Tracy asked.

"Yep. Dug down in the sand, which ain't easy. But I wasn't gettin' anywhere, just weaker, and I figured if I kept it up, I was gonna be in trouble. Then what would the rest of 'em do? So I stopped." He pounded a fist into his other hand. "Damn, I didn't have no choice!"

"You did the right thing," Tracy assured him.

"Yeah, I suppose. But when you can feel it cryin' out . . . !"

"You told us it wasn't this strong at first," Mark said. "What happened? Do you think Dr. Cooke's spirit—if it is him—started showing its anger and frustration too?"

"Maybe. But it didn't just grow a little at a time. The first I felt it like that was real recent, hardly a couple of weeks ago. I walked over, same as I did before, tried to reach out to him from up here . . . Hit me like a sledgehammer, it did. Almost couldn't get away from it. Barely even made it home; crissakes, felt like I'd walked fifty miles!"

"What do you think happened?" Tracy asked.

"Don't know; but one thing's sure, there's a soul down there in worse agony than the others."

"We have to go down," Mark said. "He has to be set free."

"Mark, no!" Tracy cried. "You can't go back there!"

"Now that we know what to expect, maybe we can deal with it better."

"That's sorta true," Old Dex said, "but it's still pretty hard. One thing I found out is it's not so bad durin' the day. Even bein' hot, that's our best chance."

"We'll start at sunrise," Mark said. "Tracy, you don't have to—"

"No, you're right," she interrupted. "We can't let that poor soul suffer any longer. I'll be fine."

"Thank God," Old Dex said. "I got all the diggin' tools we could want. We'll take my jeep. You bring food and water. I will too."

They started walking toward Bighorn Creek, curious—and frightened—to learn what they would unearth below the ruins of Concordia Sanitarium.

3

The coyote had nearly died.

One insignificant stupid creature's death was meaningless, as long as he was not a part of it. But even had Bruno been able to flee his host, the *screaming terrible outside time* would have destroyed him. For in the middle of the day, when he had fled the place of buildings, few of the desert's animals were afoot, and his passage, he knew, would have been into oblivion.

So he had let the coyote crawl into the first niche it found, not anywhere near the canyons, and he had waited within the blackness, terrified, while the creature slept; slept a long and seemingly endless sleep, panting heavily, whimpering from dreams and images. So long, all the rest of the day and into the night, until it awakened from hunger and went out, still weak, to kill for its survival. Afterward it had retreated to another niche, this time nearer its usual habitat, carrying the half-eaten carcass of a jackrabbit in its mouth, so it would not have to go out and hunt as quickly. And again it had slept all the long hot day, then fed on its cache.

Early Sunday morning, as the fleet coyote cornered its prey in an arroyo, Bruno knew the creature had recovered fully. Never again would he push the coyote past its limits; never again would he risk his own end.

He would be careful, and patient, until it was time to leave this body for good.

That, he knew, would happen soon.

No more stupid creatures, not for him. Not the people either, for they were stronger and could keep him out. They could all keep him out . . .

. . . except one.

He knew that for sure, understood why he had been there that day, watching, not only to see the woman but to know that the big man, the big man with the round face and flat nose, the *big man who looked like him*, was waiting . . .

Waiting.

. . . to be whole again, to have Bruno inside him.

And he would be patient seeking the big man out, taking no chances; he would let nothing stand in his way. And he would come so close to the big man that the *screaming terrible outside time* would be nothing, and they would become one.

And he would have the *woman*.

And he would kill again with his . . .

Hands.

And he would tear apart the man . . .

(oh mark oh mark)

. . . who had done the *Thing* with the woman.

4

Tracy and Mark drove to Dexter Jones's place before sunrise. They had loaded a large Coleman cooler with food and water, and a smaller Igloo with a six-pack of Gatorade. They transferred both to the jeep, which Old Dex had crammed with shovels, pickaxes, metal buckets, rope, and anything else they might need for the task at hand.

After last night, the glow of dawn did little to lessen the eeriness of the adobe ruins. Before unloading, Tracy and Mark followed Old Dex to the spot. Although they'd prepared themselves, they were still overwhelmed by the flesh-piercing angst from below the sand; not as strong as before, but strong enough. They absorbed it for a moment, then stepped back.

"That's . . . going to make it harder," Mark said.

"I got an idea," Old Dex told them. "If Concordia did have a cellar, I bet it was in one of the old mine shafts."

"Mine shafts?" Tracy asked.

"They had a gold rush out here before the sanitarium was built. Left a few shafts around, usually somewhere near the creek. I came across some in my time . . . too bad this wasn't one. Anyway, if I'm right, we can start diggin' farther away, where it ain't so bad, and still be OK."

He led them back to the spot, then followed a slow, straight line toward the creek. For the first couple of yards the emanation was no different; then, with each step, it lessened. At the threshold of the courtyard, it was gone.

"You may be right," Mark said, "but let's go back as close as we can stand it."

They compromised on half the distance, Old Dex marking the spot with a wooden stake.

A wooden stake, Tracy thought, *how appropriate . . .*

Circumventing the core of the emanation they returned to the jeep, which was parked in an L-shaped corner of the outer wall, a spot that would not get sun for hours. All they immediately needed was unloaded in two trips. Mark insisted that Old Dex unearth the first spadeful of sand.

Although she could not describe it, Tracy swore she sensed an expression of relief from below.

They worked hard in the comfort of the early hours, the wiry old prospector contributing a great deal. Sand was flung far away to prevent it from spilling back down, though avoiding this entirely was impossible. Before long the shaft, which they had enlarged enough to allow two people to work comfortably, was down over four feet. Old Dex had rigged a canvas lean-to over the shaft, utilizing tent poles and a couple of the taller adobe pillars.

But by mid-morning the old man began showing the strain from his efforts, and the heat. Over his protests, Tracy ordered him out of the shaft. He contented himself with keeping sand away from the rim, bringing them drinks, or whatever else was needed. Some of the color that had drained from his face soon returned; still, they worried about him.

Fourteen feet down; rivulets of sand now seemed to trickle downward from inside the hole. Before Mark could voice his concerns about this, Tracy's shovel rang against something hard. Old Dex peered down.

"The timbers of the old shaft. Has to be. You find your footing on them, but be careful."

"We will," Tracy told him, "but wouldn't these supports have been built pretty strong?"

"Yep, prob'ly so; but if the fire got down there, who knows what shape they'll be in?"

"I'd forgotten about that."

"My guess is it didn't happen," Old Dex went on. "If anyone died down there, it might've been from the smoke; or maybe they got buried alive."

They established tentative footing atop the beams and brushed away more of the crusty sand. It appeared that—here—no flames had touched the wide, three-inch-thick pine timbers. Kneeling, Mark peered through the cracks between them.

"Looks like what you thought it was," he told the prospector. "Sand has fallen in, but I think we can get through."

They dug out more of the brittle earth on both sides of the timbers, hoping to find a wider space through which they could work their way down. But however temporary the shaft had been, the miners who'd shored it up had taken no shortcuts in their labors. The widest gap was less than an inch; nor did the timbers appear rotted in any place.

Tracy persisted at brushing more sand away and finally found a section that yielded when she stepped on it. Old Dex passed a crowbar down to Mark, who managed to work it into a crack. He could not pry the board loose, but noticed the metal chipping away some of the wood. He concentrated on this, taking advantage of an existing knothole. Soon he had gouged out a hole two inches in diameter.

"So now what?"

"Try this."

Old Dex handed him a well-tempered keyhole saw. Starting the cut was difficult; but once in, the teeth cut swiftly through the beam.

"We're in," Mark said.

"Wait up, I'm comin' too."

Earlier, when they'd reached a depth of six feet, the prospector had secured a length of rope to one of the sturdy pillars above and dropped it down the hole. Now, he descended with surprising agility. They assisted him the last part of the way.

Deeply embedded nails groaned as the two halves of the severed beam were pushed in, leaving a wide enough opening. Mark, tossing the crowbar down, was first to lower himself to the sandy floor, four feet below. The others followed.

Perhaps it had been their preoccupation with the morning's hard labor that enabled them to temporarily deny the force from below. Now, it overwhelmed them again, at once repelling and summoning them with great urgency. Had they been in total darkness, with no prior sense of direction, they would still have known the way.

"Down here." Old Dex shone his flashlight along the tunnel.

Hunched over, they moved slowly toward whatever it was that had drawn them below the ruins of Concordia Sanitarium.

The shaft remained narrow, little more than a yard across. At times the ceiling rose higher; or more precisely, the sandy floor sloped down, though at no time could they stand upright. Tracy's hand tightened in Mark's as each step took them closer to the source.

Ten feet ahead, the shaft ended at what appeared to be a solid wall.

Pine timbers, the same as those shoring up the rest of the tunnel. Assuming there was some kind of chamber on the other side, the builders of the sanitarium had more than likely raised an effective barrier against anyone even thinking of using the old shaft as a means of escape.

Tracy scowled. "Did we do all this for nothing?"

"I don't think so," Mark said. "Look here."

A dark spot in the wood, about knee-high, did not appear to be a knothole. Mark tapped the spot with the end of the crowbar, then leaned hard on the metal. It punched through as though the barrier were made of cork.

An acrid, crematory stench, long pent-up, hissed through the hole, overwhelming them.

The timbers had been charred on the inside, burning nearly three-quarters of the way through before something—lack of oxygen, probably—had extinguished the flames. Mark, overcoming his revulsion, chipped at the blackened wood, until the ragged opening was large enough to crawl through. Taking the flashlight from Old Dex, he probed inside with the beam.

A chamber, much wider than the mineshaft. To reach its floor they would have to lower themselves two feet. Somehow, the fire that had razed Concordia Sanitarium in 1878 had found these depths, destroying everything—everyone—within its thick walls. Hardly a square inch of wood had escaped the devastation.

The emanation throbbed strongly within this place.

Mark took a deep breath. "I'm going in."

The floor was specked with fine ash, most of it lying so

tentatively on the sand that, when disturbed by those intruding upon the stillness, they rose in small whorls of protest.

They looked around the charred room.

"Oh my God, what's that?" Tracy cried.

The skeleton sat upright, chained to the wall, five feet to the left of where they had broken through. Not a gleaming white, college lab skeleton; nothing that ever danced or dueled to the special-effects strings of Ray Harryhausen. This was something black and obscene, bones scorched and seared from the cranium to the metatarsi. Its fleshless wrists and ankles could have easily slipped through the brackets that still held it there. Nor had the fire, which had made the chamber a furnace, burned long enough to reduce this unfortunate soul to a few grams of ash, allowing it some other form of release.

Without question, the force that had drawn them there emanated from this eternal captive.

Tracy hugged her arms. "That can't be . . . Dr. Cooke."

Mark agreed. "One of the inmates, I'd guess. This is like a dungeon or something, probably where they put—*damn!*"

The urgent cold ripped into them, first thrusting, then pulling, wanting them nearer.

Wanting to tell them . . .

Something.

"This *is* Dr. Everett Cooke," Old Dex said, staring at the charred thing.

Tracy's arms fell to her sides. "I . . . think you're right."

Old Dex approached the skeleton. "About time we got you out of those chains."

"Dex, no!" Mark exclaimed.

Dex glanced over his shoulder. "It's OK; yeah, it is. This is what he's been wantin'." His own hands shaking, he slipped one of the bony wrists through the bracket. "This is what Jacob sent us down for." He did the same with the second, then lowered the skeleton gently and pulled both legs out of the chains. "There now, yer free."

The piercing chill relented; the spirit—aloft, or afoot—swirled around them in a dizzying circle, sometimes brushing past with a feather's touch. Free now, free; exultant, dancing a dance of joy . . .

No, not joy, because in this entity there was only the cold; diminished now, but cold nevertheless, no thread of warmth, which existed in even the most tormented of those who walked above.

No warmth at all . . .

"Somethin's wrong," Old Dex said.

"What is it?" Tracy asked.

"I gotta talk to him."

The prospector held out a hand; the entity touched it. Old Dex's body heaved, shuddered. He stared, wide-eyed, at the others.

"Dex!" Mark exclaimed.

The spirit backed away, widening its circles around the chamber. Old Dex was shaky; Tracy and Mark held his arms.

"Jesus," the old man sighed.

"What happened?" Tracy asked.

"When he touched me, I . . . crissakes, I don't know exactly *what* he was tryin' to tell me, but . . ." He shook his head.

"Dex?"

"He . . . wants us to know somethin'; he wants us to know it mighty bad."

To confirm this, the spirit swirled strongly around them before retreating. Tracy swore, in that instant, she too could sense its devastating need to communicate with them.

"It's on the other side of the chamber," Old Dex said. "Let's follow it." He pulled free gently. "I'm OK, I can walk."

He led them across the sand floor. Halfway, when he staggered and nearly fell, they thought his efforts had finally become too much.

They were wrong.

Old Dex had stumbled over a human skull, barely charred, that had been all but concealed beneath the sand. Standing over it now, they noticed long, bony fingers protruding, blindly pointing upward.

"It's Jacob," the prospector said, "has to be."

"Over there!" Tracy exclaimed.

A white mist floated in front of the wall across the chamber; a narrow, undulating vapor, so maddeningly ethereal that it threatened to dissipate in a gentle breath of air. Unlike those above, who appeared briefly to dance in their endless caucus-race, the mist could hold no form, could assume no recognizable feature . . .

Except for one thing.

An . . . appendage, something long, serpentine, more a tentacle than an arm or leg. Stretching from the "torso" of the insubstantial mass, waving . . .

. . . beckoning to them.

They obeyed, moving closer; two yards away now, where a charred pillar of wood, once part of stairs that led out of the dungeon, rose a foot above the sand.

Another blackened form lay just beneath the surface. Before dying in the airless tomb, the flames had carbonized much of the bones. Abnormally large fingers, part of what remained, had been reaching for the stairs.

"Then . . . someone else died down here," Mark said.

"But who?" Tracy asked. "One of your spirits from above?"

Old Dex shrugged. "Could be. I don't suppose it's important, unless . . ." He glanced at the hovering mist. ". . . unless this is what *he* wanted us to see."

The vapor faded so suddenly that it startled them. Almost immediately they felt it swirling around them, thrusting its cold, indecipherable message into the marrow of their bones.

"I . . . think you're right," Mark told the prospector.

"Dex, you have to talk to him," Tracy said. "We have to know what he wants."

He shook his head. "I tell ya, touchin' him wasn't like it was with the others. And even if it was . . . they seem to understand me a lot better than I understand them. Nah, it won't work."

The chill grew. "Then what can we do?" Mark asked.

"There is one thing, but . . ."

"What?"

"Tracy, remember what you told me about your ma, when your dad described her as *not quite bein' herself?* You know why now, because it wasn't your ma talkin', but whoever was passin' on—"

"Wait a minute," Mark interrupted. "You're not suggesting we let him inside one of us!"

"Before you argue about it, let me have my say. First off, I've been around 'em long enough to have figured out a few things. They can only get in if you let 'em, or if you're too weak to keep 'em out; same goes for 'em *stayin'* inside. So we call the shots. Second, I don't know what's troublin' this poor soul, but I got a hunch it's somethin' real important, somethin' we ought to know about quick-like."

"Something about this third body," Tracy said, shuddering.

"Yeah, maybe. Anyway, I'm not askin' either of you to do this. *I'll* let Dr. Cooke in."

"Dex, no!" Mark exclaimed. "OK, now you hear *me* out. Crazy as it sounds, I agree with most of what you said. We do have to find out what Cooke wants. But as far as you being the host . . . Dex, you're exhausted! From what we know about Jack, and Mrs. Singer, there has to be some trauma involved in letting the spirits in. And those two were getting ready to pass on over; they weren't like this tortured one! Damn, this could kill you!"

The old man shrugged wearily. "You're prob'ly right, but—"

"Then it's settled," Mark said. "*I'll* do it."

Tracy put a hand over her mouth, stifling anything she might have wanted to say. The entity's cold emanations lessened. Old Dex clapped Mark on the shoulder.

"Yeah, well . . . thanks," he said. "Listen, I'll talk to him first, try to make it easier. Wait over by Jacob. I don't think we should be doin' it near this body."

They walked to the middle of the oppressive chamber. Old Dex sat on the sand, an arm outstretched. Tracy and Mark could not hear the words he uttered during the next minute. His body trembled.

Finished, he rose shakily and joined them. "I said my piece, and I think he understands, but I can't swear he answered. Mark, clear your mind, try to relax; just keep tellin' him it's OK to come in."

Mark nodded. Tracy kissed him, backed away and stood beside the old man. An icy throbbing let them know the spirit was near. Mark looked at Tracy one last time before shutting his eyes.

"It's all right, you're welcome in," he said, feeling—at once—foolish and frightened. "You can come in and share what you have to tell us. It's all right."

Closer now, circling him, pausing briefly above what had once been Jacob Owen's body.

"You can come in," Mark continued. "It's all right."

Swirling next to him, brushing past; touching . . .

"It's all . . ."

Touching.

". . . right."

Passing through his flesh.

"It's . . ."

The cold.

". . . all . . ."

Inside him.

Mark's eyes snapped open as his hands went to his head, his face a mask of terror as he stared past Tracy and Old Dex.

"Pain!" he cried. *"Oh God, the pain!"*

"Mark!" Tracy exclaimed.

"So much pain . . . so much . . . !"

"Mark!"

His head snapped from side to side. *"OH DEAR GOD THE PAIN THE PAIN THE—!"*

His face went blank; he lowered his hands. Two seconds passed, seeming longer, as he stood there, uncomprehending.

Then, dropping to his knees, he let out a bubbling shriek that bore only a vague resemblance to a human sound. His jaw fell.

The dark cavern of his mouth erupted in a red-black geyser that muddied the sand before him. Another sound came, a low, continuous moan, like a great beast dying in agony.

"MARK!" Tracy wanted to go to him, but Old Dex held her arm.

"Tell us what's troublin' you," the old man said in a loud voice. "Dr. Cooke, tell us!"

"The hell with that!" Tracy screamed. *"Mark—!"*

"He'll be all right! Please, Dr. Cooke, tell us."

Mark's eyes found them. Blood continued to gush from the black pit as he extended a hand. His lips moved, and more sounds came, but unintelligible, gurgling.

"Please, tell us!" the prospector continued to urge.

Agonizing frustration. Mark/Cooke tried, but the sounds were the same, and he pounded a fist on the bloody sand in his anger.

The sand.

"Tell us!"

He poked a trembling finger at the sand, drew a quivering vertical line, painstakingly added a double arch.

"A letter!" Tracy exclaimed. "I think it's a B!"

"Please, Dr. Cooke, tell—!"

Mark's body jerked to rigid attention; hands again reached for his head. He shook violently.

"NO NO THE PAIN OH DEAR GOD THE PAIN—!"

Tracy ran to him but was knocked aside by his uncontrollable flailing. *"Dex, help him, pleee-ase!"* she screamed.

The prospector knelt in front of Mark. "Dr. Cooke, you're hurtin' him!" he exclaimed. "This has to stop! You gotta get out, now!"

"THE PAIN THE—!"

"Let the boy go, *now!*"

Another sound, like the unbroken wail of a squaw mourning her fallen brave. Borne by a freezing wind, it careened crazily through the chamber.

No blood stained the sand where Mark lay, motionless. The blood disssipated with the wind.

Tracy fell beside him, cradled his head. "Oh Jesus, how could we have let this happen!"

His eyes fluttered open. Old Dex said, "You all right?"

"Yeah, great," he muttered, trying to raise himself up, failing.

"Mark, listen, when he was inside, did you find out—"

"Leave him alone!" Tracy snapped. *"Hasn't he done enough?"*

The prospector shrugged. "Yeah, he sure as hell has."

Mark looked at Tracy. "God, what that man must've suffered . . ."

She kissed his forehead. "Be still now. We'll get you out of here."

The cold, angry spirit whirled amid the three, then continued its rampage through the dark place where it had been entombed for over a century. Old Dex shook his head sadly.

"No more sufferin' for him; he's had enough. We'll see he passes on over quick. But before that happens, we'll find out what it is he needs to tell us so bad. We'll find that out tonight."

"How?" Tracy asked, afraid of the answer.

"I know what to expect now, so I'm gonna let Dr. Cooke come inside *me*."

C H A P T E R   S I X T E E N

Message

1

Harry Keller's old copper/redwood Cadillac El Dorado—his "battleship," he called it, since it took about as much fuel to run—cruised up Oasis Drive at five-forty. He pulled alongside the curb. Gary Masten scrambled out of the back seat on the driver's side and hurried around to render assistance to any of the seniors who needed it. The six travelers—tired but happy after their weekend in San Diego—exchanged brief pleasantries. Gary hugged Muriel Findley, pumped the hands of her husband and Carl, and lifted the laughing Joey Russell in the air about as easily as one would a tennis racquet. He and Harry climbed back into the battleship and left for their own place.

Bruno watched the people from the safety of dense brush. The eyes he used remained mostly upon one.

He had allowed the coyote to hunt when it wanted to hunt, rest when it wanted to rest, had made no demands upon it—until now. Poised, he waited to make sure the big monster-thing was turning around, then began a steady lope through the cactus and scrub

along the perimeter of the Estates. No need to overtax the animal's
sleek body. He would reach the big road in plenty of time to see the
monster-thing; he knew that.

Las Palmas Road dead-ended just past the palm-lined entrance
to the Estates. Bruno had already reasoned the monster-thing would
not be turning that way. He could see it now, coming down Smoke
Tree Road. Running faster, he gained another hundred yards before
the shiny reddish *coach* turned south on Las Palmas Road.

Harry was a cautious driver. Too slow, some would say, although
in Smoke Tree that wasn't much of a problem. Other drivers usually
did a double take when they pulled next to the battleship. Harry's
hands were always high up on the wheel, above the top of his gnomelike head. At first glance there appeared to be no one driving the car.

Past the Valley Clinic, then a left turn on Cahuilla Lane. Good,
Bruno thought, he wouldn't have to cross the big road. The street was
a short one; not like on the other side, where there were more streets,
more houses.

Their house was at the end of the street. Even better. Circling
around, the coyote chose the concealment of some dense brittle-bush.
On its stomach, hardly panting, it watched the monster-thing being
swallowed by part of the house, something that Bruno could not begin
to understand.

The coyote inched closer to the dead-end barrier, stopping fifty
yards away behind a clump of buckhorn cholla. Not very dense, but no
matter; there was little chance of it being seen.

It waited.

2

Gary wasn't sure what he was more excited about: all his new
baseball cards, or the visit to Sea World, or the cool games he'd seen
over the weekend. The Padres had beaten the Cardinals twice; Mr.
Singer and Joey hadn't been too happy about that, but the Padres were
his team, so he was glad. He finally decided on the cards, because—
after all—the other things sort of came and went, while baseball cards
were forever.

His most prized purchase had been a Willie McCovey card when he'd worn the uniform of the Padres. Sure, he'd found a Reggie Jackson, a Rickey Henderson with the Yankees, a not-so-mint condition Carl Yastrzemski that he'd gotten for a steal, and some others. But the Willie McCovey, oh man! Joey had lots of new ones too, thanks to his grandfather. Tomorrow, Gary decided, he would bring his collection over, and they would look at them after he finished his work.

One of the first things Gary had done when they got home was to put a load of laundry in the washer. Now, forty-five minutes later, that load was in the dryer. Gary went looking for his guardian, who was thumbing through yesterday's mail in the kitchen.

"Anything you want me to do, Harry?" he asked. "Make dinner or something?"

"No, you got the wash, so I'll get dinner. That's fair. How about just sandwiches tonight?"

"Sure. I'll be outside till it's ready."

Harry grimaced. "I swear, why you like being out in that heat is beyond me. Well, at least we came to the right place."

"It's not so bad now, Harry," the youth replied with a smile. "Temperature's down, because it's so late in the day."

"Yeah, big drop, from a hundred-nine to a hundred-four." He winked at Gary. "I'll call you when dinner's ready."

Gary's Tony Gwynn pro model glove was on the kitchen table. He'd taken it to the stadium, ever hopeful; but the closest foul ball all weekend had landed five rows away. Picking it up, he went outside.

Harry had been wrong: the thermometer on the garage said it was only ninety-eight. A regular "cold snap," that's what Harry called it. Gary found a bright orange tennis ball amid the honeysuckle in the front yard. There were always a few balls around. He took it out in the street; no concerns about traffic on Cahuilla Lane. After bouncing it twice he threw it high in the air and caught it easily in the big glove. Last year he'd done it over four hundred times in a row before finally misjudging one. No records tonight, though; he was tired from the weekend, and Harry would be calling him in soon anyway.

Yeah, he thought, we sure *did* come to the right place, like

Harry said. It was hard being ... different; not that he had any choice. But it was OK here, because he had Harry, and because the old people were mostly nice and seemed to like him, and the guys at Rainbow Tree Farm were his friends and they kidded around with him just like real friends did with one another. And he was learning so much from Harry, and he was making his own money, doing good work.

Yeah, it was OK here ...

But why did he have to be different?

He threw the ball so high that, despite its bright color, he lost sight of it for a couple of seconds. It came down near the dead-end barrier, hit a chink in the asphalt and bounced into the sand beyond a clump of creosote bush. He chased it down.

The coyote stood motionless, ten yards away, watching him.

Gary grinned. "Hey boy, how ya doing? Good boy."

He loved animals. All he had at home was a tankful of fish, because poor Harry was allergic to anything with fur or feathers. But he *really* loved animals. Last year the Findleys had taken him to the San Diego Zoo; he didn't stop talking about it for weeks.

The coyote should have turned and run; they usually did. A few times, riding his bike along a trail, he'd seen them dart across his path. But this was the closest that one had ever come to the house.

"What's the matter, fella, you hungry or something?"

The coyote took a few steps toward him, stopped.

Gary patted his leg. "I won't hurt you, fella. It's all right."

He chanced a tentative step of his own. The coyote did not run. He took another long, slow stride.

They stood five yards apart.

"I can get you a bowl of milk," the big boy said, "except I'm not sure you'll wait around if I leave."

The coyote walked again. Three yards, two ...

Gary's innocent smile grew wider. "Yeah, good boy. Wow, wait'll I tell Harry!"

The animal lay on its belly, its muzzle atop the sand, mournful eyes looking up at him.

Like a big old friendly dog, Gary thought, taking another step. Just like a—

The coyote suddenly jerked onto its side, legs stretched out, rigid. It emitted a pathetic whine as its tan body shook in some sort of palsied fury. Flames of terror burned in its eyes.

"Wh-what's the matter?" Gary said, frightened. He was a foot away from the flailing thing. Don't get too close to a sick animal, Harry had warned him many times. Rabies, you could get rabies or something.

He stood over it now.

Screaming . . .

"What's . . ."

. . . terrible . . .

". . . the . . ."

. . . outside . . .

". . . matter . . ."

Hands to his head now, staggering backward, as though pulled by an invisible string. Helpless against . . .

What?

INSIDE NOW . . . INSIDE . . . WHOLE AGAIN . . . OH THE SAME . . . THE SAME LIKE IT WAS . . . WHOLE . . .

Hands fell to his sides.

Hands.

He studied them through Gary's eyes, flexed the fingers.

Big hands.

The coyote scrambled to its feet, terror still in its eyes as it stared at the hulking human, then turned and bolted into the desert, dodging the bristling spines of a jumping cholla.

Bruno watched it flee and made a grunting sound that might have been one of appreciation.

Meager resistance; he could feel the other push against him, but he pushed back, and was much stronger, and the other stopped resisting.

WHOLE AGAIN.

He started toward the house, first stepping over the discarded baseball glove, then going back for it, thinking it would be what the other was expected to do.

A house not like anything he remembered, things as strange as he had seen rolling on wheels outside, a box with colored pictures that moved and talked and . . .

He let some of the other free, so he could understand, and not be so frightened.

"Well, good timing, I was just about to call you in."

He spun around, startled. The small old man was standing in the doorway to the kitchen. Bruno stared at him.

"Something wrong?" Harry said.

Bruno took a step toward him, clenching his . . .

Hands.

"Gary?"

Not yet . . . not yet . . . have to find out more . . . about this time and place and . . . not be so afraid . . . not afraid of talking windows and riding in the monster-thing and . . .

"Hey, Gary!"

Let more of the other free . . . find out what to say . . . what to do . . . learn about this world . . .

Gary shook his head, smiled. "Hot out there, Harry. You were right; should have stayed inside. Wow, I'm hungry!"

"Figured you'd be," Harry said. "Come on, it's ready."

He put a hand on the big boy's shoulder; Gary did the same. They walked into the kitchen.

3

Tracy had been home for over an hour when her family returned from San Diego. She and Old Dex had found it hard to move Mark through the narrow shaft below the ruins of Concordia Sanitarium, even harder lifting him to the surface. Mark, while protesting the whole time, had been of little help.

Leaving the "digging" as it was, they had driven back to Old Dex's place and transferred Mark to Tracy's car. The weary prospector, Tracy believed, struggled to stay on his feet. She had told him to rest, that she would come back tonight, at sunset. Maybe, she thought, to talk him out of what he had in mind.

She'd taken Mark to his apartment, cooled him down, sat with him while he slept. He'd been adamant about rebuffing her suggestion to go to the emergency room at the Valley Clinic. Watching him sleep, his breathing heavy, she had been angry with herself for listening to him. But his color returned by the time he awakened at four, and he assured her that he was fine, that he would be going back with her later. While she scolded him for the suggestion, she was also greatly relieved.

He had not talked about the experience with Dr. Everett Cooke; she had not asked.

If Carl Singer noticed how wan his daughter looked, he said nothing. They ate the dinner she had prepared, the excited Joey doing most of the talking. On Saturday, before the card shops and the game, they'd gone to Sea World, where Joey and Gary had been splashed by Shamu, fed the dolphins, and made ominous faces into the shark enclosure. His first visit to a major league ballpark other than Busch Stadium had been a treat.

And how had Tracy's weekend gone? Carl asked.

"Well, not as . . . exciting as yours," she said. "We rode our bikes, went to the pool, watched movies, talked a lot."

"You were with Mark the whole time?" Joey asked.

"Pretty much."

"I hope you marry him."

Tracy choked on her diet Seven-Up, then blotted it up from the table with her napkin. "Why . . . do you say that?" she exclaimed, as Carl chuckled. The boy, as befitting his maternal ancestry, was prone to straightforwardness, but was usually not *that* blunt.

Joey thought a moment. "Because he's cool, and then I could have a father and a friend at the same time."

The immensity of his usually well-concealed hurt affected her deeply. *God, he's right: Mark Alderson would be both, and he'd be damn good at it.*

"I love you, champ," she said softly.

4

Joey was exhausted from the weekend. He nodded off on the couch halfway through a *Star Wars* movie. Tracy carried him in to bed and tucked the covers up under his chin.

When she emerged from her room carrying a jacket, Carl said, "I didn't know you were going out tonight."

"Just for a little while. You don't mind, do you?"

He shrugged. "I . . . feel like I haven't seen you much lately."

Tracy smiled. "That's not a little jealousy I'm hearing, is it?"

"We-ell; that's a father's prerogative, I suppose."

She hugged him. "This is Mark's last night off until next Friday. We'll have lots of time during the week, I promise."

"You mean . . . you're staying another week?"

"Maybe more; that's OK, isn't it?"

"Are you kidding!" he exclaimed happily, returning the hug.

Mark hurried down the stairs at ten minutes to eight. If there were any aftereffects from the nightmare "possession," they were not evident. Climbing in next to Tracy, he noticed a large sketchpad on the backseat, and a box of Joey's Crayola markers. He knew what they were for.

"You look good." Tracy kissed him.

"I feel fine. We better hurry."

They said little on their way to Old Dex's place, Tracy concentrating on the trail. At times she drove too fast, jarring them.

Old Dex waited for them outside. Unlike Mark, the prospector did not look better.

"Get in, I'll drive," she told him.

"Well, OK, if you don't care about riskin' your axles." He climbed into the back seat, holding the pad on his lap. "You brought what we talked about."

The trail remained a challenge. Fortunately there was still enough daylight, even though the sun had dipped behind the coastal mountain range. Coming back would be another story.

For the first time, Mark related in detail what had happened to him. He spoke tentatively, unsure how to express himself, or if it made sense.

"As soon as he went inside me, the pain was blinding. I could hear—feel—his screams, but no words, nothing I could understand. He wanted to talk, but when he tried . . . *Jesus, his tongue had been pulled out!*"

Tracy shuddered. "We know that. Go on."

Mark glanced over his shoulder at the prospector. "Through all the pain I could sense that—like you said—he was trying desperately to tell us something, to . . . *warn* us. Even his relief over being freed was not enough to calm him. There is something we must know."

Old Dex stroked his chin thoughtfully. "And even then you couldn't get a hint of it?"

"Once, I thought maybe . . . but the pain, that awful pain! Dex, you're certain the spirit is Dr. Everett Cooke. OK, I believe you; but even if it is, I sensed that whatever's left of him is as mad—maybe more so—as those walking above. The horrible way he must've died, entombed for decades, awakening to find himself still in agony, confined in chains . . . *Christ, I'm not even sure what I'm saying!*"

"I think I know what you mean," Old Dex said calmly.

"We haven't mentioned one thing," Tracy interjected. "If that *is* Dr. Cooke, how did he wind up that way? Who did that to him?"

Old Dex patted the sketchpad. "Maybe that's what this is all about."

The ruins looked more foreboding than ever in the copper-streaked dusk. Tracy left the car in the same corner where, earlier, the jeep had stood. They walked to the site of the dig.

The emanation was gone.

Mark thought about climbing down, going into the ash-black chamber to make sure. But they knew; all of them knew.

"Dr. Cooke came up," Old Dex said. "Thank God for that."

"But where did he go?" Tracy asked.

"He joined the others, like Jacob did."

They continued on through the rubble to the communal hall. Shadows engulfed the ruins of the sanitarium.

Halfway there, they felt it.

"You were right," Tracy told the old man.

Though strong, it did not have the same intensity as in the confining chamber. Darkness was nearly complete now, but as yet nothing—not the frost-wall, not the raging spirit from below—was visible. Old Dex, kneeling on the sand, removed a red marker from the box, uncapped it, handed the rest to Tracy. He opened the pad before him.

"You'd best stay back for now," he told them. "But later on I'll prob'ly need one of you to flip the pages."

"Dex, are you sure—?" Tracy began.

"We ain't discussin' it no more, pretty lady," he said. "It has to be done. Besides, I'm sure of what's comin' and I think I can handle it."

They sat down across from him. The presence grew stronger. Old Dex held out his left hand; the other gripped the marker.

It was visible now, a thin, vaporous pillar, swaying pendulum-like a foot above the sand. Tracy, already wearing her jacket, pulled it tightly around her.

The entity whirled twice around Old Dex.

"Well, come on, friend," he said calmly, "no sense dallyin' around."

The rigid pillar became a twisting, snakelike thing as it floated toward him, disappearing like a corkscrew into a wine bottle.

"Oh Dex," Tracy whispered.

The lean body stiffened; he pulled back his left hand, clamping it over his mouth to keep it shut.

Blood trickled between his fingers. Tracy swallowed a rising scream.

His body shook as violently as a drenched animal throwing off water. Against the unbelievable pain, he struggled not to open his mouth. He dropped to his knees before the pad, which had been well positioned. The red marker cut the air like a spastic wand.

They were aware of the hoar-frosted wall, a smaller portion of it, which had taken form farther back from where it usually did.

His right arm fighting for control, Old Dex lowered the marker to the pad; the felt tip touched the paper to the left of center. An insignificant long serif, then a quivering letter, a second and a third, connected by briefer serifs: B-R-U.

The marker reached the edge of the pad.

"We have to turn it!" Tracy exclaimed.

Pulling free of his torpor, Mark knelt by the top of the sketchpad. He reached around and quickly flipped the page.

Two letters, larger, sans serif: N-O.

Another page: F-R.

The letters growing smaller: E-E-B.

Writing faster now: R-U-N.

Still smaller: O-F-R-E.

Even faster: E-B-R-U.

The letters becoming elongated, more wavy: N-O-F-R.

Almost illegible: E-E-B.

The felt tip stabbing at the paper, meaningless spirals and concentric circles and blood-red spider webs.

"Dex!" Mark cried.

No more writing. The marker dropped to the sand. Old Dex toppled over, writhing, flailing, one hand still—somehow—clamped over his mouth.

The frost-wall fell back, wavered.

Mark grabbed his arm. "That's enough!" he exclaimed. "Leave him now! *Leave him!*"

"Dex, please!" Tracy cried.

Through the pain, his eye found her. He pulled his hand down from his face. His mouth snapped open.

They recoiled instinctively from the expected torrent.

The scream came, loud, agonizing, but no blood.

The spirit careened madly through the portion of the ruins that had been the communal hall.

The frost-wall dissipated.

They made Old Dex as comfortable as possible. The prospector pointed a shaky finger at the pad.

"Did you . . . get it all?" he gasped.

Tracy flipped through the pages. "They don't mean anything!"

"Write them down on a single line," Mark said, "in that same order."

She ripped pages off until there was a blank one, and started copying the letters. Even before she had finished, they saw it.

"Two words, over and over," Mark said. *"Bruno Free."*

Tracy repeated it. "What does that mean? Dex, could you sense anything else from him?"

"Nope, it was all I could do—*oohh*!"

"Dex!"

The pain twisted his face grotesquely. "We have to get him to the clinic!" Mark cried.

Old Dex shook his head. "I'm finished, in case you couldn't tell. Been sick for a long time now. I was hopin' to hold on till this work was done, but . . . At least I can take poor Dr. Cooke with me, end his sufferin'."

"Oh Dex," Tracy sighed.

He beckoned them closer. "Listen to what you gotta do: this message, it's important, damn important. Talk to Jacob, find out . . ."

"Dex, no-oo!"

Overwhelming *pain*. Tracy held his hand, but the fingers were limp.

The entity floated above; unseen, but they knew it was there. In the past minute the raging thing had been forgotten. Now, its emanations were softer, and through the cold they sensed the first threads of warmth from this tormented soul.

It had delivered its message; now it was time to pass on over, and even through its rage, and agony, it knew this.

The emanations were gone.

The old prospector's face became smooth as the entity took his pain.

He smiled, squeezed Tracy's hand.

Dexter Jones said, "Take care of the rest of my friends, will ya?"

CHAPTER SEVENTEEN

Changes

1

Joey Russell first saw Gary Masten on Monday morning through the front window of his grandfather's house. Gary was working on the Gibbs's yard. Fifteen minutes later, when he'd finished breakfast, Joey hurried across the street.

"Hey Gary," he called, waving.

The big boy looked up and saw Joey but did not smile. "Oh, hiya," he said.

"You bring your cards over?" Joey asked.

He shook his head. "No, forgot."

"You wanna play ball later?"

"Can't; I'm working all day. Gotta go out to the tree farm."

"You usually have time in-between."

Gary resumed what he'd been doing. "Harry's taking me home for lunch."

"You can have lunch with us. Grandpa won't mind. We'll call Harry and—"

"I have to work now," he interrupted.

"Yeah, sure. Well, see you later." Dejected, Joey walked back across Oasis Drive.

2

Tracy had been on the telephone in her father's room for a while. Long distance, she had told Carl, offering to pay the costs. He had advised Tracy what she could do with her money—in a fatherly way.

She was surprised to find Joey moping on the sofa, absently pounding a baseball into a mitt. This was not her son's usual demeanor. She sat down next to him.

"What's doing, champ? They cancel the rest of the major league baseball season? They decide to stop making horror movies? What?"

"Leave me alone!" he pouted.

"Well sor-*eee*. Come on, what's wrong?"

He shrugged. "I don't know . . . Gary, I guess."

"What about Gary?"

"He's kinda different today."

"Different in what way?"

"He didn't smile; you know, like he always does when he sees you? And he's sort of grumpy?"

Tracy nodded. "And you're not used to seeing him like that, huh?"

"Nuh-uh."

"It's true that Gary Masten is 'special.' But he's also just a person, and like all people he has good days and grumpy days. Whatever's bugging him, it has nothing to do with you."

He looked up. "Yeah, but aren't friends supposed to help each other when one's having a grumpy day? That's what you always told me."

"Sure, and you might talk to him later. Just don't be surprised if he doesn't respond. He may have to work it out himself, or with Harry's help, and he will; you'll see. Tomorrow or the day after he'll be the same as always."

He changed the subject: "You gonna be with Mark all day?"

"Just for a little while this morning; he's working today. Wanna do something?"

"Yeah!"

"I have some errands to run, but I should be finished in a few hours. We'll have the whole rest of the day and evening. If they changed the movies over in Borrego Springs, maybe we'll go."

"Can we eat at that Mexican place?"

"Sure."

"Aw-right!"

The boy pumped a fist and ran off to challenge his grandfather to a game of Scrabble, Jr. for the undisputed world's championship.

3

Mark swerved on his bike when the gust of wind caught him but had no problem keeping his balance. He was pedaling up Oasis Drive, and these intermittent gusts had worried him since leaving his apartment. Ribbons of sand had blown across the Seaway, Las Palmas Road, all of Smoke Tree's thoroughfares. And this was nothing compared to what winds coming down over the coastal mountains could cause when fully unleashed. Hopefully, the gusts were not a portent of that.

He had slept late, till nine-thirty; Tracy had insisted he do that, and his body would not allow him otherwise. Yesterday had drained him.

Yesterday had changed him.

Last night they'd taken Dexter Jones's body out of the ruins and driven it to town. Mark had been behind the wheel, negotiating the car over the rugged jeep trail, Tracy too distraught to drive. Not sure what to do, they had stopped at the Valley Clinic, where Dr. Hoberg was still around, checking on patients. Hoberg had the body moved from the car and promised he would take care of everything else. A niece in Arizona, Old Dex's only relative, would be notified.

If the doctor wondered what Tracy and Mark had to do with the prospector, he didn't ask.

Tracy had driven Mark home, and they'd lain together in his

for

bed, not making love, not talking, just holding each other, waiting for the trembling to subside, trying to understand what had happened, what was still to come.

Bruno free.

Mark left his bike in Carl's garage and hurried to the front door. When Tracy let him in, he was still brushing wind-blown sand from his face.

"You look tired," he told her.

"Didn't sleep much. The dreams . . ."

He nodded. "I know. Anyway, I spoke to Jerry before. He thought I was calling in sick . . . sounds like a great idea. I told him you were interested in the old asylum, wanted to do a paper on it or something. Asked him who around here might know about it."

"And?"

"According to Jerry, Smoke Tree's founts of information about Concordia Sanitarium were Jack Redmond and Dexter Jones."

"Oh, that's great," Tracy muttered. "We already know Dex hadn't a clue who or what Bruno was. No one else?"

"He couldn't think of anyone but he suggested we try the library in Borrego Springs."

"So, that's where I'm headed."

"You be careful. It can get bad out here when the wind starts blowing like this."

She looked at her watch. "You still have a few minutes before work. Come sit down."

4

Harry Keller had run out of ham and wasn't about to have Gary miss out on his favorite lunch. Not today. Not with the boy being so out of sorts, like he'd been since last night. Heck, you don't spend all those years around a Down's kid without the least change of behavior being obvious. He'd tried to talk to him earlier, find out what was wrong; they could always talk before. But this morning Gary had been sullen, and for a moment verged on belligerency, but caught himself.

Harry was concerned.

Parking his battleship in front of Rusty's Market, Harry saw Chief Donald Upton outside the police station. They played poker together at least once a week, sometimes more, whenever the lawman could get away from his duties to join the retirees. Upton's new full-time deputy, Danny Martinez, an enthusiastic twenty-six-year-old from Indio, had just driven off in the Chevy Blazer that had sat in Steve Cornwell's driveway on the day of his death.

"Hello, Don," Harry called.

"Harry, good to see you." They shook hands. "Here, let's move out of this damn wind."

They stepped into a narrow alley between the two boxlike adobe buildings, out of the stinging whipcords of sand. Harry said, "You showing up Wednesday night so I can lighten your wallet of some of the big bucks we pay you?"

Upton grinned. "Wouldn't miss it. How's the boy?"

"Fine, he's . . . fine."

The chief looked at him curiously. "What's wrong?"

"I don't know. He's not exactly himself today, not since last night, after we got back."

"From where?"

"San Diego."

"What'd you do there?"

"Card stores, the beach, Sea World, couple ball games."

"Well, there you are," Upton said sagely. "The poor kid's on overload, trying to sort it all out. He'll be fine."

"I guess so," Harry said, not convinced. "But knowing that kid so well, I'd almost swear . . . Nah, that's crazy."

"What? Tell me."

"It's like . . . it's not Gary at all, but someone else inside him."

"Someone else inside . . ." Upton smiled. "That's strange talk, Harry."

"Alzheimer's talk, huh? Maybe I'm finally losing it."

"No, Harry, not you. Come on, stop worrying about the boy. He'll be all right by dinnertime, you'll see."

"Yeah, thanks. Speaking of food, I'd better get what I need so I can make him lunch. See you Wednesday, Don."

Chief Upton watched Harry go into Rusty's Market. He thought: someone else inside him.

Someone else.

That morning in the jail . . .

Must get inside . . . can't stay . . . out . . .

. . . when that drifter was in the cell . . .

Let . . . me . . . in . . .

. . . and there was something . . .

Too strong . . . can't get inside this one . . .

. . . that only the drifter had seen, and that pathetic-looking boy had said . . .

I was walking along the road . . . in the daytime. That's the last thing I knew until I . . . woke up just now.

An hour later the boy was carrion on the desert floor.

Someone else.

Crazy shit. What the hell was he thinking? Crazy . . .

Chief Donald Upton hated when the sand blew like this. He pulled down the brim of his Resistol hat and went inside the station.

5

Gary had worked on the Gibbs's yard first, and would have washed their car, had the wind not begun. Mr. Gibbs had called him into the garage, where they had begun work on a redwood planter. Now, with the wind relenting a bit, he was outside again, putting the finishing touches on the yard.

Across the street, the woman came out of her house.

The woman . . .

. . . who had done the Thing *with the man at the Bad-Tasting Water place.*

The woman . . .

. . . was smiling at him, waving, from her driveway.

Bruno wanted her. He wanted her more than he had wanted the woman in San Francisco.

He stared at her with Gary's eyes, his moon-face a mask of desire and confusion. She called out something . . .

Hi Gary.

. . . waved again. His eyes bore into her across the distance, reaching under her flesh, twisting gelid fingers around her bones. He clenched his . . .

Hands.

Her smile faded as she stared back, puzzled, something disturbing her thoughts.

Let some of him go, let him . . .

Gary grinned, waved. "Tracy! Hiya, Tracy!" he exclaimed, hurrying toward her, stopping to look both ways on Oasis Drive, as Harry had taught him. At first he'd called her Mrs. Russell, but Tracy had corrected that.

"Hi, Gary." Smiling again, she met him at the curb. They hugged, the embrace lasting longer than usual.

The woman who had done the Thing *with . . .*

He squeezed her tightly.

In his arms . . .

One hand slipped down to her buttocks, tightly packed in cut-off jeans. She stepped out of his hold gently but purposefully.

He's kinda different today.

Jesus, so that's his problem, Tracy figured. *Puberty coming a bit late. He must be confused as hell.*

"I have to go now, Gary," she said.

He grinned again. "See ya later, Tracy."

Gary was still on her side of the street, waving, when Tracy pulled onto Oasis Drive. But his smile was gone.

6

Mr. Gibbs paid Gary in cash, as he always did, while Harry Keller waited for his charge at the curb. Gary pocketed the money absently. Since the woman had left, nearly half an hour before, he'd thought of little else. The woman . . .

Tracy.

He wanted Tracy, wanted to touch her again, to watch her take off her clothes so the two of them, *she and Bruno*, could do the *Thing*, wanted . . .

"Come on, Gary, lunchtime," Harry called from the leather interior of his battleship.

The *monster-thing* again. Before, when the old man had driven him there, Bruno had receded deeply into the depths of his unwilling host's mind, for he had been terrified. Now, climbing in, he felt more curious than afraid, and allowed a little of Gary out.

"Great job on the Gibbs's lawn," Harry said, and when Gary only nodded he asked, "You OK?"

"Sure, Harry," he replied. "I'm just real hungry." That was true.

Harry hardly said anything on the ride home. He was concentrating even harder on his driving, the wind having renewed its assault, swirling sand across the road, raising dust devils amid the scrub, blowing tumbleweeds and broken pieces of cacti. Winds like this often blew across the desert, though the onslaught of sand and dust, or lack of it, was dictated by the amount of rainfall in the prior year. Since last summer, less than five inches had fallen on Smoke Tree.

Bruno, one white-knuckled hand gripping the shoulder harness, looked at the odd array of things with numbers and letters and such in front of Harry, watched his foot shift back and forth from the accelerator to the brake as the big old Caddy lurched along.

Finally approaching the house, Harry picked up a small box and pointed it out the window. A wide door began to open with a protesting clatter. Gary slunk down in his seat, eyes closed. This was what had happened yesterday, Bruno thought, and it was too terrifying to watch.

The descending door fell noisily behind the monster-thing, leaving it in the blackness of the cave.

Blackness.

Bruno was determined to remain inside until he could see, but Harry, tapping the steering wheel impatiently, said, "Come on, let's go. You want to sit here all day?"

Let more of him through. Let more . . .

Gary nodded and climbed out of the car. His eyes half-shut, he waited for Harry to come around then followed him to a smaller door, not far away. He sidestepped the old man and threw the door open quickly. Light, beautiful light from the well-illuminated kitchen washed around him in waves, cleansing him of the blackness, pushing it far back. He smiled; Harry shook his head.

"What's for lunch?" Gary asked.

"Your favorite." Harry opened the refrigerator. He was going to reach in when the phone rang. "Go on, help yourself."

Harry answered the phone, listened for a few seconds, then said, "That's great, thank you very much," and hung up. He had been watching Gary grope around in the refrigerator; so far the boy had taken nothing out. Harry picked up a can of Coke and a plate with the sandwiches and orange wedges, and put them on the table.

"That was Dorothy, from the farm. She knows I don't like to drive in this kind of weather, so she's sending Jorge by for you."

Gary nodded absently. He looked at the lunch.

Within, Bruno probed.

"Where are the cupcakes?" Gary asked.

"Something special today," Harry said. "I picked up a quart of pistachio almond ice cream at Rusty's Market. It's in the freezer."

Bruno probed again. "Pistachio almond, yum."

"On one condition: you tell me what's wrong today."

Sullenly: "Nothing's wrong."

"Come on, boy, I know you better. You've been acting weird ever since we got back from the city."

Gary sat down at the table, picked up one of the sandwiches. "Nothing's wrong," he said again, taking a bite.

Harry Keller's smile, which had warmed generations of Los Angeles schoolchildren, shone brightly as he put a hand on the boy's shoulder. "Listen, pal, we've always talked about stuff, right? When did I ever keep a secret from you? So why don't you tell me what's bothering—"

Gary shrugged the hand off and pounded a fist on the table. "Nothing's wrong!" he exclaimed. "I want to eat my lunch."

Harry was losing patience, something he rarely did. "Blast it, Gary, that's enough. What's gotten into you anyway? I'll find out, one way or another. And you can forget about the ice cream!"

He turned and walked to the refrigerator. Gary dropped his sandwich on the plate, stared at him.

What's gotten into you?

He knew; this bent little man knew! But how . . . ?

Gary stood. "Nothing's gotten into me."

"Yeah, right," Harry said, chuckling without humor. "I know better."

He knows he knows.

The room, the house, the world spun crazily around him. The old man kept his back turned disdainfully as he looked in the cold box. Over and over he clenched and opened his . . .

Hands.

The woman in San Francisco.

The woman who had done the Thing with the man at the Bad-Tasting Water place.

Tracy.

What's gotten into you?

Hands.

He knows, he knows.

Hands.

"NOTHING'S GOTTEN INTO ME!"

The bellowing voice startled Harry. He turned. Gary stood over him, cold eyes piercing like stilettos, the moon-face twisted in something more feral than human. In his decades of teaching, Harry had broken up fights between switchblade-wielding punks, had been threatened many times. Never had he known the fear he felt now, staring up at this leviathan of rage.

"Gary, stop it!" he said firmly. "You—"

A massive hand grabbed him around the throat, lifted him as effortlessly as, a day earlier, the coyote had done with a pack rat. Harry's eyes bulged; arthritic fingers clawed helplessly at his captor's forearm.

"Nothing's gotten into me," the voice said.

The other hand suddenly shot up to his head. His grasp on the old man eased; confusion replaced the anger on his face.

Not Harry not Harry please let him go don't hurt Harry please get out of me.

Harry was thrown back, slamming hard against the open refrigerator as Gary clutched his head with both hands now. *No no can't be he's pushing me he's pushing me out no can't be . . .*

Don't hurt Harry please don't hurt him won't let you—

"NO-OOOO!"

The rumbling sound was that of a deep-throated jungle predator, temporarily cornered but unwilling to remain in that helpless position. He stood tall; hands were lowered, and he darted glances with his questioning eyes.

Something between a sneer and a smile grew on his face.

The body, the mind, were his. The other was gone, beaten back, sunk in the darkness of near-oblivion.

He, Bruno, had won, and the *screaming terrible outside time* would not have him.

Harry, dazed, reached blindly for something to try and pull himself up. Bruno grabbed the hand, yanked the arm free of the body as easily as pulling a petal from a flower.

The old man shrieked.

Bruno thrust four fingers into Harry's mouth, pulled up and down, snapped the jawbone, continued to pull, left it hanging by a few threads of flesh and cartilage.

Blood soaked the refrigerator and the oak veneer cabinetry and the shiny floor tiles, and Gary Masten's favorite pair of Levis 501 jeans.

The gurgling, mewling sounds from the dying man were barely audible.

He thrust two thumbs into Harry's neck, widened the hole, tore out his throat, which made the sounds stop for good.

He went on savaging the body with his . . .

Hands

. . . and he was complete, and the rush within him was an orgasmic flood tide, something long unfelt, something he had almost known in San Francisco, something that, he now understood, had to do with the *Thing* itself.

He stopped tearing at the body, and the flood tide receded. This was good, but not as good as it would be with . . .

Tracy.

He would save it for her, and it would be the best of all.

He shuddered, spent. Sitting down at the table, gazing with admiration at his work, he finished the sandwiches and fruit, downed the can of Coke in a few deep swallows.

Probing deep into the blackness for the other, he learned what to do. He showered, discarding the bloody clothes on the bedroom floor, then dressed in almost identical jeans and shirt. Returning to the kitchen, he stood amid the slaughter and ate the quart of pistachio almond ice cream, which was good. He was careful not to get any blood on his work boots.

At ten minutes past one, with the wind still swirling through Smoke Tree, he went outside in response to Jorge Montoya's three long blasts on the horn.

CHAPTER EIGHTEEN

"Big Idjit"

1

This kind of weather made Tracy long for cold, wet Midwestern nights, even energy-sapping, humid days along the muddy Mississippi.

The wind, increasing soon after she'd left Smoke Tree, buffeted the Cressida. Twice, she swerved onto the stony shoulder. Fortunately, traffic along the Borrego-Salton Seaway was light. She drove with caution, the normal ten-minute ride to the eastern limits of Borrego Springs taking nearly twice as long.

The Borrego Springs branch of the San Diego County Public Library was housed in a small storefront along Palm Canyon Drive, near the Christmas Circle—the hub of the town. Inside, Tracy approached Edna Markey (the woman wore a plastic name tag), fiftyish, bookish and prim. Gold-framed bifocals, perched on the end of her nose, were connected around the back of her head by a Florentine chain. Her mouth was puckered in what Tracy, as a girl, had called shush-mouth, a rare disease afflicting those who worked in libraries or attended operas. Despite the seriousness of her mission,

Tracy struggled to keep from laughing when Edna turned toward her and peered rodentlike over her glasses.

"Can I help you?" Edna asked in a barely audible voice.

Tracy glanced around quickly. One other person was in the library, an old man sitting and reading a *Wall Street Journal.* He wore a bulky hearing aid.

"Uh, yes," Tracy whispered, bending over like a conspirator, "I'm doing some research on Concordia Sanitarium. That's the old asylum over near Smoke Tree?"

Edna's pucker grew tighter. "I've lived in the valley most of my life," she huffed, "so I know where Concordia Sanitarium stood."

Jesus, strike one. "Sorry, I mean . . . Do you have any background information on the place?"

"Not much written about it; footnotes in a few texts. If you read any of the brochures available in Smoke Tree, you've seen it all. But I can guide you to those references, if you want."

"No historians around, amateur or otherwise, who might know something more?"

"Well, there's always Phillip Lantz."

"Phillip Lantz. Where can I find him?"

"You can't. He died in 1977."

Tracy's eyes rolled back in her head. *I'm being tested, right? That's what this is all about.*

"He was never published, not formally," Edna went on. "But Phillip must have written hundreds, maybe thousands of pages on valley history; clipped newspaper articles, that sort of thing. His widow donated all his papers to the library after his death. I doubt whether anyone knew more about Concordia Sanitarium." The shush-mouth became a wry smile. "Some say that's because Phillip Lantz was a little crazy himself."

"Can you get them for me?" Tracy asked.

"Sorry, but they're in the back room, and as you can see, I'm the only one here. That back room, it's in such a state! We keep meaning to do something about it . . . I'm afraid I'd have trouble finding them anyway. Now Kathy Curry—she's our head librarian—could probably lead you right to them."

"What time will she be back?"

"She won't. Monday is her day off."

Tracy gnashed her teeth. "Then may I look for them myself? It's very important, and I won't be in town long."

Edna thought for a moment. "We-ell, I suppose it would be all right." She opened a drawer and withdrew a single key hooked to a rabbit's foot key chain. "Go down that second aisle, past Biographies. You can't miss it."

Even unlocked, the heavy door groaned open; it had been a while since anyone had been in here. The back room, permeated by a not unpleasant old-paper smell, was in something worse than a *state*; more like a whole *country*, Tracy thought. Ancient books with cracked spines and torn or broken covers were stacked everywhere, perhaps waiting to be re-bound; magazines were plentiful. About half, Tracy noticed, were the yellow, ubiquitous *National Geographics*. Boxes marked "Donations" or "Friends of the Library" flanked another door. There were at least ten file cabinets scattered about, some of them the old, fireproof four-drawer kind that weighed a ton even when empty. Scores of other vaguely marked boxes rounded out the back room, which, owing to the dry desert climate, had not suffered the ravages of mold and mildew, although there was more than enough dust.

"Gee thanks, Edna," Tracy muttered as she started poking around.

If the woman was right, Phillip Lantz's contribution to the library would have been voluminous; probably delivered in a box or boxes that, after all these years, might still be unopened. But narrowing her search down to old boxes did not seem like narrowing anything at all, considering most of them looked old. Besides, the boxes were stacked two- and three-deep in places, meaning that many would have to be moved out of the way. For more reasons than one she wished Mark were with her.

OK, forget the boxes right off; try the filing cabinets. Fortunately they were all unlocked, which prevented her from having to ask Edna Markey if she would hunt down the keys. A couple were empty; others contained long-forgotten supplies: metal bookends, index cards, plastic dust jackets, magazine covers, a broken three-hole punch. One drawer, marked *Personnel*, held records of those who had worked at the branch in the past—a thin file.

The cabinets yielded nothing; nor did the boxes within easy reach. *Figures.*

She thought of Joey and looked at her watch: ten minutes to one. *Oh damn. Sorry, champ, but this might take all day.*

All day. What was so important about doing this?

Bruno free.

The answer was somewhere in this room; it had to be, she decided.

All day. And longer, if need be.

Outside, wind-blown sheets of sand scratched against the windows of the library's back room.

Tracy breathed deeply and began moving boxes aside.

2

Jorge Montoya hadn't said much on the way over to the tree farm. It was all he could do to keep the old Ford pickup on the road against the relentless lashing of the wind. Once, a confused driver on her way up Las Palmas Road drifted over the yellow line, coming dangerously close to the truck. And with dust beginning to rise, Jorge did not see a westbound car on Carrizo St. until it was nearly on top of him. Had it been going any faster than 10 mph, it would have struck him broadside.

The Mexican's only comments were how ill tempered *el jefe* was today, how he wanted to see Gary as soon as he got in, and how, despite the building storm, they had been so busy today. Bruno only half-heard the man's words. For the first time in . . .

How long? He didn't know.

. . . he had killed again with his hands, and he should have felt gratified, fulfilled, but he did not, because some part of him still drifted in a void, an emptiness with distant, barely discernible borders, like the finely stitched edges of huge, sky-filling blankets, and he needed to reach out and draw these blankets tightly around him, until that nothingness had been pushed away, and he was safe in its folds, and that couldn't be, he knew, until he had her, until he had the woman.

Until he had *Tracy*.

They would find the old man he had killed; sooner or later they would find him, and they would know who did it, and they would come looking . . .

. . . for the big boy named Gary.

Looking for *him*.

A small part of him regretted what he had done, because now his time was shorter, and he could not think of what to do. Why was it so hard to think? Why did thoughts come so slow, so confused? And the other, he couldn't use him, because he was the same. *Damn him, damn* . . . But then, if he wasn't the same, how else would Bruno have him, using his eyes, his tongue, the rest of his body . . .

His hands.

Once, before they reached the tree farm, he had clutched at the head that held the offending brain, and Jorge had glanced at him, asked what was wrong, but he had muttered something and sat up in his seat, and it was over.

Why couldn't he think?

Big idjit. That was what they had called him in San Francisco. Other names too, bad names, but he remembered that one more, because it was what the woman had shouted in his face when he tried to do the *Thing* with her.

Big idjit.

The woman . . .

Tracy.

Couldn't think, just couldn't think . . .

Jorge turned off the road onto the tree farm, driving the pickup to the door of a modular office. As Gary climbed out, the Mexican grinned at him.

"Hope he don' chew your ass out too bad! Me and the boys, we meet you over in the barn, you tell us wha' happen."

Gary hurried through the door and out of the wind. Dorothy Reed, Terry Cooper's secretary of fifteen years, sat at a small desk; two other office workers were absent. The petite woman, approaching sixty gracefully, liked Gary, often joked with him; but not this time.

"Watch out, he's in a snit today," she warned him in a hushed voice. "Don't take whatever he says too seriously; you know him."

"Yeah, sure, Dorothy," Gary said. "Thanks."

Terry Cooper was a great guy when things were going right, which was most of the time, this being a successful business. There wasn't much he wouldn't do for his friends or employees. But when he was in a "snit," watch out; you wanted to be as far away as possible. Later on he would apologize for what he said, buy you a soda or beer, something like that.

Everything had gone wrong that day, from sunrise on. First, and worst, had been an unannounced pesticide storage check by the Agriculture Department. Cooper hated those. Next, a few sick calls. Then, the Mexican workers had nearly set a few acres of jacarandas ablaze with a fire they'd kindled to heat up their mid-morning meal. And of course the damn wind out there . . . Cooper liked the desert, and for the most part could live on its terms; but he really hated wind. At least they'd gotten the trucks loaded and on the way before it got bad. But then, one of the drivers had called in from Brawley with engine problems; he'd be stuck there overnight, at least.

When Gary entered the cluttered office, shutting the door behind him, Cooper was gazing sourly through the window. His scowl remained frozen when he saw the big teen.

"Did Jorge say anything to you on the way over?" he snapped.

"Uh, just about how busy it was."

"Yeah, that's for damn sure. But nothing about last Thursday?"

"Nuh-uh."

"Probably too damn stupid to even figure it out," Cooper muttered. "When you left at the end of the day, you forgot to move those flats from the greenhouse to the shade house to be hardened off. Do you know how far behind production that put us by the time we found out on Friday?"

"Whoops, sorry."

"'Whoops, sorry,'" he mocked. "Only an idiot would do something like that!"

Gary looked at him coldly. "Wh-what did you call me?"

"Tried to get a hold of you all weekend," Cooper went on, "all I ever got was Harry on the answering machine!"

"We went away. What did you call me?"

Big idjit.

"I—what?" The hyperactive man flailed his arms. "I said only an idiot would forget to move flats!"

You tore my dress, you big idjit.

"Don't call me that."

Cooper glared at Gary, who had never stood up to him. "I'll call you what I damn well please!" he exclaimed. "Or did you forget who you're working for?"

Gary took a step closer. "Don't ever call me that."

Cooper thrust his face defiantly into Gary's. "Then don't do idiotic things like forgetting to move flats!"

Don't touch me there, you big idjit.

Gary grabbed the man's throat with his left hand, squeezing tightly as he lifted him off the ground. Cooper, wide-eyed, tried to fight back but was defenseless, even though he was a strong man.

"Don't ever *ever* call me that."

He drove the palm of his right hand with great force above the bridge of Cooper's nose. The head snapped back; the skull shattered, and shards of bone ripped into the brain, and after a violent, spastic shudder the body was still.

Dorothy had opened the door and was standing there, hands over her mouth, watching the big, gentle boy she'd known for years thrust fingers into Terry Cooper's dead eyes, then tear up, removing the forehead flesh and most of the scalp to reveal the splintered bones underneath.

He threw the body against a filing cabinet.

He caught Dorothy easily, for she was too terrified to run. She did not deserve the same as this man.

He snapped her neck like a twig and left her lying where she fell.

The compelling rush brought about by having killed with his . . .

Hands.

The need, the desire . . .

Don't touch me there, you big idjit.

. . . to have . . .

Tracy.

More people dead. Others didn't like that, and soon men in uniforms would come looking for him, and there would be no more time . . .

No more time.

He would have her now, right now. The little dark man (Jorge?) would take him there in the monster-thing.

Right now.

He left the office and moved sidelong through the hot, stinging sand. The barn, thirty yards away, was a large, corrugated storage building where irrigation and other plumbing supplies were kept, containers were built, and anything mechanical was serviced. With the wind rising Jorge, Pedro, and Jaime had been working outside for the past hour amid the containered trees, which offered more shelter. Now, they had come in to await their friend.

"Look like *el jefe* not bite your ass off, eh?" Jorge said, laughing. "So now you goin' do some work!"

"Hey, *El Gigante*," Pedro called, "c'mon, we mess you up!"

He ducked and feinted in his best Oscar de la Hoya imitation. The three circled Gary, sparring playfully. Bewildered, he turned clockwise, eyes darting between them.

"*El Gigante!*" the gentle Jaime exclaimed, moving in to land a series of featherlike blows against the big man's left arm.

Gary put a hand behind the small man's back. Jaime stopped; his smile grew.

His heart exploded when Gary's fist, propelled by a ramlike arm, was driven into his chest. Blood erupting from his nose and mouth, Jaime Alvarez fell to the sawdust when Gary let him go.

The other men stopped their game and stared in disbelief at the body.

Gary drove their heads together, shattering them like overripe watermelons, grinding the flesh and hair and bone and blood into a pulp even as the reflexively jerking bodies were lowered to the floor.

He shouldn't have killed the one called Jorge, he thought afterward, when the rage had passed. Now, who would take him to the woman?

Tracy.

He had to have her, *had to . . .*

Take one of the monster-things himself, Bruno thought.

No, the other could not make it go, he quickly learned.

Without glancing back at the three bodies, he walked to the door. The wind whistled shrilly around the building, through its loft. He reached into his pocket and withdrew a handkerchief, folding it in a triangle and knotting it in back of his head so the widest portion covered his mouth. Among other tools and things hanging on a pegboard near the door were a few pairs of goggles, something unfamiliar to Bruno.

Seconds later he understood what they were for and removed a pair.

The woman . . .

Tracy.

He went outside, into the searing wind.

3

It was a good day to be inside, Carl Singer thought.

He and Joey had run the Scrabble, Jr. set into the ground, and afterward the boy had whipped him soundly at gin rummy, a game Carl had taught him only last week. Now, they were going to make an indecent amount of Orville Doofendurfer popcorn and catch a ball game on ESPN. If the boy was disappointed about his mother's phone call a while ago, he was handling it well.

Tracy. He wished his daughter wasn't out in this miserable weather. What was so important to make her go? What was so important that she had to let Joey down, after promising him . . . ? And was he wrong, or had she been acting . . . weird? Where had she gone last night? Surely it had to do with Mark Bradley; but he was working at the club right now, wasn't he? After all, he had called Tracy before.

Carl had never tried to meddle in his daughter's life, but this wasn't like her. He was more concerned than curious. Suddenly, he wished she were home, so he'd know she was safe.

"Grandpa, I'm gonna start melting the butter now," Joey called from the kitchen.

"OK, pal. Do it on a real low flame."

There was a loud knock on the front door. Carl jumped to his feet, startled. Tracy, he hoped. No, she wouldn't knock. Even if she didn't have her key, the door was unlocked.

The knocking persisted as he went to the door. "All right, all right," he muttered.

He pulled it open. A towering figure stood before the gusting sheets of sand.

"Gary? What the devil are you doing out in weather like this?" Carl asked.

CHAPTER NINETEEN

Wall Of Sand

1

At 2:45, with the magnitude of her task becoming more evident, Tracy had gone across the street to a phone outside Village Liquor and called her son. Tomorrow, she told Joey, she was all his, morning till night, no ifs, ands or buts. She prayed she would be able to keep her promise.

Twenty minutes later she had found the box.

It was in the stack against the wall, of course, and on the bottom, of course; but it could have been one of many others still left in other corners of the library's back room, which meant it could have been worse. Unlike the other boxes, this one had no designation either on top or on the side facing her. She had to extract the dusty carton, which had once held cans of Carnation evaporated milk, from between others and turn it around before she could read what had been written in blue ink, quite small, in the middle: *P. Lantz.*

Not thousands of pages, as Edna Markey had guessed, but without a doubt, hundreds. Unlined paper, mostly, the kind often used for stationery, with a high rag content. The oldest ones had yellowed a bit, and some edges had frayed, but for the most part the unbound sheaves were in good shape.

Phillip Lantz's lifelong hobby: a history of the sprawling but lightly populated Borrego Valley, his home for three-quarters of a century, surely with countless personal anecdotes. Hundreds of thousands of words, scrawled first in fountain pen, later in ball point or felt tip, on pages that were sometimes numbered; small and wavy script, legible, but with effort. Some day it would be a patient research historian's dream. But Tracy had no patience, no time ...

Was *this* what she had spent all these hours looking for?

Bruno free.

Somehow, she sensed time was running out more quickly than she'd first thought.

Under the sheaves was another layer, this of tan, nine-by-twelve clasp envelopes. The one on top, thick, was marked *Borrego Springs I*. Next, logically, was No. II, thinner. Another said *Pegleg Smith*, which Tracy remembered as the name of a monument east of town. The next few, all skinny, said *State Park, Early Ranchers, Earthquake & Weather*, and *Wildflowers*.

The next one was marked in red pen: *Concordia Sanitarium*.

Tracy's hands shook as she undid the clasps. There was an old table in the back room, and three chairs, all in lousy condition. She chose one that wobbled precariously but held her, and spread the contents of the envelope out.

They were articles from old newspapers, either copied on the shiny paper of copiers from decades past, or actual yellowed clippings, mounted between plastic inserts. Enough of the pages had been cut out to include the names of the periodicals, as well as the dates, most of which were from the 1870s. *The Los Angeles Star, Santa Monica Outlook, San Diego Union, Visalia Weekly Delta, Sacramento Bee* were all represented, as well as a number from San Francisco, including the *Chronicle, Call*, and *Examiner*. Tracy selected one at random and began reading.

At first the articles seemed little more than indirectly related to the sanitarium. But after a half-dozen or so, a pattern began to emerge. They were about the social elite of their time: the matriarch of a well-to-do family, the young heiress (Tracy noticed her name: Sarah Pruett) to a banking fortune, the founder of a steamship line, and so on. All similar in that respect, and in that, one way or another, they had become either a burden or an embarrassment to their families, the articles reporting unseemly behavior in public and the like. And while the families had struggled to keep it a secret, journalists had learned that these poor souls were being sent to a new asylum, somewhere remote; in the desert, they heard.

Concordia Sanitarium, founded by Dr. Everett Cooke, had been a nineteenth-century haunt of the very rich.

Dr. Cooke. An article in the *San Francisco Chronicle*, at the time he left Livermore Sanitarium to take up the directorship of his own facility, could not have lauded his capabilities in any more reverent terms.

Dr. Everett Cooke, the tortured soul from the dungeon of sand and charred wood, for whom Dexter Jones had sacrificed his life to pass along a message, the brief, urgent, *damned message.*

Bruno free.

A headline in the *Examiner* caught Tracy's attention:

CONVICTED MURDERER WILL NOT BE HUNG NEXT THURSDAY.

Bruno Josef Leopold, eighteen, who had been sentenced to death last month for the brutal slayings of four family members, and another child, at a Geary St. boardinghouse, has been temporarily spared the hangman's noose, according to police officials. A new date of execution was mentioned as being "Later this year, around May or June," although as yet this has not been confirmed.

While no explanation for this unprecedented action has been given, it is believed that Leopold, a dullard of immense strength who murdered his victims with his bare hands, has been sent to an insane asylum for the purpose of becoming a subject of some research into his aberration. Officials from Livermore Sanitarium, it has since been learned, had been petitioning for this action, and it is safe to assume that this is where he has been taken, although the proximity of this institution might cause problems with the people of San Francisco, already angered by the brutality of Leopold's misdeeds. Lynch mob talk had begun, but was silenced upon discovering that Leopold had already been removed from his cell in the night.

The article went on to include quotes from irate citizens, but Tracy had seen enough. Struggling to control herself, she pushed the plastic-sheathed clipping away.

Bruno Josef Leopold.
Convicted murderer . . .
. . . brutal slayings . . .
Bruno Josef Leopold.
Bruno free.

"Oh my God," she said, the words no louder than a soft breath.

Whoever had written the story guessed correctly: Bruno Leopold had not been taken to Livermore Sanitarium, where a threat of mob violence would have existed. The officials there would have helped Dr. Everett Cooke . . .

Dedicated Dr. Cooke.

. . . spirit the murderer away, far away from the Bay Area.

All the way to the southern desert, to Concordia Sanitarium.

Bruno free.

If any doubt remained, another article from the *San Francisco Call* dispelled it. Dated a few months later, it reported the tragic fire in the asylum, listing names of the dead from the Bay Area. But much of the article was about Bruno Leopold, whose incarceration there had first been confirmed by the *Call*. Since no one within the walls had survived the blaze, and since the terrible desert surrounded the asylum, it was a certainty—the story said—that the "Monster of Geary Street" had met his deserved end.

Someone like that would have been confined in the dungeon for sure.

The third body under the sand . . .

Bruno free.

Confused, scared, Tracy flipped hastily through the remaining articles. They were mostly obituaries from the hometown papers of the elite who died at Concordia. She'd already found what she came for. Sliding them into the envelope, she returned them to the carton, along with all the rest of Phillip Lantz's work. She left the back room of the library in disarray; if Edna Markey swore at her somewhere down the road after discovering the offense, then so be it. There was no time now.

Suddenly, she had to be back in Smoke Tree.

The old man had gone, leaving Edna as the only one in the main room. Still, she spoke in hushed tones.

"Did you find what you were after?" she asked.

"Yes, I think so." Tracy tried to be calm as she handed Edna the key.

"You be careful out there, miss. It's blowing harder than before."

Her concern seemed genuine. Even more, Tracy regretted leaving the back room as she had.

"I will. Thank you, and thanks for your help."

The wind tried to hold her back as she struggled to reach the telephone across the street. She could see parked cars—her own included—swaying slightly.

Tracy first dialed her father's number; the line was busy. She tried the club; seven rings, before Jerry Zirpolo answered.

"I sent Mark home a while ago," he told her. "He caught a ride with one of our suppliers' trucks. No one's coming out in this crap. I'm just holding down the fort."

"Can you give me his landlady's number?"

"Yeah, sure."

Tracy dialed, let the phone ring eight, ten, twelve times. No answer.

"Damn!" she exclaimed, disconnecting the line.

She called her father's number again; still busy. Odd. Carl Singer almost never spent any time on the phone.

As soon as she pulled out on Palm Canyon Drive, Tracy knew how difficult and dangerous the return trip was going to be. Almost immediately a strong gust pushed her across the median with no more effort than it would take a child to divert the course of a Tonka toy.

Squeezing her hands white as she gripped the wheel, she managed to keep the Cressida on the right side of the road, most of which was obliterated by drifts of sand. Even driving snail-like she missed a turn at the Christmas Circle and lost a few minutes in backtracking.

Sand, even when carried by gusts, was heavy, and usually swirled no more than a couple of feet off the ground. But the relentless wind had lifted it more, and had thrown the lighter, choking dust so high that visibility in the gray murk was all but non-existent. Along the snaking Montezuma grade, large stones and even small boulders had been blown onto S22. Valley residents knew to stay off the roads during times like this.

Past the Pegleg Smith monument at the outskirts of town, Tracy swore the assault was easing. Her thoughts returned to the back room of the library. She tried to assimilate more of what she'd read, make sense of it, relate it to everything that had happened since the night she and Mark had found Dexter Jones in the ruins of Concordia Sanitarium.

The third body below was almost certainly that of Bruno Leopold. He had been chained there . . .

Dr. Everett Cooke and the man called Jacob had come down to free him, probably because of the fire raging above. But the murderer had turned on them, killing Jacob, putting the doctor in the chains that had held him . . .

Pulling out his tongue.

After that, Bruno had hurried to the steps to try and get away. But the fire consumed the dungeon, and all within.

Jacob's spirit had arisen first . . . about a year ago, Old Dex had said. Later on, the prospector had become aware of another entity below the ruins. Always a strong emanation, but nothing like it had been . . .

. . . just recently, since two weeks ago, perhaps less.

Cooke's spirit had awakened but remained trapped by the presence of chains. Most of the time, it had been crying out for its own salvation.

Then, it had seen something, or sensed it . . .

Bruno Leopold's malevolent essence had awakened, and was

moving away.

Bruno free.

Surely not above, not with the others, for Dexter Jones would have known, or Jacob.

Then . . .

Where?

A brutal mass murderer's spirit, *free.*

There had been two violent deaths in Smoke Tree last weekend. A coyote did it, they said.

No, not a coyote. They are wrong, Gary Masten had insisted, *I know they are wrong.*

And maybe Tracy didn't know her desert animals that well, but she too felt . . .

Gary Masten.

A dullard of immense strength . . .

Gary Masten.

His eyes . . . his hands on her . . .

Gary Masten.

He's kinda different today.

"No oh no . . . *oh dear God no!*" Tracy pulled off onto the shoulder, for the moment too shaken to drive. What she'd just thought was crazy, right? But all of this had been crazy since that first day, nearly two weeks ago, when her mother had spoken to her in someone else's voice.

. . . kinda different . . .

Sweet, gentle Gary Masten.

. . . immense strength . . .

She began driving again, barely looking to see if any other vehicles were coming, challenging the desert's wind-whipped fury in her puny vehicle. Too fast, as she learned when a hard gust nearly spun the Cressida. Then slower, wrestling with the steering wheel, swerving, stalling once, cursing the slow pace, not even thinking about her windows opaquing, or the exterior finish of her car being marred by the abrasive zephyr.

He's kinda different today.

Thirty-seven minutes to drive the short distance to Smoke

Tree's town limits . . . the longest thirty-seven minutes of Tracy Russell's life.

The downtown streets were as deserted as Borrego Springs. Tracy pulled into Ironwood Terrace, staggered up the stairs and hammered on the door. Mark opened it almost immediately.

"Thank God!" she exclaimed, throwing her arms around him.

Mark smiled. "Hey, I'm glad to see you too. What's—"

"Just come on! I'll tell you everything on the way."

"Where are we going?"

"Dad's house, first." She handed him the keys. "You drive, please. I-I can't anymore."

They hurried down to the car. "You found what we were looking for?"

She nodded. "Yes."

Sirens rose above the howling winds as they turned onto the Seaway. Tracy tensed, her hands clutching the dashboard.

"Oh please, no," she muttered.

Mark had stopped the car. Ahead, they could barely discern two sets of flashing lights as the Smoke Tree police force turned south on Las Palmas Road, the opposite direction from the Estates. Tracy sighed deeply, sat back.

"Start talking," Mark said, driving off.

It was hard to listen when battling the elements. Tracy's voice straddled the tightrope of rationality as she related what she'd found in the back room of the library, and what she'd concluded afterward. Mark did not interrupt once.

By the time they turned onto Oasis Drive from the security kiosk, she had told him everything.

From the street they saw that the front door of Carl Singer's house was open. Mark pulled into the driveway. Tracy jumped out before he turned off the engine. He hurried after her. They stepped over a mound of sand that had blown into the living room.

Carl lay face down on the carpet, across the room. He'd been reaching for the telephone on a small desk, but had only managed to pull the receiver off.

Tracy held back a scream and they ran to her father, turning him over gently. He uttered a soft moan; his eyelids moved.

"He's alive," Mark said.

"Joey! Where's Joey?" Tracy cried.

Hurrying from room to room, then out to the garage, she called his name. When she returned to the living room, terrified and helpless, her father's eyes were open. He raised a feeble hand.

"Gary," he said weakly. "Gary took . . . the boy. Left message. Must tell . . ."

"Dad!"

Carl Singer's eyes rolled back in his head.

2

They had loaded the five bodies from the slaughter at Rainbow Tree Farm into one ambulance for the ride to the morgue, in back of the Valley Clinic, where autopsies would be performed some time during the next twenty-four hours.

Chief Donald Upton, looking twenty years older, had accompanied the death wagon and was on his way out of the hospital. Tracy and Mark, who had been sitting in the hall by the emergency room door for what seemed forever, saw the lawman and waved him down.

"Folks, I'm not having what you'd call a good day," he said impatiently. "What is it you want?"

They'd heard about the murders from the hospital staff. "We know about your day, Chief," Mark said. "We also know . . . who killed those people."

"I think we got that under control too, son. There's an APB out right now for Gary Masten."

Tracy glanced at Mark, then turned again to the cop. "You're right . . . I guess. He hurt my father—that's what we're doing here—and he's taken my son."

Upton's face softened. "Christ, I'm sorry, miss. Do you have any idea where they might have gone?"

Mark shook his head. "We believe he told Mr. Singer, which is why he's still alive. As soon as Dr. Hoberg brings him around, we'll find out."

"Chief, there's something else you ought to know about this," Tracy said.

"Yeah?"

She looked at Mark again before saying, "You're going to think this is crazy, that we're distraught or something, but Gary . . ." She hesitated.

"Tell him," Mark urged.

"Gary Masten isn't responsible for any of this. Someone or something inside him forced him to kill all those people."

"Oh Christ, *not again*," Upton muttered.

"What did you say?" Tracy asked.

The cop shrugged. "Nothing . . ."

"You know about this, don't you?" Mark snapped. "If you do, now is not the time to deny it!"

"I think maybe we got some talking to do—" Upton began, when the walkie-talkie on his belt crackled. He excused himself and walked a few yards down the hall, spoke into it briefly, then listened. When he returned, they noticed his face was drained of color.

"What is it?" Tracy said.

"I sent some men to Harry Keller's house, told them to wait for me before going in. But the county boys got there first and took care of that."

"Was Gary there?" Mark asked.

"No, but they found Harry . . ." He bit his lip, hesitated.

"Please, tell us!" Tracy exclaimed.

"They found him in *pieces*, all over the kitchen."

Tracy raised a hand to her mouth as she stared, wide-eyed, at Upton. The long and terrible day overwhelmed her. She shook uncontrollably; her legs were like rubber. Mark and the lawman helped her to the couch.

"We have to find out where . . . Gary went with your son," Upton said. "I'll let Doc Hoberg know how urgent it is that we talk to your father." He patted her arm. "You pull yourself together, miss. I don't think he's hurt the boy, truly I don't."

His smile, though strained, had a calming effect on Tracy.

When he returned a few minutes later, she was standing at the emergency room door. Dr. Wayne Hoberg followed the lawman out.

"Your father will be all right," he told Tracy. "He has a bad concussion, some internal injuries. There'll be discomfort, but we'll minimize that. He's sedated now; shouldn't really talk, but the chief was insistent. OK, you have one minute."

They followed him through the door and down a short hallway to the last room of the small unit, where Hoberg had tended to Carl Singer. His head bandaged, tubes running from his veins to IV bottles, Tracy's father—the man of the bone-crushing embraces—looked old, helpless. It broke her heart to see him that way.

While the others waited by the door, Tracy went to his bedside and took his hand. His eyes had been closed, but fluttered open when she called to him.

"That you, prin . . . cess?" he asked weakly.

"Yes, Dad, I'm here, and you're going to be all right."

A grimace was either from the pain or his recent memories. "Gary . . . he . . . hurt me . . . don't understand . . ." His eyes opened wider. *The boy . . . what about . . . Joey . . ."*

"Dad, we need to know where Gary and Joey went," she told him. "You said he left a message. Please, try to remember what it was."

"Come alone . . ."

"What?"

"He said you were . . . to come alone . . ." Carl shut his eyes as he wrestled with drug-clouded thoughts. "Come alone to the . . . Bad-Tasting Water place. Anyone else follows, he'll hurt the boy. Just you . . . alone . . ."

"Dad, *where*? I don't understand!"

"Bad-Tasting Water . . ."

She glanced at the others; they shook their heads. "Dad, *please!*"

Carl was agitated now. "Come alone . . . Bad-Tasting . . . he'll hurt . . . *oh God he'll hurt my . . . !*"

"Dad!"

Hoberg came forward. "All right, that's enough. Chief, I want everyone out of here, now!"

Upton, with Mark's help, led the struggling Tracy out of the emergency room, down the hall and around to an adjoining wing, where there was a small cafeteria. Only the presence of some staff made Tracy relent. While Mark sat her down at an isolated table, Upton brought them strong coffee.

"What was he talking about?" Tracy exclaimed, ignoring the drink. "My dad . . . what was he saying?"

Upton shook his head. "Nothing that made sense. He must've been delirious."

"I'm not sure about that," Mark said. "I think Mr. Singer was repeating exactly what he was told."

"The Bad-Tasting Water place." Upton shrugged. "There's nothing I know of around here with a name like that."

"Me neither," Mark said. "But I doubt if it's a place name. Probably it's how Bruno perceives something. Remember, he's in the wrong century."

Upton scowled. "Bruno . . . OK, you going to start explaining this to me?"

Tracy slammed a fist on the table, startling the two. "Why are you sitting here and talking?" She glared at Upton. "You should be out looking for this madman, for . . . *my son!*"

Upton faced her sternly. "You listen to me, miss . . . Tracy, right? I've got six bodies on my hands, some good friends among them. If you don't think I want to catch this sonofabitch . . . And there's something real different about this case, so I've got to find out everything you know in order to understand what in hell we're dealing with. It might be the difference that saves your son."

Tracy sat back in her chair, subdued. "I'm sorry."

"Another thing," Upton went on, his tone less harsh. "In case you haven't noticed, it's hell out there. Old-timers I talked to today, folks who've lived in the desert a lot longer than me, say this is the worst they can remember. Portions of the interstates are shut down. Earlier, they had a chain-reaction accident on I-10, north of Palm Springs. Over two dozen vehicles involved; couple of folks killed, lots injured, cars flipped over."

"Jesus," Mark muttered.

"OK," Upton said, "so who or what the hell is Bruno?"

While Tracy sipped the bitter, bracing coffee, Mark told Chief Donald Upton everything about the tormented spirits of Concordia Sanitarium, about the work of Dexter Jones—and about the malevolent thing called Bruno Leopold. Tracy filled in details regarding the latter. Upton listened, barely raising an eyebrow.

When they were done, Upton revealed what had happened during Scott Millard's imprisonment. And if what Tracy and Mark had just told him was anything close to the truth—his expression still said otherwise—then the deaths of his deputy and the drifter had not been the result of random attacks by an animal.

"You were able to keep Bruno out," Mark said, after Upton was done. "That's what happened, Chief. But how?"

"I think I know," Tracy said. "Old Dex said something about them only being able to stay inside someone if they were allowed, or if the mind was too weak to keep it out. They didn't have a name for it a century ago, but from the descriptions I read of Bruno Leopold, I'm sure what he had was Down's syndrome, same as Gary Masten, or some other form of retardation. He isn't strong enough mentally to take over a normal mind, but that wouldn't be a problem with poor Gary."

Mark shrugged. "I remember what Dex said, but I don't know. What about this . . . Scott? He wasn't retarded, was he?"

"Scott Millard was an exhausted, half-starved boy," Upton said, "and despite what he told me, I'm sure he did his share of drugs in the recent past. I think someone like that would be just as . . . susceptible. Jesus, listen to what I'm saying!"

Tracy downed the last of her coffee and ignored his disbelief. "I agree. But do you realize what *we're* saying? The only way of putting an end to the spirit of Bruno Leopold is by destroying its host, and that means . . ."

Mark finished it for her. "Killing Gary Masten. Shit!"

Upton looked at them helplessly. "This Bruno, or Gary, or whoever, won't go down easy, so blowing him away is almost a given."

"But even if you order your men to try and take him alive," Mark said, and they shoot out Gary's kneecaps or something, Bruno's spirit still gets away. Poor Gary burns for something he doesn't even understand, the murderer is free, and *no one* will believe anything we try to tell them!"

Tracy sighed. "Right now all I care about is the safety of my son."

The lawman stood and tried to shake off his jumble of thoughts. "I'd better get out and see what's going on. Will you be here at the hospital?"

"Either here or the Singer house," Mark said.

"I'll be in touch." He put a hand on Tracy's arm. "Getting back your boy is our top priority, please believe that."

She nodded. "Thank you, Chief."

Upton started to leave. Halfway across the cafeteria he stopped, and for a few moments appeared to ponder something. Finally, he rejoined them.

"What is it?" Mark asked.

"Maybe nothing, but . . . Let's say I buy some of this—which I ain't saying I do yet."

"Yeah?"

"When . . . Bruno was pounding at my head, and I was resisting him, it felt like . . . his big hurry was not as much getting inside as it was getting away from being *outside*. Hell, I don't know if that makes any damn sense. But I'm sure of it, because I remember him screaming—or something—when he left the jail, and it sort of went on and on, like . . . he was scared."

Mark nodded thoughtfully. "Then leaving Gary might not be so easy for him, no matter what's happening. It could help."

This time, Upton left. Tracy and Mark followed shortly after. The ER nurse said that Carl Singer had been moved to the second floor. They went upstairs, found him sleeping comfortably, although his face wore a troubled expression. Dr. Hoberg's prognosis for Carl's recovery was a good one.

Nighttime soon came, but the transition was barely noticeable in the gloom of the blowing dust. Upton stopped by once, when the remains of Harry Keller had been brought to the morgue. So far, they'd found nothing. At the moment they were conducting a house-to-house search. No way did they get out of Smoke Tree, not in this storm, he said; this goddamn storm . . .

At 8:45 a fatigued Tracy was nodding on a chair beside her father's bed. She had agreed—reluctantly—to let Mark take her home at nine, not sooner, as he'd asked.

Mark was outside, pacing the length of the hallway, which he had done many times in the past hour. Something, some inexplicable thought lay so teasingly close, but not close enough, just beyond the grasp of memory. It was driving him crazy. Then . . .

Tracy sat up when he pushed the door open and hurried in. "What is it?" she asked.

"I know where the Bad-Tasting Water place is," he replied.

Bad-Tasting Water

1

Joey Russell was not as scared as he had been a few hours earlier. His greatest fear had been for his grandfather. When he'd first seen him lying there . . . But when he realized it was important for Grandpa to live so he could deliver Gary's message, he didn't worry as much, except about Mom and what she would think when she came home.

Gary . . . It hadn't taken him long to figure out this wasn't Gary Masten, his friend. Because Gary wouldn't hurt Grandpa, and Gary wouldn't take him away like this; no way.

He's kinda different today. Yeah, really.

Joey was blessed in a number of ways, first with the intelligence and common sense both inherited and absorbed from spending the majority of his young life in and around his mother, next with the rich, unfettered imagination of a nine-year-old. Although he might not have been able to explain it, he'd had no trouble reaching his conclusion about Gary, something grown-ups would not have done as quickly, if at all.

But there had been no chance to find out who this guy was. He'd been told to pack food and water then was taken outside, into the awful blowing sand and dust, and up the street, the wind nearly sweeping him away, until *Gary* had taken him around the wrist, often too tightly. Out of the Estates, along the creek, *Gary* sometimes carrying him against the worst gusts. To the mouth of Madhouse Canyon.

The canyon's walls had offered shelter from much of the dust and sand, making the rugged climb less difficult than passage through the wind. Responding to Gary's insistent grunts, Joey had kept up with the big man, slipping only once and skinning an elbow. Then, in the grotto past the waterfall, Gary had sent the boy scurrying up the rock wall first, following close behind.

Bruno stared at the boy across the hot spring. Joey stared back at him. Since coming there they had eaten fried chicken and candy bars, but they had said nothing.

Joey glanced up at the sheer walls of the depression, then faced Bruno again. "How come we came here?" he asked.

"Had to," was the sullen answer. "Waiting for somebody."

"Who are you?"

Bruno had not expected the question. He cocked his head. "You know. I'm Gary; can't you see?"

"You may be inside Gary, but you're not him; you're not my friend. Who are you?"

He knows. How could he know? He's just a child; a little boy. But a smart child, not a child like he had been, not a . . .

Dullard.

Idjit.

Half-wit.

Idjit idjit idjit.

Why couldn't he have been a child like this? Why couldn't he have been smart, always known what to say?

He clenched and unclenched his . . .

Hands.

"What's your name?" The boy was persistent.

"Bru-Bruno," was the subdued answer. The hands dropped to

his sides.

"Bruno," Joey repeated. "You said we were waiting for somebody. Who?"

"Just . . . somebody."

"It's my mom, right? You want to see my mom. Hey, you'd better not hurt her!"

Too smart. "Won't hurt her. Now you shuddup."

"Did you suck out Gary's brain or something? Or is he still in there?"

His hands clenched again. *Too smart too smart.* "Gary's still here."

"Can I talk to him?"

. . . hear you Joey I hear you but so far away so far Joey . . .

Can't let him say no more . . . too smart . . .

He thrust an index finger at the boy. "You don't say nothing. Any more talk, I put you in there."

Bruno lowered his finger toward the hot spring. Joey leaned back against the wall, silent. A few minutes passed. Joey began to squirm, finally stood. Bruno stiffened.

"I hafta pee, OK?" the boy said sourly, unzipping his fly.

The big man eased. Joey finished his business on the rock wall and sat down again. Gary/Bruno lay on his side, his head on the only backpack they had brought, his ample bulk more than filling the narrow defile. The spent body then conceded to the events of the long day; the eyes fluttered closed, and seconds later he was breathing loudly.

Joey glanced quickly around the depression, even though he already knew there was only one way out. He could climb over Gary, maybe get past before he was awake enough to grab him. But he would chase Joey, probably catch him before he got down to the waterfall, and then . . . Could he knock him out when he was sleeping, maybe? Always worked in the movies. Yeah, get real; this wasn't the movies. Even if he could lift something big enough to do the trick . . . but there wasn't anything that big or heavy around here, except maybe in the backpack, which he couldn't get to anyway.

Joey was scared again; scared for himself, first. He wanted his mom, his grandfather, Mark, wanted so much for them to come get him.

But he was also scared for them, scared that if they came, this crazy *man* inside Gary Masten would hurt them. He would hurt them real bad.

Fatigue and despair took Joey into slumber.

2

"You're not going out there! Are you nuts?"

Tracy had left a backpack and other things in the living room of her father's house, near the front door, and was filling a canteen in the kitchen. She had changed into the same clothes she'd worn on their first hike to Madhouse Canyon.

"I can't stand around here and do nothing."

She screwed the top of the canteen back on and went into the living room. Mark was at her heels.

"Did you forget the drive back from the hospital?" he said. "All that time to go a mile; and we were *inside* something!"

"Mark, I—!"

A loud knock on the door startled them. Mark opened it. Chief Donald Upton and five pounds of sand blew in before he could get it closed.

"Damn!" the cop exclaimed, brushing himself off. "That's about the worst . . ." He saw the equipment. "What's this?"

"She wants to go out," Mark said.

Upton shook his head, sending more sand to the floor from the brim of his hat. "Miss, if there was any way humanly possible, I'd be out there with you right now, and I sure as hell know Mark would. I was about to say, this is the worst it's been all day, if that's possible. Spoke to the weather people in San Diego a while ago and they confirmed that the wind's hit a peak; should probably start blowing itself out during the night. We'll be OK by dawn. And believe me, we got plenty of people ready to go into the canyon."

"No!" Tracy cried. "No one else. You heard what my father said!"

Mark held her gently. "He knows that; he only meant for backup. Right?"

"Yeah. And in the meantime, if you want to be of any help tomorrow, you'd better get some rest. We're going to keep searching the town, just in case . . ."

"They're at the hot spring," Tracy insisted. "I know it."

Upton nodded. "OK. Now, you do like I said." He started for the door. "I'll be back before sunrise."

"You come when the storm stops!" Tracy exclaimed. "Please?"

"Yeah, sure."

"Even if it's a couple of hours from now?"

A couple of hours. Midnight, one a.m. Upton glanced at Mark; both knew what it was like trying to boulder-hop a rugged canyon in the dark. But go and explain it to this exhausted, distraught woman. Besides, it would be many hours before the wind subsided, so he was safe.

"I promise," he told her.

Upton sidled out into the wind-blown fury. Tracy stood at the window for a while, finally sat down. Mark held her, but they were mostly silent. Occasionally she would go to the window again.

An hour passed; the storm, truly at its height, continued to lash the house. Mark had left Tracy, who sat cross-legged in front of the sofa, to go down the hall and use the bathroom. Tracy had pulled off her hiking shoes, dropping them on the floor.

When Mark returned, the shoes—and Tracy—were gone.

"Damn!"

He ran outside, concern momentarily dulling his caution. Sand lashed his body, dust got into his mouth and nostrils. He blew it out, then knotted a handkerchief in back of his head.

Tracy had not taken the Cressida out of the garage. More than likely she would follow the creek. Turning his shoulder against the storm, Mark started up Oasis Drive.

Less than a minute later, he found her.

On her knees, head down, shaking, sobbing; overwhelmed by fear, frustration, rage, and the storm itself. Far past her own limits, and the limits of most, but still trying. Mark took her hand, asked her to stand, but her legs would not obey. So he lifted her up in his arms, difficult in the swirling sand, and she did not protest, instead burying her head against his chest. Staggering, he went down the slight grade of Mortero Hill to the Singer house, gratefully slamming the door behind them. He put her on the couch, brushed away most of the sand, got a wet cloth and blotted up the rest. Tracy opened her eyes for a moment before she was finally taken by sleep, anguish etched on her face, a face that had aged in the past twelve hours.

Some time later—as predicted—the tempest began to blow itself out. By 3:30 a.m. road crews began converging upon the worst hit portions of the interstates, county and state highways, and other desert arteries. Still, it would require most of the day to make them drivable.

Mark had fallen asleep sitting on the floor, his head on the sofa alongside Tracy's. He awakened briefly after four, acknowledging the fact that, in her hard sleep, Tracy had not even shifted her position.

When he next opened his eyes, at 5:05, he was immediately aware of the stillness engulfing the house. He stared up at the ceiling for a few moments, not yet wanting to confirm what he already sensed.

Again, Tracy was gone.

3

Chief Upton had come alone in response to Mark's call. He would have been there anyway in the next half-hour, he'd said. He wanted to get this business done as quickly as possible. Hell, by dawn lawmen from all over would be showing up to assist in the hunt for the killer and the boy he'd kidnapped. Bloodsucking reporters from every newspaper, television and radio station in the southern half of the state—and elsewhere—would try to get there with mini-cams and microphones, because by now word of the six brutal murders in a quiet desert community had leaked out, and *that* of course was *big* news. Only the terrible road conditions might quell the onslaught.

Mark was silent, grimly determined, as Upton's Blazer jounced wildly along the sand-strewn jeep trail between Dexter Jones's place and the old ruins. It was commendable that the cop could even stay on the path. The pre-dawn light was a hazy slate-gray from the dust that, despite the storm's abatement, had not yet settled.

This time, Mark had not gone after Tracy. She'd gotten sleep, and enough of a head start, and the storm was over. He would probably not find her along the way. No sense stumbling after her by himself, ill-equipped for what he would have to face in Madhouse Canyon—both along the way and above the grotto. So he had been waiting—impatiently—for Upton outside the Singer home.

Waiting for the police to pick me up, he had thought. *Have I forgotten what I am . . . or does it really matter anymore?*

The ruins of Concordia Sanitarium brooded in the dawn haze. Here, the monster had been reborn. Mark wondered what Tracy's thoughts had been when—perhaps minutes earlier—she'd passed the place.

Ordinarily, Upton would have been able to maneuver his 4x4 at least part of the way into the canyon. But sand had piled high at the mouth. He stopped and radioed his men for the first time, letting them know where he was, telling them to wait for him there.

Upton gave Mark one of the two canteens he'd brought. In addition to his service revolver he'd added a weapon from his personal collection, an imposing .457 Magnum, but he offered neither to Mark. They started into the canyon, the waffle prints of Tracy's hiking boots evident in the sand.

All along, Mark had been concerned over Upton's ability to climb the steep, boulder-strewn canyon. Middle-aged, a bit overweight, his leisure activities—Mark guessed—would have been things less strenuous. But he maintained Mark's fast, sometimes breakneck pace with surprising agility and never complained.

An hour after entering Madhouse Canyon they had negotiated a considerable distance. Still, they caught no glimpse of Tracy. Moonlight Falls was not far ahead. But for the last fifteen minutes Upton had been laboring. He'd fallen once, had an ankle shredded by catclaws. Now, he lagged behind nearly ten yards when Mark thought to turn. He hurried to the red-faced lawman.

Upton had dropped to one knee. "You . . . go ahead. I won't be any damn good for a while."

"I'm . . . not armed."

Upton pulled the service revolver and leveled it at Mark. "My deputy had a thing up his ass about you, son. Was he right?"

"Yeah, he was," Mark said.

He nodded, twirled the gun and gripped it by the barrel as he handed it to Mark. "You be careful. I'll get there when I can."

4

Moonlight Falls seemed to be running sluggishly.

Probably choked with sand somewhere. Sand, miserable sand. Heat and wind and dryness and scrub and cactus.

And sand.

God, she hated the desert.

Tracy had deceived Mark by slipping out of the house while he still slept, and she was not proud of herself, but she had to come here alone . . .

Come alone to the Bad-Tasting Water place . . .

. . . because that was what he said, w*hat the monster wanted,* and he would kill Joey if she brought others. Still, she wished Mark was with her, because she was so alone, and she needed him . . . *oh God she needed him.* If—when—this ended, and they were together again, all of them together, she would never . . .

But this, first. She had come here, to the grotto, hardly remembering a detail of the rugged journey; along the creek, past the ruins, through the canyon with its steep walls and catclaws and boulders. Water, surely she had sipped some water on the way.

Now, she splashed her face from the cascading flow, noticing no grittiness. Perhaps that had been her imagination, a trick of the dim light.

She looked up. Somewhere above, *he* was there, at the hot spring, the Bad-Tasting Water place; Bruno, or Gary, or both, or neither. What did it matter? Because Joey, *her* Joey, was there too.

Leaving her canteen and backpack, she started up the steep rock wall. The climb had not seemed nearly so hard when she'd made it with Mark. Niches were few, and widely spaced; a growing numbness in his fingers did not make feeling for them easier. But she ground her teeth against the effort, and eventually pulled herself atop the narrow ledge. Though this close now, she was unable to move for a minute.

They were waiting for her on the other side of the hot spring.

Sitting a yard apart, facing the defile. Joey saw her first, wanted to stand, glanced to the side and thought better of it.

The cold, probing eyes of the other found her, explored her body, penetrated her flesh. After a moment she averted her own eyes, looked at Joey.

"Did he hurt you, champ?" she asked.

"Uh-uh. What about Grandpa? Is he . . . ?"

"Grandpa's OK; he'll be fine." She looked at Bruno again, scowled. "All right, I'm here, and I came alone, like you said. First, you let my boy go, then tell me what you want."

She had come the woman had come Tracy had come. He had wanted her to come, wanted it so bad, but had feared it as much, or more, feared what he would do or say—feared what he would be unable to do or say—when he saw her. Just like he had been so afraid of the woman in San Francisco.

Just like he had been so afraid of doing the *Thing*, even though he had heard others talking about it, and even though he   had seen . . .

He stood, towering above the hot spring, hands clenching . . .

"Well, what do you want?" Tracy asked again, taking a step toward him.

Not smart; idjits can't think quick.

"You be quiet," he scowled, waving a thick finger, "or—"

Joey jumped up. "Hey, you said you wouldn't hurt my mom! That's what you said!"

"Joey, no!" Tracy exclaimed.

Won't hurt Tracy won't hurt her only want to touch her only want to do the Thing *like she did with the man . . .*

(oh mark oh mark)

. . . here at the Bad-Tasting Water place . . .

Confusion and rage became interchangeable on the moon-face

as he glanced from the woman to the child. Ham-sized fists smacked against his sides.

"No-oo don't hurt my boy!" Tracy suddenly screamed, running at him, aiming a blow with her foot at his genitals. He twisted, absorbing the brunt with a meaty thigh, then knocked her down with the back of his hand, nearly into the hot spring.

"Gary, he's hurting my mom!" Joey cried. "You gotta make him stop! Please, Gary—!"

Hurting her he's hurting Joey's mom but I can't stop him Joey I can't . . .

Bruno reached a hand to his head; a shadow of uncertainty fell across his face.

"Gary, you gotta listen, you gotta—!"

The other hand grabbed the boy by the throat, lifted him like a blade of grass. Cupping her hands, Tracy scooped up water from the spring and threw it in his face. It stung his eyes, and he dropped Joey as he wiped them. Gasping, Joey tried to scramble away but was taken again, this time by his left arm, which was nearly torn off.

"Mom!"

That wavering a moment ago, Tracy thought. "Gary! Gary Masten!" she cried. "Can you see what he's doing to your friend Joey? Can you see him hurting Joey, using you to hurt him?"

Hurting Joey my friend Joey . . .

The shadow again; his other hand went to his temple, but he held the boy.

"Gary, I know you can hear me!" Tracy went on. "You can't let him use you anymore to keep hurting! He's hurt so many, *oh dear God so many!* And he killed Harry! Don't you remember? *He killed your Harry!"*

Harry I love Harry but Harry's dead because . . .

He looked at Joey, squirming in his grasp, and let him go. Both hands went to his head; he rocked from side to side. Joey scrambled over to Tracy, and she held him tightly, but her eyes remained on the hulking figure as they backed toward the defile.

"Gary, you must force him out!" she exclaimed. "He's made you do bad things. But you're strong, Gary, and you can make him go, you can make Bruno go! You must!"

Killed Harry you killed . . .

No you're weak don't listen to her you can't . . .

Killed Harry killed my friends hurt Joey hurt Tracy . . .

I'm stronger than . . .

Mark burst through the defile, pushing Tracy and Joey aside. *"Look out!"* he exclaimed, leveling the .38 Special in two shaky hands.

"No Mark, no!"

Tracy deflected the gun, jarring Mark's finger on the trigger. The explosion was deafening in the narrow, rock-lined place. High up on the cliff, near a niche that an animal might have once used, the bullet struck, whining numerous times, the echoes melding into one another, eventually fading into the more dominant stillness of the desert.

The hulking figure had dropped to both knees by the spring, its weaving more animated.

Don't want you in me anymore . . . get out . . .

No . . . can't go . . . the screaming terrible . . .

Get out of me . . .

. . . outside . . .

NOW.

The body stiffened, then eased; eyes from a face filled with anguish gazed at them.

"Joey?" Gary Masten whispered.

"Gary!" the boy cried.

He rose unsteadily. "M-mark? Tracy?"

SCREAMING . . .

Tracy grabbed her head suddenly, nearly falling. "No! Oh no, you get away from me, you bastard!"

TERRIBLE . . .

Mark went rigid, his fingers white around the butt of the pistol. "Yeah, that's what you think," he muttered. "Stay out there and rot!"

OUTSIDE . . .

Joey had run to Gary, who gathered the boy up protectively in his massive arms. "Y-you can't have my friend either," Gary snapped.

"I sent you away, and you better not come back."

They stood together now, the four of them, made stronger by their proximity, and their defiance of the entity, which they heard/felt/sensed swirling helplessly around them, perhaps ricocheting off the stone facings, as the errant bullet had done earlier.

Chief Donald Upton staggered through the defile, eyes glazed, blood streaking his face from a cut on the head, the big gun held limply at his side. His efforts of the past few minutes had further weakened him.

The frenzied flight of the entity ceased abruptly.

Weak minds, Mark thought, *it can only occupy weak minds.* "Oh Jesus, no!" he exclaimed. *"Chief, don't let it in!"*

Upton's body straightened; the barrel of the Magnum tilted up. He took another step toward them, gritty sand crunching beneath the souls of his heavy boots.

Tracy dug her fingers into Mark's arm.

Halfway between the spring and the defile, a three-inch-long, straw-colored scorpion crawled purposefully, its curved stinger moving rapidly at the bulbous base of the poised tail. Against the sandstone floor, it was nearly invisible. Its goal was a small crevice, less than a yard away, which would take it into the mountain, and from there, anywhere it wanted to go.

Upton raised a foot, brought it down upon the creature, ground the life from it.

The scream was brief, distant, and faded so quickly they wondered if they'd heard anything at all.

"Is . . . it over?" the lawman asked.

Mark looked around, nodded. "Yeah, it's over."

"You all OK?"

"I think so."

He glanced at Gary. "How're you doing, boy?"

"Harry's dead," Gary Masten said.

The lawman put a hand on his shoulder. "Yeah, I'm sorry."

Gary fell to his knees and sobbed. Tracy and Joey tried to console him. Upton took Mark aside.

"And *that's* who everyone is waiting to hang for the murders," he said bitterly.

"We can't let it happen!" Mark exclaimed.

"It won't happen, I swear to God it won't." He shrugged. "I'll think of something. In the meantime, we have to get out of the canyon, and from the look of this sorry band that's going to be a worse job than getting here. Come on."

"Chief, what . . . about me?" Mark asked.

Upton stared blankly at him. "What *about* you, son?"

Mark handed him the gun. "Thanks."

He led them through the defile, Upton at the rear. They did not look back at the Bad-Tasting Water place.

CHAPTER TWENTY-ONE

Passages

1

The trek out of Madhouse Canyon was as difficult as Upton had predicted. If their numerous cuts, scrapes, and bruises were not enough, they sustained more. Exhaustion owned them. But Gary Masten, despite his grief, seemed tireless and even carried those who momentarily refused to take another step, quickly jarring them back to the reality of what had to be done.

Two and a half hours later, they reached the canyon's mouth. Upton's deputies were there, other lawmen, concerned members of the town council. A few enterprising reporters in 4x4s had actually made it to Smoke Tree but were being kept at a safe distance, back along Las Palmas Road. The furor over Gary's appearance was immediately quelled by Upton, who told them the young man had nothing to do with the killings, that like Joey Russell he too had been a hostage of the murderer.

And what about this madman? he'd been asked. Yes, after separating him from the hostages, Upton had pursued him far back into the canyon, you know, where it has all those crazy forks and such.

(He said nothing about the hot spring, which he'd never even known about, despite living in Smoke Tree since just after the town was built.) Anyway, the bastard must've gotten tired of running, because he'd waited in ambush up around those old Cahuilla Indian fire pits, then came at him with a knife. He'd had to shoot him, and damned if the body hadn't tumbled down one of those splinters of the San Jacinto fault. Hell of a place to have to recover a body from, that fissure. No hurry though, because the whole blessed thing's over. Yeah, they'll do it some day. But in forty-eight hours or less, whatever scavengers could get down there will have picked the body clean. So again, it's over; I'll make a statement, then everyone can go home.

But who was the killer? they persisted. Who knows? Some crackhead drifter, chose our town to lose his mind. Maybe an escapee from a mental hospital, or one they just released because he was doing so nicely, thank you; check it out, happens all the time. Hell, there'd been a drifter through not too long back, got himself killed near the edge of town. Anyway, right now we got folks who need medical attention, so let's break it up, OK?

The five were driven to the Valley Clinic. Some county lawmen actually mulled over the idea of going up to the Indian fire pits and looking for the body. But it was one hundred and seven degrees, and the locals assured them the place was a bitch to get to anyway.

Joey protested against treatment until he could see his grandfather. When Carl Singer opened his eyes to find the boy standing there, his broad smile broke free of his pain.

Bending his own clinic rules, Dr. Hoberg had a cot set up alongside Carl's bed. After the mandatory visit to the emergency room, Joey went to sleep there.

Tracy had broken a small bone in her wrist (she had no idea how, or when). Chief Upton had a mild concussion, among other things. Mark would not be sitting down comfortably on a badly bruised rear for a while. Gary's physical injuries were minor, but his fatigue, and grief, left Hoberg concerned about shock. They were treated, given rooms, and left alone to sleep the sleep of the dead, all day and well into the evening.

Donald Upton was well respected, both as a cop and a person.

If that was what he said about the incident in Madhouse Canyon, then that was what happened. The reporters hung around for follow-up stories, filed them, eventually left. No more news here, and it was so damn hot.

By dusk a minimal calm had settled over the quiet retirement community of Smoke Tree, California.

2

Mark had not heard Tracy come in. She could have been there an hour without his being aware of it; for that matter, she could have danced on his bed and not drawn him from sleep until he was ready, as he was now. He rose from it slowly, like walking through a long and dark but otherwise unimposing tunnel toward a myriad of twinkling carnival lights at one end. When he reached the midway those lights exploded, becoming Tracy's face. He smiled.

"What time is it?"

Tracy glanced at her watch. "After nine. I thought I'd outsleep you by a week, but I've been up a while."

"How are the others?"

"Chief Upton's giving the staff a hard time, wants to be back at work. I don't know why; he'll be filling out paperwork until this town freezes over. Joey and Dad are watching a baseball game.   Gary . . ." She grew somber. "He's having a bad time. But someone's been with him constantly. The staff really cares about him."

"I wonder what will happen to him."

"Upton and Harry Keller were friends. The chief has spoken to Gary a couple of times today, told him not to worry about being sent away, that he'd look after him if need be. Gary's of legal age anyway, and according to Upton, he's got a nice nest egg from Harry's estate. He can stay in the house—that might be hard—do what he was doing before. The tree farm will probably continue operations, so he'll have a job there. I think Gary will be OK."

Mark held out a hand. "And what about you, lady?"

She took it. "I'm . . . fine. First thing I did when I woke up was tell myself it was all a weird dream. But that only made it worse." She let go of his hand, walked to the window. "So it happened, and we got through, and it's done, and I'm glad, and that's— Oh my God, Mark, *look*!"

Mark leaped from the bed . . . too fast, his throbbing head told him. Tracy was pointing down into the parking lot, where an elongated, mistlike figure drifted slowly toward the building. A tank-sized Olds Delta 88, swerving to miss it, braked to a stop inches from the bumper of another car. Beyond the specter another floated, this one shorter, its shape that of a stalagmite from a deep ice cave. There were more of them, four, five, the line—it was jagged, but it was a line—stretching across Las Palmas Road and into the desert. Another car screeched to a stop on the street, its horn blaring.

"They're coming in on their own!" Mark exclaimed.

"No one's been there for two nights," Tracy said. "They didn't know what to do, probably thought they were abandoned!"

"We've got to make them go back. They don't understand—"

There was a crash, and the sound of broken glass, from outside the door. They ran into the second floor hallway. A wide-eyed orderly hurried past them. Down the hall Chief Upton and a nurse stood outside room 214, the lawman trying to calm the hysterical woman. His head was bandaged, and he still wore his pale green hospital gown, over which he'd pulled his trousers.

"You know what's happening?" Upton asked as Tracy and Mark joined him.

"We have a good idea," Mark said.

"Then get in there and do something about it!"

They pushed open the door to room 214. Another orderly stood just inside, staring at the patient, who sat bolt upright in bed. Mrs. Blythe Kennedy had had minor surgery the previous day, was doing nicely, and was scheduled to be released the next morning. Now, she wore a misty, purplish-blue aura around her head, which swelled, shrank, swelled again, while she held out her hands, terrified.

"What's happening to her?" the orderly exclaimed.

"We'll take care of it," Tracy said. "Why don't you wait outside?"

"You got it!"

The man left. Mark went to one side of the bed, spoke soothing words to Mrs. Kennedy. Tracy, opposite him, reached a hand out to the mist.

"You're scaring this lady, and that's not right," she said softly. "You shouldn't have come here; it's not time yet. Let me take you back."

A tendril of the mist flicked out, touched her, withdrew, touched her again. Tracy backed away, and the mist rose above Mrs. Kennedy, then followed. Mark helped Mrs. Kennedy lay down. Briefly, a face took form in the drifting haze; an elderly face, but smooth, unlined, mostly with a blank expression, though upon occasion sparked by curiosity, seeking answers to unfathomable questions. Then, the image faded, but the mist continued to follow Tracy as she moved to the door.

"Will she stay with you?" Mark asked.

"Yes, I'm sure of it."

He held the door for her. When the nurse saw Tracy step out, she hurried back to her station. Upton shook his head in disbelief.

"Is it actually . . . *following* you?" the cop asked.

Tracy nodded. "We'll have to get them all, one by one, and lead them back to the ruins. Actually, if we can find Jacob, it might be easier."

"Jacob," Upton muttered. "Anyway, most of them are still downstairs. Come on."

He started for the elevator, changed his mind and walked to the stairwell. Tracy turned slowly, as though she were wearing a heavy backpack, and glanced at Mark. He was grinning.

"What's so funny?" she asked.

"*Who you gonna call?*" he said, and broke up, the infectious laughter spreading to Tracy, who stopped after a few seconds, concerned about frightening her 'passenger.'

The Valley Clinic's first floor was bedlam. Helpless, misguided spirits explored halls, rooms, probed the wills of patients and staff. A couple of the latter had fled out into the night, which seemed almost as terrifying. But most stayed with their charges, despite this incursion by something of which they had not the least bit of understanding.

Tracy and Mark reached out to the spirits; soon, frost-walls had formed behind each of them.

Dr. Wayne Hoberg had joined Chief Upton. The physician had no clue what was going on in his sometimes chaotic, but otherwise orderly domain, but was eager to help nonetheless. They met Tracy and Mark in the lobby, where Upton was called away by the security guard. An important phone call from his deputy, the man said.

"The first floor appears to be clean," Hoberg told them. "What now?"

"We take them outside and start back," Mark said. "Any others that are coming, we'll pick up on the way."

Hoberg shook his head. "I hope someone will explain to me what happened in my hospital tonight."

They passed through the automatic doors, the loud *whoosh*—or perhaps a static charge—startling the frost-walls, causing them to waver. In the parking lot, Mark paused to retrieve another spirit. So far, they had not yet found Jacob. Ahead, one lone entity crossed Las Palmas Road.

"How many do you have?" Mark asked.

"Six, I think."

"And I have seven or eight. That's only half."

"The rest are probably still at the ruins."

"Let's hope so. I'd hate to think—"

Upton burst through the doors, a clucking Doc Hoberg behind. "Hey, wait up!" he called. "Seems like we got another problem."

"What is it?" Tracy asked.

"More of . . . them. At the country club! Come on, I need at least one of you."

"Don, you're not going anywhere!" Hoberg exclaimed. "You shouldn't be out of bed—"

"Aw, can it, Doc. I'll be back later."

Mark looked at Tracy. "I'll go with the chief. Can you take all of them?"

"Sure, the more the merrier. I'll wait for you there."

Tracy's frost-wall grew as she continued across the parking lot.

3

Upton had compromised and let Mark drive his Blazer. They pulled in front of the clubhouse less than two minutes later, passing a few erratically driven cars on the way. An old woman, having fainted, lay on a couch in the central hall. A man sat on the carpeted floor, favoring an ankle. Other patrons, oddly, were still around. It had been a busy evening for the restaurant and the Arroyo Lounge, in the wake of both the storm and the murders.

A spirit wafted inside the pro shop. Noting it, Mark followed Upton to the lounge entrance, where Jerry Zirpolo, Rita Vasquez, Ray Clifton and Danny Martinez stood. The deputy, wide-eyed, held his gun poised.

"Oh for Jesus' sake, Danny, put the gun away!" Upton snapped.

The deputy holstered his .38 Special. "Chief, it's the craziest damn thing—!"

"Yeah yeah, I know. We'll take care of it. You get folks with no business here on their way home."

Jerry looked at Mark curiously. "Why are you here? You got something to do with this?"

"Guess so. When did they get here?"

"They . . . It started about ten minutes ago," he said, glancing at his Rolex. "Barful of people, too. Cleared out like—"

"Wait here," Mark told them. "I'm going in the pro shop first."

It was Jacob; he knew that, even in the brief passing. He touched the entity and felt disjointed thoughts about how afraid they had been when no one came, and how they would have to walk the ruins forever unless they overcame their fear and left on their own. And how Jacob had told them they had not been abandoned, that someone would come, and to wait, keep waiting, but after a while he had wanted to leave too. They had gone in two lines, one following the creek, the other the trail. Now he was wondering if they had done the right thing. No, Mark told him, because people didn't understand, and they were scaring them, and it wasn't anyone's time yet to pass on over, and they didn't want to be hosts, and the probing was scaring them even more. They had to go back now, and Mark needed Jacob's help.

Jacob agreed. He followed Mark across the central hall, people giving them a wide berth. Into the Arroyo Lounge, which had suffered minimal damage, mostly from the exiting stampede.

A milky-white frost-wall—seven or eight of them, Mark guessed—wavered near the bar. They had followed the creek like this, or had come together afterward, frightened by the people and the lights and the things they didn't understand. One tendril wafted amid the tables; another floated above the jukebox. Snaking down, it probed the neon contrivance tentatively, then disappeared within.

Frankie Laine's "Mule Train" filled the lounge. Mark jumped; the frost-wall wavered.

Frankie Laine became Dinah Shore which became Perry Como which became Peggy Lee. Two lines of a song, one, a few words, parts of syllables.

Peggy Lee became Frank Sinatra which became the Andrews Sisters.

The entity streaked from the jukebox, which hissed and sizzled and popped and coughed out a few last bits of 1940s and '50s nostalgia before the bubble lights dimmed, and it fell silent.

He didn't like "Mule Train" either, Mark mused.

The entity quickly rejoined the others. Jacob communicated with the last straggler, as he'd already done with the frost-wall. They followed Mark outside, into the desert. Upton stayed behind to try and calm the people at the club.

Later, when the residents of Smoke Tree tried to explain that July night, they would be at a loss. What really *had* happened? What had they seen? At their age, with specters of words like *senility* and *Alzheimer's* and *infirmity* hanging about, perhaps it was best not to talk about such things at all.

4

Tracy, approaching the ruins of Concordia Sanitarium, saw the single entity hovering shakily along its perimeter. She led the others back to their place—their prison, but where they must be for now—and walked over to it.

Kneeling, extending a hand, she said, "Hello, Sarah. You did good to stay here. How frightened you must have been. I'm going to see you don't endure this much longer. Come now, come back with the others."

A wispy tendril brushed her, and this time held on. She took Sarah into the ruins, separated from her, sat down amid them.

Mark arrived not long after. The shorter frost-walls joined, swirled for a few moments, then faded into the quiet darkness of the ruins.

Hand-in-hand, Tracy and Mark returned wearily to the hospital. Chief Upton was back in his bed: "Making Doc happy as a clam." No need for Tracy and Mark to stay, but they were welcome to, Hoberg said. They decided to go home but first checked on Gary Masten, found him sleeping comfortably. Joey wanted to stay the night with his grandfather, who was doing fine.

They slept in Tracy's bed, holding each other. Not making love; not needing to. Glad, simply, to be together.

5

On Wednesday morning, Tracy officially checked Joey out of the Valley Clinic. Even so, the two of them spent much of the day in Carl Singer's room. His recovery, Doc Hoberg said, was amazing. He kept it up, he'd be home by the weekend.

The hospital seemed back to normal. So too the country club, where any talk of the strange event was done in hushed tones. Except for Jerry Zirpolo, who was still livid over the damage to his magic jukebox. He hurled a thousand questions at Mark, and would have asked more if they hadn't been so busy. Mark's vague, Gee-I'm-not-sure-what-happened-myself-Jerry answers only soured his boss further. When he found few others willing to discuss it, Jerry finally gave up.

That same day, Tracy received a call from Preston Gruber, who had been Dexter Jones's lawyer for decades. Old Dex had left most of his estate to his niece, but just last weekend had amended his will to include a generous sum of money for Tracy and Mark. A note, attached to the amendment, was a request that they "finish up my work," which the attorney did not understand. It was not a condition of the inheritance, since there would be no way for him to monitor it. Tracy assured Gruber she and Mark knew what it meant, and would do what had to be done. Afterward, she called Mark with the news.

On a visit to the hospital that afternoon, Tracy was invited into Doc Hoberg's office. A much-recovered Chief Donald Upton was present. While she listened, the physician offered his observations of what had been going on in Smoke Tree, specifically at his clinic, for some time now. Dexter Jones's endless probing into the condition of his patients, some things Hoberg himself had seen—and of course last night—had allowed him to reach some amazingly accurate conclusions. Tracy needed only to fill in a few of the blanks.

When she left Hoberg's office, Tracy knew all about Mrs. Ethel Fricke. The poor woman's heart had been deteriorating for a long time. She'd been admitted again on Monday, during that awful sandstorm, and had been on life support since then. Poor dear; doubtful she'd make it through tomorrow. But she'd lived a good eighty-seven years.

Late that night Tracy was able to draw Sarah . . .

Sarah Pruett, young heiress to a banking fortune.

. . . away from the ruins of Concordia Sanitarium. Soon the tormented girl had found eternal peace.

6

Friends and neighbors of Gary Masten had joined together under Chief Upton at Harry Keller's house to scrub, paint, or otherwise eradicate all physical evidence of what had occurred there. Still, when Upton brought Gary home on Thursday morning, he was worried about how the boy would deal with it. True, he had been doing well in the hospital, had even shown a good deal of understanding about what had happened to him; but . . .

Gary seemed glad to be home. Sure, something bad, real bad, had happened here. But most of his life with Harry, a wonderful time, had been lived in this house, and even though the bad memory would bother him sometimes, the good memories would always be strongest here. He would stay, and he would be all right. Upton believed him. All that Harry Keller had done through the years to make Gary a self-sufficient young man had worked. Harry would have been damn proud.

That same morning, Tracy had a long talk with Joey. When she was done, the boy knew exactly what his role in the day's events would be. Next, she called Jerry Zirpolo.

When Mark stopped by the Singer house on his way to work, Tracy was gone. Joey said she'd be back about one-thirty. Nope, don't know where she went. There was a message to call Jerry at the club. Feeling magnanimous, Jerry was giving Mark the day off; yeah, that's right, with pay. Sorry Marco, too busy to talk right now.

"So you get to hang around here," Joey said, dragging Mark to the couch. "Here, put your feet up, take a load off, relax."

"Take a load off? What is this?" Mark asked.

"I'm being your . . . lackey, I think." Joey saluted. "That's my job."

Mark grinned. "I see. So what do we do first?"

Joey held up a video. "Dinosaur movie, cool one. Hey, you want some Orville Doofendurfer?"

"Some *what?*"

"Popcorn! I make it pretty good. Not as good as Grandpa, but his is the best in the galaxy."

They ate popcorn, watched movies, rode their bikes, went to the pool, came home and had lunch while another film was rolling. Once, Mark threatened to beat the boy to a pulp if he didn't tell what was going on, and Joey had made the sign of sealed lips and tried to escape between Mark's legs, but Mark had pulled him back and they'd wound up wrestling on the floor, laughing their heads off.

At one-forty, Tracy walked through the door, followed by a short, silver-haired man, conservatively dressed in a dark, rumpled suit and tie. Mark stood.

"Julius?" he said. "My God, Julius!"

His eyes on Mark, Julius Mandell hurried forward. They embraced, pounded each other on the back, sobbed. Standing off to the side with her son, Tracy grinned as she sparred with her own tears.

"You did good, kid," she whispered. "He didn't suspect a thing."

They finally separated, and Tracy guided them to the couch. Flustered, Mark said, "What are you . . . I don't—"

"Let me talk, and I think all your questions will be answered," Julius said.

"Just one. Anna . . . ?"

"She passed away five months ago."

"I'm sorry."

"She went as painlessly as they could make it for her. But it was before she died that she made me realize what a fool I had been."

"I don't understand."

"When you had the trouble and ran away, I didn't even *know* about it. I didn't know a *thing* until nearly a week later! Only reason I found out then was because Anna—in all her suffering—asked about you, asked why you hadn't been by. So I looked into it, found out what had happened. It wasn't good, but I was sure there was a lot of it I didn't know, things I should've heard from your own mouth. Anna was so angry with me! How could I let this happen? she said. Go and help the boy, stop moping around here!

"Things looked real bad. The drugs they found in your apartment . . . Unbelievable! As far as the police were concerned, it was an open-and-shut case. All they had to do was pick you up . . .

"But I checked around, found out about the pressure Tony Vincent was putting on you. Then, before I could do anything else, Anna died. After the funeral I tried to find you, but you'd done a hell of a job of disappearing off the face of the earth!

"When Tracy got a hold of me last week, I was thrilled." He smiled at her. "I wouldn't have doubted for a minute that two people like you could find each other, even under the circumstances. I asked her not to say anything, that I wanted to come out here and do it myself."

"That was hard," Tracy interjected, "but I agreed."

"This is all great," Mark said, "but the bottom line is, I still did what I did and I'm in big trouble, right?"

Julius shrugged. "Maybe not."

"Mark stared at him, wide-eyed. "What?"

"No promises; I'm still working on it. Called in a few favors, both before and after we caught up with Tony Vincent."

"Tony's in the slam again?"

"Actually, he's dead. Mortally wounded resisting arrest. I went to see him in the hospital, before he died, a few days ago. Tracy, I hadn't told you about this yet. Being a step from the grave must've given him a bad case of guilt. He not only confirmed the pressure he put on you, but also admitted the fall you took for him years ago."

"What . . . does all this mean?" Tracy asked. "Is Mark still in trouble?"

"He still has to go back and face the charges, but the people I spoke to said that, considering the facts, the penalty may be light."

Mark frowned. "But I'll still have to do time if I go back."

Julius put a hand on his shoulder. "Son, you did six years for nothing. Far as I'm concerned, they owe you! And I think the DA will agree."

Tracy cried and hugged Mark; Julius and Joey grinned at each other.

"Some of the favors I called in included getting all of this taken care of fast," Julius said, "as soon as we get back to New York. Look, I'd be lying if I said everything was a slam dunk. But it's real hopeful."

Mark was still standing with Tracy. "I'll go with you. Julius, I don't know how—"

"You be quiet, son," Julius scolded. "This was my pleasure. And I'm sure Anna is resting peacefully in her grave right now. So, if all goes well, what plans do you have?"

"Oh wow, plans . . ." Mark shrugged.

Joey stood at his side, looked up. "Hey, you wanna be my dad?"

Tracy groaned. Mark said, "You want me to?"

"Yeah."

"Fine."

Joey turned calmly, took a few steps, leaped a yard above the floor, threw a fist in the air and ran whooping into his bedroom.

"That OK with you, lady?" Mark asked Tracy.

"Only if you trade in your Mets cap for Cardinal red."

"Tough choice . . . but whatever. Anyway, if I survive New York,

St. Louis will have to wait. It might take the rest of the summer to finish our work in Smoke Tree."

"This is true."

Julius was puzzled. "What kind of work are you two doing in *this* town?"

"That, Julius, is a long story. Ought to make for an interesting flight."

ABOUT MIKE SIROTA

Mike is the author of nineteen published books with houses that include The Berkley Publishing Group (Penguin-Putnam), Bantam Books, Pocket Books, Kensington Publishing Corp. and now ZOVA Books. For fourteen years he was an award-winning feature writer and editor for a Southern California newsmagazine. Mike has facilitated many read and critique workshops, and has taught seminars and classes for various educational systems. He is an instructor for the University of California, San Diego Extension and is presently a workshop leader for the Southern California Writers' Conference, the La Jolla Writers Conference, and the Alaska Writers Guild Conference.

Mike's journalism honors include a prestigious Simon Rockower Prize for investigative reporting, and an award from the San Diego County Medical Association. He was also honored as the first "Person of Letters" by the 2002 La Jolla Writer's Conference "for his ongoing and unselfish contributions to and support of the writing community."

Visit Mike Sirota at
www.mikesirota.com

ZOVA BOOKS

ZOVA Books is an independent publishing company serving discriminating readers and booksellers of quality. We strive to create dynamic and successful partnerships for our authors, vendors, and retailers.
ZOVA Books seeks to build the next generation publishing firm.

Visit us at www.zovabooks.com